To Faith

MOONSHINE IN THE MORNING

Andrea McNicoll

ALMA BOOKS

ALMA BOOKS LTD
London House
243–253 Lower Mortlake Road
Richmond
Surrey TW9 2LL
United Kingdom
www.almabooks.com

Moonshine in the Morning first published by Alma Books Limited in 2008
Copyright © Andrea McNicoll, 2008

Andrea McNicoll asserts her moral right to be identified as the author of this
work in accordance with the Copyright, Designs and Patents Act 1988

The author wishes to give special thanks to the Scottish Arts Council for the
bursary under which this book was written.

Printed in Great Britain by CPI Cox & Wyman, Reading, RG1 8EX

ISBN: 978-1-84688-067-4

For my father, with love

MOONSHINE IN
THE MORNING

List of Characters

Mother Pensri – the lottery ticket seller
Uncle Nun – her husband
Kwan – their daughter

Mother Noi – the deep-fried pumpkin vendor
Uncle Daeng – her farmer husband
Tuptim – their daughter

Sergeant Yud – a policeman
Mother Nong – his wife
The novice – their son
Maew – their daughter

Aunty Wassana – the noodle soup stall owner
Uncle Ong – her husband

Mother Suree – the green papaya salad stall owner

Gimsia – the Chinese grocer
Mother Pon – his wife
Dee – their son

The Chief – the Chief of Police
Madam – his wife
Panit – their maid

Uncle Moon – the dustcart driver

Gop-Guu – the madman

Mali Foi Thong – the butcher's daughter

The Shan Fortune Teller

Sia Heng – the Chinese entrepreneur

Sergeant Pan – a policeman

Bee, Lek and *Jai Kham* – migrant workers

Jamu – a tribesman

Lai – the moonshine stall owner

The Abbot

The Schoolmaster

The Headman

The District Officer

The Forestry Officer

Prologue: Lottery Day

At six o'clock in the morning dawn was sneaking through the chill of night. A mountain mist lay over the village like a damp cloth; dogs lay curled nose to tail on steps and under houses, too cold to bark. Along the main street shops and businesses were stirring, creaking and clattering their shutters and opening their doors. A thousand small birds prattled in the ancient banyan tree in the temple grounds, while cockerels stretched their scrawny necks and crowed in the backyards of sleepy householders who shivered, washed their faces and spat out the staleness of the night's sleep.

It was the first day of December. Mother Pensri yawned noisily and stretched. While dressing, she pondered the unfolding day and how different her life could be by late afternoon. She washed her face and swept her black hair back with both hands, expertly making a neat bun. Peering into the mirror, she powdered her nose and cheeks, pursing her lips and applying a dash of lipstick for respectability. She moved through the house towards the door, frowning at the few particles of dust that had dared creep inside overnight. Once outside, she plucked a jasmine blossom from the bush in the yard, inhaled its scent and tucked it into the folds of her bun before mounting her bicycle. The front wheel wobbled as she found her balance in the dawning day and pedalled past the district office, oblivious to the pink and purple bougainvillea that flourished luxuriantly in the gardens. She turned left on to the main road.

"Where are you going?" called her neighbour, Mother Nong.

"To market! Are you coming?"

"What are you cooking today?"

"*Nam prik ong!*"

"Isn't it cold!"

"Oh, colder than last year… but then, we had so much rain in September!"

Bellows of laughter rang out from the market entrance. Standing amidst the mopeds, bicycles, barrows and baskets was Uncle Moon, the dustcart driver. Clutching the neck of an almost empty bottle of rice whisky, he staggered from stall to stall, berating the market vendors good-naturedly on the price of their goods.

"*Aow,*" he shouted, "three baht for one lime! You are all thieves! No one will buy your tomatoes at the prices you ask!" He took another swig of whisky. "*Oh-ho,* Mother Pensri! Good morning!" He bowed elaborately as she went past him into the market. "How do you stay looking so beautiful?"

Mother Pensri clicked her tongue against her teeth. Uncle Moon had never married. Some of the villagers dismissed him as a drunkard and a ne'er-do-well, but with the older women he was a favourite: they understood he drank to forget the death of a young girl with a strawberry birthmark on her cheek many years before.

The market was set out in three long rows of wooden tables, covered by a makeshift roof of corrugated iron to keep out the cool winter mists, the hot summer sun and the rainy season downpours. It began in darkness at four o'clock when the first vendors arrived to set up their stalls, donkey baskets full of goods slung across the backs of their mopeds, balaclavas over their heads to keep out the cold. A couple of the vendors sold their products wholesale. They drove out before midnight to the nocturnal city markets to buy fresh squid, meatballs, egg noodles, dried shrimps and yellow slabs of tofu, which they piled into trucks and brought back over the mountains, a three-hour drive along a narrow switchback road with hairpin twists and turns. In the old days the road was a rough dirt track, cut through the north-western highlands by the Japanese during the occupation to improve their trade route from Thailand into Burma. In those times the villagers had to walk to the city in the rainy season, camping in the forest, lighting fires to scare away tigers and bears. But as the village expanded much of the forest was felled to make way for concrete roads, and the tigers and bears were hunted down or chased away.

Sometimes vendors would come from outside the province with goods that the villagers couldn't find easily in the northwest of Thailand: pungent, prickly durian fruit from the south, bales of shimmering homespun silk from the north-east, cigars and face powder from across the nearby Burmese border, garish Chinese blankets. But most days the vendors were local women, Shan or northern Thais with noisy, teasing voices and pale, smooth skin. They brought fruit and vegetables, bunches of neatly bound holy basil, sweet basil, mint and coriander, homemade sweets and sour pickles. Some came only with the meagre produce from their backyards, a handful of tomatoes, a bunch of lemon grass, beans or morning glory. Others collected wild plants and roots from the dwindling forest, spending hot afternoons climbing steep mountainsides, their arms and legs scratched by thorns and bitten by fierce red ants. They would wade patiently through the river with nets, catching whitespots and shark minnows, or they would lay traps for field frogs, which they sold speared on to sticks, three in a row, ready to barbecue. Sometimes they even daubed glue on to bamboo poles near the river to catch the cicadas flying in over the water in the evening, selling them by the kilo for villagers to fry.

The vendors sat cross-legged on top of their wooden tables, gossiping, complaining, and rearranging bundles and packets in front of them with innate tidiness. A few of the older ones were smoking cheroots. The women who had come to buy walked around with baskets on their arms, rubbing their eyes, planning meals. A straggle of men sat around Lai's moonshine stall and his selection of herbal whisky contemplating the red-and-orange firebrand liquors, such as "Eleven Tigers" and "Chinese Man Who Can Carry a Water Buffalo over His Head". Eyes bleary and bloodshot from a night spent arguing and gambling, the men knocked back shot after shot, hoping the moonshine would give them the courage needed to go home and face their wives. Mother Pensri sniffed and walked past them: her husband was safe in bed, for once. She stopped to buy some coconut cakes, leaning over the wooden table.

"What numbers do you want, Grandmother Gaysuda?" she asked the tiny woman who was scooping the hot cakes from a griddle into little boats made from banana leaves.

"Three and four, for sure!" answered the old woman, pausing to relight a hand-rolled cheroot. "My grandson bought a new moped yesterday and the last two numbers of the licence plate are three and four."

Mother Pensri nodded and put the cakes into her basket. She moved among the stalls, prodding and picking at the vegetables, complaining wildly at the prices. Gold bracelets and rings set with Burmese rubies and sapphires twinkled on wrists and fingers as deft hands packed wares in banana leaves and in packets folded out of old newspaper. A small group had gathered around the fried pumpkin stall.

"What's going on?" asked Mother Pensri, elbowing her way in.

"Mother Noi had a dream!"

"Yes!" confirmed Mother Noi, pulling her sarong more tightly around her waist. "I was sitting under a tree, eating mangosteens. It was a big banyan tree, like the one in the temple grounds. I was very full and sleepy. I was about to close my eyes and take a nap when a tiger appeared in front of me! I didn't know what to do!" She paused for dramatic effect. "But it only looked me straight in the eye and then turned and walked away. And then I woke up! What do you think, Mother Pensri?"

Mother Pensri wrinkled her nose. "A banyan tree in full bloom is a... nine. A tiger is a two or a seven. But mangosteens... I'm not so sure."

The chatter resumed as the women began clamouring for Mother Pensri to take their bets, noting down numbers on small slips of paper, tucking them inside pockets, bras and shoulder straps for safe-keeping. Mother Pensri continued through the market, making a mental note to look up the significance of mangosteens in her book of dreams when she got home. She bought ingredients for the morning meal: some fermented soy bean cakes, a slice of pork, cherry tomatoes, a bunch of red shallots and some coriander tied into a spray with spring onions.

Outside the market a row of seven monks had stopped to receive their daily alms. Barefoot on the cold cement they clasped their bowls, chanting a blessing as some of the women knelt to offer food. Mother Nong was first in line, as usual. Since her son had become a novice monk, she never missed the morning alms round and was always first up at the temple on Buddha days. Mother Pensri peered at her. *Oh-ho!* she exclaimed to herself, *surely that isn't another new silk sarong she's wearing?*

Mother Pensri, bags and parcels dangling from the handlebars, pushed her bicycle past the monks and along the road. The Chinese merchant, Gimsia, called out to her from his grocer's shop, just across from the market.

"Hey, Mother Pensri, buy some bananas! Only six baht a bunch!"

"Your bananas are too expensive! Everyone else sells a bunch for only four baht!"

"But my bananas are more delicious! Good enough to eat with sticky rice; a meal in itself!"

Mother Pensri laughed. Gimsia smiled and his eyes disappeared. He smoothed down the front of the faded pyjamas he always wore, regardless of weather or occasion. His only concessions to the cold were the socks he wore under his rubber sandals and the old scarf around his short neck. His eyes darted for profitable opportunities everywhere. The hairs sprouting from a large mole on his chin were proof of his shrewdness in business. He had migrated to Thailand during the fifties on the advice of an uncle, nothing in his bag but a change of clothes and a small roll of banknotes, his heart full of the steadfast Chinese will to prosper and succeed. He and his wife, Mother Pon, had run the grocer's shop for almost thirty years. Despite the fact that Gimsia sat on a comfortable fortune, he still kept his old newspapers and cardboard boxes to sell, and he ate rice porridge with salted cabbage twice a day. His money, he liked to boast, had all gone on sending his only son, Dee, to the very best university in the nearby city.

"What numbers will you buy today, Gimsia?" asked Mother Pensri.

"*Aiya*, no dreams, no deaths, no new cars or special signs. Why should I throw good money away when I am certain not to win?"

He shook his head and bent down to pick up the yellow cat lying across his feet.

Mother Pensri swung on to her bicycle, heading home, past Aunty Wassana's noodle soup stall, Mother Suree's green papaya salad stall, the newsagent's and the police station. Mother Pensri had only caught sight of the handsome new Police Chief a few times but from what she'd heard around the marketplace he was planning to come down hard on illegal gambling. Busy worrying whether his crackdown would affect her underground lottery sales, she had to swerve suddenly to miss Gop, the madman who wandered around barefoot, collecting rubbish.

Once home, Mother Pensri unpacked the coconut cakes, placing three of them on to a small silver plate, and filled a small china cup with water. She took three incense sticks and a thin candle out of a silver bowl and holding everything carefully she padded across the living room to the small red and gold shrine affixed to the south-facing wall. She placed the cakes and water in front of the bronze statue of Buddha at the centre of the shrine. Buddha was seated, head erect, eyes closed, legs crossed, one long, elegant hand resting palm upwards on his lap and the other resting across his knee, fingers pointing down towards the earth. As Mother Pensri knelt down, the candle and incense unlit between the palms of her hands, she meditated on the significance of the Buddha's pose. The Buddha had reached a state of enlightenment in the forest, when Mara, the devil, jealous of the Buddha's wisdom and serenity, sent a great army of demons to destroy him. Buddha, unperturbed, pointed down at the earth, calling her to witness his goodness. Up rose the earth goddess, Mother Thoranee, wringing the water out of her long hair, creating a great flood that washed away the army of demons. Mother Pensri thought about the story as she bowed to the floor three times, her feet tucked as neatly behind her as her short, fat legs would allow. Then she prayed the special prayer she reserved for the first and the sixteenth of every month: lottery days. She prayed to win. She prayed to win so that her daughter, Kwan, could give up work canning fruit in the city factory, come back and live at home, find a good husband, and settle down. She prayed to win just enough to make life a little easier and she promised to spend some of her winnings on religious offerings and merit-making ceremonies. If she won a lot she would order a new Buddha statue for the big temple, or new robes for all the monks.

"*Saddhu, saddhu, saddhu!*" she concluded, lighting the incense and candle in front of the Buddha.

She was feeling lucky as she went about her daily chores, sweeping and polishing the wooden floors of her house, pestling garlic and chilli, toasting the soy bean cakes, chopping the vegetables she had bought from the market that morning, steaming and frying until a delicious aroma filled the house. Her mind was busy considering the numbers she had heard at the market. Mother Noi's dreams were often worth following, and Mother Pensri reminded herself about the mangosteens. She consulted her book of dreams and jotted down numbers furiously. Lighting a cigarette, her eyes were caught by two small house lizards chasing one another fitfully across the wall next to the shrine.

Seven for the lizards, she thought automatically, *two because they are a pair.*

"*Tch, tch, tch, tch, tch*," said the lizards, rolling their tiny eyes and flicking their tiny tails.

Tickets had to be bought before two o'clock in the afternoon. Some people bought the official government lottery tickets with six numbers, hoping for a jackpot. However, most of the villagers bought tickets from the underground lottery organized by Sia Heng, a rich Chinese entrepreneur. Mother Pensri had been an agent for Sia Heng for nearly ten years. The underground lottery used the same numbers as the government, but the chances of winning were greater because the gambler could choose to gamble on only one or two numbers.

Mother Pensri spent the rest of the morning going around the homes and businesses of her regular customers, advising on numbers and collecting bets. From her book of dreams she had found that mangosteens signified numbers one and three, so she had chosen these numbers for herself. Nevertheless, she advised her regular customers to buy nines, threes and fours, sensing that if too many people knew about the mangosteens then the portent wouldn't come true. Twice a month she made a small amount of commission on the tickets she sold and, despite fervent resolutions to the contrary, reinvested most of it in her own lottery numbers.

By two o'clock the sun was high. Balaclavas and scarves had been discarded and the women who had risen early to go to the morning market were lying down inside cool houses, on wooden floors, catching an hour or two of sleep before children came back from school and husbands returned from the fields. Mother Pensri returned home and lay down on her side, her hands clasped under her head as a pillow, her mind a confusion of money and mangosteens and what to make for the evening meal.

Around four o'clock all ears turned to the radio as the winning numbers were announced from Bangkok. Word of the numbers spread through the village and across the whole country like a trail of firecrackers, an explosion of whoops and groans as the villagers pulled scraps of paper from pockets. One farmer had won a small amount on the last two numbers and was already on his way to order the celebratory bottle of herbal whisky, a mob of men clustering round him, eager to share the good luck. "I knew it!" he cried. "I dreamt I saw the numbers painted across my rice field by the hand of Mother Thoranee herself! Sure enough, seven and two! Didn't I tell you?"

Mother Pensri was not alone in feeling envious. *Why*, she thought, *that farmer is drunk every evening and never goes to the temple to make merit and yet he wins quite often!* Mother Pensri couldn't understand where all the luck she had enjoyed last year had gone. "Maybe," she said to Mother Nong, over her backyard fence, "we should start drinking to see if we have auspicious dreams!"

The afternoon ended in another upsurge of noise as children came home from school, riding too fast on bicycles, walking in small gangs and talking in loud voices. Along the main street Aunty Wassana's noodle soup stall was closing up, stools stacked on tables, the big pot all but empty. Aunty Wassana's latest Burmese worker was crouched over the huge basin of dirty bowls and chopsticks. Mother Suree, face grimly set, was still pounding green papaya salad in her huge wooden mortar. Every so often she would pause to wipe a hand across her eyes: rumour had it her husband was seeing another woman. Gimsia was out on the street, turning a water hose first on his plants and then on the road, washing away the dry season dust. People stopped to chat to one another on their way home, about the weather, their day, and the lottery results. Those who had won were laughing, explaining how they had known which numbers to buy, describing their dreams from the night before. Those who had lost were shaking their heads because it seemed they had come so close to winning, just one or two numbers away from a jackpot. "Never mind," they said to one another, "what we have lost this time we will win back in the next lottery!" As the sun slipped behind the mountains, basking the valley in a brief golden glow, the villagers hurried home to bathe and change before the chill of dusk set in. The steady *pok-pok* of marble pestle on mortar could be heard; the smell of deep fried garlic, chilli, fresh herbs, barbecued fish and mouth-watering omelettes. After the fading smells of dinner came the sharp aroma of the mist mingled with the perfume of wood smoke. Men gathered around small fires at the edge of the road, toothpicks between their teeth and cigarettes hanging off their lips, grumbling about their rice fields and their wives, dredging their pockets for the price of a glass of moonshine, the possibility of a game of cards. Televisions echoed channel seven, the only channel the village could pick up, as families settled down under quilts to watch serial dramas.

All was quiet in the old temple: the monks were already sleeping. Gop, the madman, had fallen asleep under the old banyan tree, near the *chedi*. In front of the *chedi* a statue of Mother Thoranee gazed patiently over the temple grounds, hands elegantly grasping her long black twist of hair, as if wondering when the villagers would start paying attention to her again.

Mother Pensri loved the cold evenings. She sat on her porch smoking a cigarette, checking over her notebook of lottery bets to see who had won. Her commission was all spent as usual, lost on mistaken interpretations of the signs and portents. Mother Pensri knew she could have won, if only she had been paying attention to all the signs. *Tho-oei! Two and seven: how foolish of me!* thought Mother Pensri, one eye on the notebook and one on the persistent house lizards.

"*Tch, tch, tch, tch, tch,*" laughed the lizards, chasing insects on the wall in front of the shrine, rolling their eyes in derision. Somewhere in the nearby jungle the ghost of a tiger roared.

Pumpkin

The stranger sat at Aunty Wassana's noodle soup stall in the morning market, his truck parked across the street where he could keep an eye on it. He was a long way from home, and mountains made him wary. Too much open space and sky. He had driven all the previous day and through the night, reluctant to stop on the twisting road, feeling trapped by the cold, silent mountains that loomed under a huge, watchful moon. He was dressed in the leather jacket, tight corduroy jeans and brown suede boots he had recently purchased in a Bangkok department store. Foreign brands. He believed in spending a little extra money in order to buy good quality, stuff that would last. On the little finger of his left hand he wore a large blue sapphire set into a thick gold ring. His nails were clean, and trimmed to the quick. As he tucked into a bowl of steaming yellow noodles, he listened to the group of local farmers gathered around the herbal whisky stall. Heads and bellies suffused with the whisky's mellowing magic, the men were oblivious both to the stranger and the early morning chill; by now they seemed to care little whether they had won or lost at the hands of poker they had spent all night in playing. Their easy, familiar bluster told the stranger they were all neighbours, brothers: the greatest of friends.

"My wife won't tell me off! She's got money of her own now!" One of the farmers chuckled and sucked on his cheroot, spitting out the stray tobacco stuck between his teeth.

"How much did your wife get for that old piece of silk then?"

"Ten thousand baht, that's how much! And I haven't seen a single baht of it; she's got very sticky fingers when it comes to money!"

"Who can blame her, with you as a husband!"

"I wish my wife had something of value," said another, taking off his hat to scratch his head, "I'd sell it like a shot! Buy some pigs, that's what I'd do. There's money in pigs."

"Buy some whisky more like!"

"*Aow*, you'd sell your own wife if you thought you'd get a good price for her!"

The stranger smirked into his noodles. Laughing loudly and knocking their glasses together, the men drew disapproving looks from the market vendors busy behind their stalls. The women vendors raised their eyebrows, shook their heads at one another and prayed their husbands hadn't been out losing at cards too.

One farmer was laughing a little less loudly than the others. Daeng was a quiet man: always the last to find a space to sit among the circle of card players and whisky drinkers. He didn't win or lose that much, told few jokes, and was never so drunk that he couldn't walk. That morning, he knew his wife had seen him. She was in the far corner of the market, selling strips of pumpkin deep-fried in a golden batter. Twelve baht for a small bag, twenty for a large. Daeng had watched his wife and daughter cutting up the pumpkin the night before, whispering together about some story of their own as the pale yellow pumpkin seeds spilt out of the orange flesh, sticky, spread over an old newspaper on the kitchen floor. They had hooted with laughter and he had got up then and gone out, round to Uncle Nun's house. Just for something to do and a bit of male company. Spending the whole day in the fields made a man lonely. He hadn't really wanted to join the poker game but sometimes it was difficult to say no. *A few deals,* he had thought, *then I'll go home.*

Daeng looked over at his wife. She always had something to sell – banana fritters, steamed taro, deep-fried pumpkin, pickled bamboo shoots, fruit – depending on the season. He stood up and tucked his shirt into faded indigo trousers, pushed his bare feet back into his rubber sandals, knocking his stool against the stranger at the next stall. The man looked up, nodded at Daeng's apology, and turned back to his bowl. He shovelled the soup quickly into his mouth with chopsticks and a spoon, making smacking noises with his lips as he sucked the noodles in. The circle of red faces around the herbal whisky stall turned towards Daeng.

"Where you off to, Daeng? Back home to sleep?"

"Work to be done. Field needs clearing."

"Your head needs clearing, more like! Don't worry, your wife will do that for you!"

Another round of back-slapping guffaws rang out through the market. Daeng smiled wanly, hands in pockets, and threaded through the stalls to stand next to his wife. Her tray of deep-fried pumpkin was almost empty. She was stirring the remains of a bowl of peanut sauce, lips pursed, eyes down.

"How much have you made?" he whispered, the vendors around them falling silent, exchanging glances.

"How much have you lost?" Mother Noi hissed scornfully, glancing up.

"Only a couple of hundred." Daeng fumbled in his empty pockets, brought out his hands and folded them across his chest. "Look," he said, leaning over towards her, his voice low, "I need some money to buy weed killer. I can't clear the field without weed killer."

She shook her head, wiping her hands down the sides of her apron. From the apron pouch she pulled out the coins and notes from the morning sales and shook them out furiously in front of him. "Take it," she said, fixing him in her gaze, "why not take it all?"

He scrabbled with the money, counting out the hundred and fifty he needed. There was just enough. He looked around to still the curious gazes of the other women and saw his daughter moving through the stalls towards them. Tuptim had just turned sixteen, and was fresh with the same prettiness her mother once had. Mother Noi was still staring at him.

"Well, what're you waiting for? You got what you wanted, didn't you?"

"Ssh, Tuptim's coming."

"Hey Mama, haven't you finished yet? I've steamed some rice and fried the leftover pumpkin with some egg for breakfast. Papa, there's a packed lunch for you to take to the field."

Daeng put out his hand to cup his daughter's smooth cheek and turned to leave, passing on his way the man at the noodle soup stall. The stranger watched him go, sitting back to light up a foreign cigarette with a flick-top silver lighter, turning with narrow-eyed interest to watch Tuptim in the blue skirt, white blouse and short socks of her school uniform. She was helping her mother to pack up the stall.

* * *

It wasn't far from the house to the field, three kilometres at most. His old motorbike had broken down again so Daeng walked, carrying the weed killer and his lunch in a cotton bag slung across his chest. The sun was glowing through the cold morning mist, warming the landscape. Patches of fallow paddy mingled with fields of soy bean and garlic on the plain, *lamyai* and mango orchards covering the lower mountain slopes. Daeng stopped to look across the valley, the river snaking through it. Ten years ago he could have named the owner of every plot of land. But now houses had sprung up on the farmland, modern houses made from bricks and concrete, with red tile roofs. People who worked for the expanding government office had moved into them, snapping up the land from farmers tempted by the lure of a fast buck. An economic boom, so the papers said. On the opposite side of the river the new Police Chief had started to build a luxury guesthouse complex, a row of teak wood bungalows on the river's edge. Tourists had found the valley, rich people from the city in jeeps and minibuses, and even some farangs: tall and white and loud-voiced, they were, with cameras swinging from their necks. They loved to photograph farmers working in the fields, bending over the rice. Daeng sighed – he couldn't keep up with it all.

He sat down in the little bamboo shelter at the edge of his field and looked over his paddy, thinking about last season's harvest. The government had fixed the price of rice so low that small farmers like him had barely made any profit. All those months of watching and waiting for the rains, planting, transplanting, weeding, spraying, harvesting and threshing: all for nothing. He shook his head, mulling it all over. *What else could I do but store all the rice? At least I can feed my family for now but how much longer can I go on without cash? It's been months since I put money on the table. If it wasn't for the money Noi earned...*

He looked over to the next field. In the yellowing stubble of last year's crop a new house had been built. Daeng's new neighbour worked for the district office – something to do with the Forestry Department. A few months ago the Forestry Officer had made Daeng a generous offer for some land; he was keen to have a big garden round his house. He was interested in orchids, he had told Daeng, was cultivating them to sell, and wanted to grow a lot more. Rich businessmen and tourists liked the delicate, intricate blossoms. There was a future in orchids. *But where*, thought Daeng, *is the logic in selling off my field? What would I do then? Go to the city? Leave my land, my village, and the valley I was born in? A job on a construction site is about all I'd get. Someone else's lackey. Like a dumb old buffalo, good for nothing but lugging bricks.*

He had borrowed money from the Farmers' Bank to help make ends meet, to pay for the new rice seedlings, the hire of a motor plough. *It will be OK*, he told himself, *after next season's crop. The prices will be up and I can pay back the loan and the interest then. I won't sell out like all the others.* But the loan niggled at him like a mosquito buzzing in his ear; he hadn't been able to make any of the repayments yet. Letters had started to arrive from the bank. He couldn't keep it secret forever: he would have to tell his wife. Daeng licked his lips, parched now from the whisky. He lay back on the split bamboo platform and closed his eyes, one hand behind his head. *A few more shots of Eleven Tigers would be good.*

"Nice piece of land."

Daeng looked round. He must have been dozing – he hadn't heard the truck coming along the road, nor the stranger walking over, picking his way carefully across the furrows to keep his boots clean. Daeng vaguely remembered him from the market.

"Mind if I sit down?"

"Go ahead."

The stranger sat next to him in the shelter, one leg dangling, the other casually swung over it. Daeng glanced at the expensive suede boots. The stranger flicked some dirt from one of them and reached inside his jacket for a cigarette, lighting it between cupped hands.

"This your land?"

"Yes. Three and a half *rai*, all mine."

"Bet it's worth quite a lot of money now – nice location, good views across the valley."

"It's not for sale."

"Get a good harvest last year, did you?"

"Good enough." Daeng folded his arms. "What're you doing up here then? Visiting someone?"

"Mm." He pulled on his cigarette. "Pretty place. I'm just passing through. Stopped in the market for some noodles. Been driving all night, straight up from Bangkok. I'm going up to the Shan border later on to pick up a delivery for my boss. He's done a deal with a guy up there. First time I've been this far north. Cold, isn't it? But pretty. Women are pretty too."

The stranger smiled.

"What business are you in?" asked Daeng.

21

"Entertainment," answered the stranger, looking Daeng in the eye. "My boss has a club in Patpong. He's always on the lookout for new talent. And the customers love the northern girls. It's the pale skin and long hair." He took one last drag of his cigarette before flicking the butt across Daeng's field. "Girls from round here can make a lot of money in Bangkok."

The stranger pulled a half bottle of Scotch from the inside of his jacket and unscrewed the cap. "Want a drink, Uncle?"

Daeng took the bottle, reading the label. It was good stuff – foreign and expensive. He took a drink. The whisky was smooth and warm in his throat, all the way down into his belly. He passed it back.

"You recruit new staff for him, is that it?"

"Guess you could just about call it that."

Daeng thought for a moment. "Is it just girls that your boss needs? What about men? I might know someone. You know, for washing dishes, cleaning up, that kind of thing?"

"Not much call for male staff." The stranger took a long hard gulp from the bottle, wiping a hand across his smile. "But maybe you know some girls round here looking for work? I might be able to cut you a good deal. A little commission."

Daeng rubbed his face and spat on the ground. He looked over at his neighbour's fine new house. The Forestry Officer was outside, watching a worker watering his orchids with a hose. Daeng waved at his neighbour. *Maybe*, he thought, *I should invite him over? The Forestry Officer might like to talk to the city stranger. I wouldn't mind listening to them talking things over. I might have a few things to say myself.*

"So what do you think, Uncle?"

"What kind of place is it, Bangkok?"

"Bangkok? Fast and bright. Fast and bright and full of angels, Uncle. *Krung Thep*. City of Angels, just like they say. Plenty opportunities for the right girls. This delivery I'm picking up, for instance. Six pretty little angels from the Shan State, all ready to go and eager to work. Their families get a cash advance – ten thousand baht, sometimes a bit more. Depends on the girl, her age and, well, experience. And when the girls get to Bangkok they work off the advance. Once that's paid back, any money they make is their own. Good tips too now – especially from the foreigners. Listen Uncle, some girls even end up going to work abroad, all over the world. Tokyo, Frankfurt, Hong Kong, London."

The stranger had a way with words. *Fast and bright*, Daeng repeated to himself: *Tokyo, Frankfurt, Hong Kong, London.* The foreign names were exciting. Daeng stood up and shouted "Hey sir!", calling his new neighbour over to join them. The Forestry Officer looked across and turned towards them.

"Ten thousand baht, eh? And the girls just serve?" Daeng asked. "Like in a restaurant?"

"Just like a restaurant. Some singing, maybe a little dancing, if they've got talent."

"What's your boss's restaurant called?"

"Dollhouse."

The two men were silent for a while, watching the Forestry Officer walking across to them over Daeng's paddy field. The sun was through the mist now, warm and yellow. *Dollhouse*, thought Daeng, staring at his paddy. The day felt full of possibilities.

* * *

The national anthem was echoing out from the police station loudspeaker. *Tho-oei! Six o'clock, and he still isn't home,* Mother Noi fumed. *It doesn't take that long to spray a field, not a lousy three-and-a-half rai field anyway.* She yanked the laundry off the line in the backyard as though the sleeves and trouser legs offended her, folding the clothes. *He better not be out at some poker game again. And where's Tuptim? There's still the pumpkin to cut up for tomorrow morning, the batter to mix, the peanuts to roast and grind for the sauce. Am I supposed to manage everything by myself?*

She went inside the house and sat down, picking up the letter that had arrived in the morning. It was from the Farmers' Bank, addressed to Daeng. But she had opened it anyway. *A bank loan! How could he? And two months of payments missed, two whole months!* She tapped the letter on the edge of the table for a moment and then threw it down flat with a slap. *And the old fool thinks he can go out dealing poker with my money?* She got up from the chair and crouched on the floor, spreading out an old newspaper, rolling a fat pumpkin in front of her. Holding it with one hand, she drove her kitchen knife down hard with the other, plunging it through the tough outer skin. *It's not like there's anything left to pawn. First it was my gold necklace, then my ruby ring. My grandmother's old silver betel nut set. Daeng's watch. What else? There's nothing left but a scrap of land and Daeng won't sell that. Stubborn old fool.*

The pumpkin lay in two halves. She plunged the knife in again, shaking her head. She knew that the price Daeng had been offered for the land would be enough to clear the debt and set up the small business she had in mind: a few folding chairs and tables and an aluminium stove. *My fried noodles are good, people say so. And you can't lose with food, especially with all the new office workers in the area, too busy to cook for themselves. But oh no, doesn't matter how many times I try to explain it to him, Daeng is a stubborn old fool!* Mother Noi sank back on her heels, staring at the pumpkin's four quarters.

Footsteps came up behind her.

"Mama, do you need some help with that?"

"Where have you been? How come you're so late?"

Tuptim pouted. "I was talking to Aunty Wassana."

"Well you're here now so get started on the peanuts."

"I saw Papa." Tuptim slipped it out.

Mother Noi blew out a breath. "Where exactly? As if I didn't know! At the whisky stall?"

"Mama, don't get angry. He wasn't that drunk. And he seemed happy."

"Who was he with today? That good for nothing Nun?"

"No, he was sitting with the man from the Forestry Department and someone else, another man, not from round here."

Tuptim had been impressed by the stranger. He had asked her to sit down so politely, as though she were an adult. He had asked her about school, what subjects she liked, what she wanted to do when she left. And the way he looked at her – it had made her stomach lurch.

"Papa said he had some good news to tell you. He said you could stop worrying now."

"Who did you say he was drinking with?"

"I told you – the Forestry Officer, the one who's built the new house up by our rice field, and a nice man from the city, all the way from Bangkok. Do you know what the man from Bangkok asked me..."

But Mother Noi had stopped listening. *Good news? Their troubles over? Surely drinking with the Forestry Officer can only mean one thing?* She laid down her knife and wiped her sticky hands on her apron. *The field must be sold!* Mother Noi jumped up and ran outside to find Daeng, leaving her daughter alone on the floor beside the pumpkin quarters and a basket of peanuts. The girl reached into the basket and started shelling, humming as she worked. She popped a raw pink peanut into her mouth and sucked on it, rolling it round and round with her tongue.

The Novice

The novice was bored. He was supposed to be meditating in his hut, but instead was sitting idly under the huge old banyan tree in the temple grounds. He knew nobody would look for him there because all the monks were in the great hall, chanting an especially long prayer – today was the last day of the funeral of a young village woman who had died in Bangkok. Later on, after the prayer, the young woman's relatives and friends would feed the monks and all the other funeral guests, and the coffin would be driven to the cremation site just outside the village, paraded slowly along the roads on a motorized cart covered in flowers and photos of the woman. It would be hoisted up onto the concrete pyre and set alight. One of the villagers – probably Uncle Moon – would let off a few mournful fireworks, and tomorrow, at the morning market, another villager would swear the young woman's ghost had visited them in the night, a claim which would only add to the growing body of speculation on the cause of her death.

The novice, thinking about all this, sighed and picked up a small stone to throw at a stray cat sitting a few feet away, basking in the winter sun, licking its paws. The cat jumped up and ran away, out of the temple gates and across the road to Mother Suree's green papaya salad stall, disappearing from sight. *I wish I could run away*, thought the novice, *and never come back!*

But running away wasn't an option. *Where would I go?* he brooded, *everyone in the village would know me straight away. Before long Mama and Papa would be after me, shouting and crying because of all the shame I've brought on the family. All over again.* He banged the back of his head a few times on the old tree and groaned.

Now that he was a novice there was a great long list of things he wasn't allowed to do. Apart from upholding the Five Precepts – not to kill, not to lie, not to steal, not to take intoxicants and not to engage in sexual misconduct – he wasn't allowed to have any money, or eat after midday. He wasn't allowed to have possessions except his robes, a towel, and his alms bowl. He wasn't allowed to get up after dawn, otherwise he wouldn't be able to go out on the alms round, and he wasn't allowed to wear shoes, which meant that he often trod on something dirty or unpleasant.

As if the rules weren't bad enough, he thought, *my mother never misses an alms round!* He couldn't help feeling annoyed when he saw Mother Nong standing outside the morning market with food, ready to step out of her shoes in front of her son, to kneel down and wait for a blessing. After the alms round, he had to spend hours on end chanting in the main hall. Then he was supposed to meditate all afternoon in his hut. When he was meditating, he wasn't to slap the mosquitoes that landed on him because it would count as breaking the first Precept. His arms and legs were covered in itchy bites. *And then, just because I'm the youngest novice*, he fumed, *I have to do all the worst temple chores!* He had to sweep up dry leaves, polish the hall's wooden floor, wash up after meals, and put all the flowers the village women brought as offerings into vases to place in front of the Buddha statue. *Flower arranging!* This last chore, he felt, was not in the least bit appropriate for a man; it was a girl's job. Not that there were any girls in the temple. That was another thing wrong with being a novice.

He wandered over to the temple pool and sat down to watch the catfish swimming back and forth, their long tails swishing. He could hear the sound of a motorbike engine revving up along the road and knew it was his friend's bike. Before he had become a novice, they had taken the muffler off the bike's exhaust so that when they drove through the village they could startle the dogs and cats, make the water buffaloes buck around in the rice fields. They had sprayed the bike black and had decorated it with stickers bought from the city – a skull and crossbones, the names of their favourite rock bands, and the silhouette of a naked woman, one hand on her back as she pushed her breasts forwards.

The novice closed his eyes and pictured the sticker for a while, feeling sleepy. Last night he had hardly slept because of all the activity in the temple. There must have been around fifty villagers present, wrapped up in hats and scarves, towels draped over the shoulders of the old ones for warmth, all keeping watch at the funeral. Most of the women had come to help prepare food for the following day, peeling huge trays of garlic and shallots to go into the big pot to make a *gaeng hang ley*, the thick yellow curry served at funerals, weddings and ordination ceremonies. Others had turned up to take advantage of the opportunity to gamble. Gambling was meant to be illegal. Once or twice the new Police Chief, bored or short of funds, had sent his officers out on Sunday afternoons to knock on closed doors and shutters, catching a few old uncles and aunties red-handed as they dealt out the cards, hauling them outside. Those who couldn't pay the fines were marched down to the station for the night. The temple, however, was inviolable ground, so funerals presented a great opportunity for all manner of cards and dice and games of chance. The novice had watched his father, Sergeant Yud, triumphing noisily at poker early last night, then losing all his winnings later to Aunty Wassana, who owned the noodle soup stall along the road. Since her husband, Uncle Ong, had gone to work in Saudi Arabia, Aunty Wassana had turned into an infamous card-sharp. Nobody knew when she was bluffing. But not everyone came to the funeral to gamble. Others were there out of fear that if they weren't seen attending people's funerals then nobody would attend theirs.

The smell of the *gaeng hang ley*, wafting out from behind the main hall, reminded the novice of his ordination a few weeks ago. It had all happened so quickly. His mother and father had spoken to the Abbot behind his back, announcing after dinner one day that he was to shave his head and become a novice for a year! A year – it seemed like the rest of his life. Most boys only became monks for a month or two, during the Lent season. His mother had broken down and cried when he protested, while his father had shut the doors and windows, not wanting the neighbours to hear anything.

"You will do as you are told!" Sergeant Yud had said. "We are your parents and we know what's for the best!"

"I hate you! I hate you both!" he had shouted, running out of the house to find his friend. That night they had stolen a bottle of whisky from Gimsia's shop. His friend had distracted the old Chinese grocer by asking him how much his bananas cost and whether Gimsia picked them out the jungle himself, while he had pulled the whisky easily off the shelf and tucked it into the waistband of his jeans, under his shirt. They had driven away, laughing, turning the front wheel of the bike round in the road too quickly, sending a cloud of dust over the front of Gimsia's old pyjamas. Driving to the brothel at the edge of the village, they had sat on the bike drinking the whisky, clicking their fingers and watching the men coming and going, trying to catch a glimpse of the girls inside. All the boys in the village saw the girls often enough in the daytime, walking down the street arm in arm, spending money on boxes of biscuits, barbecued chicken, shampoo, soap and colourful hair clips. But the girls wore ordinary clothes during the day, T-shirts and long cotton trousers, with only a shadow of last night's rouge on their cheeks, or a stray red ribbon, forgotten in their hair. The boys would nudge one another and wink, and the braver ones would call out to them.

"Where are you going? Can I come too? What's your name? Have you got a boyfriend?"

The girls always ignored them. One older boy claimed his father had taken him to the brothel, to be initiated, at which the younger boys had sniggered doubtfully. He said inside the brothel was a big room with a long bench that the girls sat on. They wore short skirts, high-heeled boots and sequined strapless tops. Then there were some other rooms. The men would disappear into them with the girls. The older boy said he had seen Sergeant Yud in there, with a young girl on his knee, and although the novice didn't quite believe him, it was an image he found hard to keep out of his head. He wondered if the day might come when his father would initiate him too. But he'd have to serve out his time as a novice first. He looked up and saw his older sister Maew coming over to sit next to him at the edge of the pond. She had arrived from the city last night to attend the funeral of the young woman, who had been in the same class as her at school.

"Hey little brother, how does it feel to be a novice?"

"What do you think? I can't wait for it to be over! You don't know how lucky you are to live away from the village."

"It's not so bad, is it? Anyway, it's not as easy as you think – living on my own and working, trying to save money to send back home. At least you don't have to worry about all that when you are in here. No food to buy or rent to pay!"

Maew had moved to Bangkok to work as a secretary three years ago. She had been very bright at school and had wanted to attend university, but Sergeant Yud and Mother Nong didn't see the point in her wasting so much time and money. At first the great capital had depressed her, the foul air and sticky heat, the beggars languishing on the pavements and overhead passes, stretching out their incomplete limbs to collect alms from passers-by. She missed the green rice fields, the buffaloes, the smell of wood smoke and the cool breeze blowing through the treetops in the village. She had found work as a secretary in a small trading company and sent home half her salary every month. She lived in a room in a big apartment block; it was two hours' bus ride away from the trading company. The building was so damp during the rainy season that her clothes and shoes grew white with mould. But it could have been worse. She tried to be a good daughter, and knew that sending money home was one way to show gratitude to her parents. It would also earn her some merit, although not nearly as much as her brother had earned by becoming a novice.

The novice shrugged his shoulders. "Do you know what happened to her?" he asked, tilting his chin towards the hall where the coffin was.

"The last I heard she was working in Bangkok. And it must have been a well-paid job because her parents just finished building a new house!"

"Can't you get a job like that?"

"I doubt it," exclaimed Maew, looking at him, "haven't you heard the rumours?"

"What rumours am I likely to hear when I'm stuck in here all day and night?"

"Use your imagination," said his sister, getting up. "I'd best get back; I think it's time to serve the food to the monks."

Sure enough, the chanting had stopped and the monks were coming to sit outside. The women had formed a line of helpers, dishing out rice and the *gaeng hang ley*. He knew he should go over and show his face. He spotted his mother, dressed in one of her silk sarongs, pouring out water into plastic cups. He couldn't bear to see her; he knew she would say something ridiculous, and embarrass him in front of everyone. Instead of making his way over to join the monks he walked around the pond in the opposite direction, past the village spirit shrine and behind the hall where all the gambling had been going on the night before. The hall was empty now, except for the dead woman. He entered the back door and walked over to the coffin, still open. It was quite an expensive casket, made out of thin strips of wood painted white and decorated with raised gilt flourishes. The novice looked inside at the body. The young woman was hardly recognizable to him now but he remembered her from school. She had been round-faced, with eyes a little too small and a nose a little too wide. She had been almost pretty, he remembered, and good-natured enough not to mind when he wanted to tag along with her and Maew when they played at their games. He couldn't recall exactly when she left the village to work in Bangkok. He supposed she must have come back during the festivals, at Songkran and Loy Krathong and the end of Lent, but he didn't actually remember seeing her. All he recalled was that her parents spoke of her with pride, telling everyone their daughter had a good job in Bangkok and had sent them money for their new house. It was a grand enough house, with red concrete roof tiles. It had a marble floor that his mother envied quite openly. So much cooler than wood, she always said. But now the young woman was dead. Her face and body seemed thin and worn. He could see a dark patch on her skin at the collar of her dress, two other patches on her hand and her cheek.

The jasmine flowers strewn around her barely concealed the formaldehyde, yet the novice didn't feel sickened. He hadn't been so near a woman's body since he was a child, except for his mother's or his sister's, which didn't count. His eyes travelled over the woman's emaciated body. Underneath the dress he thought he could make out the shape of her collar bones, her small breasts, her hips and the swell of her thighs. His head was thumping and his skin hot and prickly with a familiar excitement. Outside the hall he could hear the monks eating, clinking their spoons against the plates of delicious yellow curry. *My mother and the other women – they'll all be serving the village elders now*, thought the novice, as he pulled his hand out from under his saffron robe and reached it over the coffin-edge, where it hovered uncertainly before coming to rest, gently, on the curve of the woman's left breast.

Fat of the Land

"Quickly," barked the Police Chief, clapping his hands, "get dressed and get out. She'll be here any minute."

He pulled the bedcover back sharply; the naked girl scuttled for her clothes. Walking over to the mirror, he watched her reflection stepping neatly into a skirt, her long hair swinging forwards. He zipped up his trousers, the ripe, sweet taste of her still on his lips. His wife could arrive early, walk in, see the girl's bare breasts, glossy hair, narrow thighs, her tight, smooth skin. *What then?* he mused. He buttoned his jacket, smoothing it down in front of the mirror with the palm of his hand, wondering why his wife had come all the way up from the city this time. She had said on the phone that it was something "important". *Tho-eoi*, thought the Chief, *to her a broken fingernail might be "important"!* The Chief caught hold of the girl's arm.

"Next time," he murmured in her ear, "why don't you bring your sister along too?"

The girl bit her lip and nodded, sliding her feet into the little red shoes she had left at the door. Spinning round to face him, her eyes teased upwards.

"So many bills to pay this week, Chief... electricity, gas, water... and I have to make merit – it's my eighteenth birthday next week..."

He pulled some money from his trouser pocket, peeling off a five hundred baht note, handing it to the girl. She placed her

35

palms together in front of her chest, bowing her head in a deep *wai*. Opening the door of his quarters, the Chief gently pushed her out.

"Find Yud. He'll get someone to take you home."

The girl stuffed the note into her handbag, turning on her high heels, strutting across the path in the direction of the main building. *A most satisfactory arrangement*, he reflected. *She's young, pretty, discreet and undemanding – I'm growing quite fond of her.* He had known before moving to the country that the girls were beautiful, but what a pleasant surprise to find one so inexpensively maintained. He'd had problems with minor wives in the past: their jealousies and tantrums, their unreasonable demands for more money, cars, jewellery, apartments, holidays, clemency for relatives in trouble. *As if*, he thought, *I don't have a wife for all that!*

Other men managed it differently. He knew of one colleague who had his minor wife move in, share the family house with his first wife, their children. *But where's the fun in that? Isn't it better*, he thought, *to keep it all separate: marriage and sex, business and pleasure? Isn't trying to guess how much my wife knows part of the fun?* The Chief looked at his watch. *She should be here by now.* He picked up his radio from the bedside table and switched it back on. Reaching under the pillow, he pulled out a pistol, tucking it into the black leather holder attached to his belt. The radio crackled into life: "Control to Chief, control to Chief, come in Chief! Over!"

"Chief here. What is it Yud?"

"Someone to see you Chief."

"Right. Have her wait in my office. And take the other one home – make sure they don't bump into each other!"

"Oh no, sir, ahem, heh-heh, it's not your wife! It's a man, won't say what he wants, says he'll only do business with you, sir. Over!"

"OK, Yud. On my way."

What now, he wondered, *some idiot farmer complaining about his neighbour's buffalo?* The Chief shook his head, chuckling to himself as he strode across the grass to the station. *Maybe*, he thought, *someone has come in to complain about the price of Gimsia's bananas!* He looked up and saw, to his great irritation, Sergeant Pan hanging over the station balcony, staring blankly into the distance.

"*Aow*! Pan!"

"Sir!"

"Go and... and..." said the Chief, climbing up the steps wearily, "cut the grass!"

"Sir!" Pan saluted, standing aside to let the Chief pass.

Sergeant Yud was sitting at the front desk, his big paw digging into a bag of banana fritters, having underestimated how long his boss would take to get to the station. The Chief cleared his throat. Sergeant Yud jumped to his feet, the chair clattering backwards to the floor. The Chief looked him up and down, taking in the crumbs around his mouth, the unbuttoned jacket. Yud was fumbling at the buttons with greasy fingers but the jacket refused to fasten. Behind him, an officer was sweeping the floor slowly, while another was peering into a mirror, plucking at some stray whiskers on his chin. The Chief sighed.

"Right! Half-past seven this evening – I want you all assembled on the front grass! Full uniforms! Jogging three times round the village!" He paused for effect. "Now Yud, who's this man who has come to see me?"

"He's... em, well, he's, heh-heh..." Sergeant Yud leant over and widened his eyes dramatically, "...he's from over the border."

"Ah," said the Chief, turning to look through the glass door of his office at the back of the man's head. "Does he speak Thai?"

"Oh yes. But if you have any problems, Chief, you know you can call on me," said Sergeant Yud, drawing himself up to suck in his belly, "I can translate for you." He started to follow the Chief over, reaching the door of the office just in time to see it close in his face. Inside, the Chief pulled a blind down over the glass door.

"Hey Yud!" called Sergeant Pan from the lawn outside, "Chief's wife is here!"

Yud went over to the balcony and looked outside, groaning. A car had swung off the main road and up the station driveway, stopping by the balcony steps. The driver got out, putting up an umbrella before opening the back door. A figure emerged, trussed up in an expensive pink silk suit. Yud and Pan gawped at the elaborate coiffure, stiff with hairspray, the heavily powdered face, the eyebrows pencilled into disapproval, the pink lips pursed in disdain. *Maybe I should go to Gimsia's*, thought Yud with a shiver, *and fetch the Chief a bottle of whisky!*

"You," said the woman, pointing at Yud on the balcony, "fetch my bags from the car. And inform my husband I have arrived."

* * *

After two hours' walk across the steep terrain, Jamu came to rest at the edge of his secret field. It stretched out along the slope

38

for about half an acre, not far from the invisible, unmarked border. Jamu looked east, at the purple mountains of the Shan State. The air was cool and fresh, but Jamu could already feel the tell-tale signs: the headache, the sickening nausea gripping his stomach. He had been up to check the plants last week; most of the petals had fallen, a scarlet carpet at his feet. He looked around. The pods were dark green, swollen, their points already curving upwards. The poppies were ripe for harvest. It was late afternoon: the sun low in the sky. Rubbing tiger balm on his temples to ease the nausea caused by the plants, Jamu walked amongst the stems and pods, deciding on the best area to start work. He reached into the elaborately embroidered cloth bag he wore across his chest, drawing out a wooden handled tool with three flat iron blades attached to it. Starting at the far corner, he began to work backwards across the field, scoring the lower, more mature pods first. That way he would avoid brushing up against the stickiness. He examined the tips of each pod carefully, holding them gently between his fingers before drawing the tool vertically across to score two or three times at the side. A precise amount of pressure was required to milk the pods to their fullest potential: too much and the opium would flow too quickly, dripping to the ground; too little and it would harden in the pods. He stood back to watch the raw white sap ooze out slowly from the wounded pods before moving on to the next one. He left the opium to congeal in the cool air, to darken under the coming night sky. As he worked his way painstakingly across the mountainside, Jamu tagged the plumpest pods with a coloured string, marking out the ones he would later cut open and dry in the sun, saving the best seeds for next year's planting.

He tried to calculate in his head how much the harvest would yield. *Two, maybe three kilos?* If prices hadn't changed from last year, he might earn about fifteen thousand baht: a lot of money. The first priority was rice: the yield from his own upland rice fields was not enough to feed his family throughout the whole year. *Without the opium*, he thought, *how could we manage?*

A few winters ago government workers had come up from the district office down in the valley, promising Jamu's village a new irrigation system. You tribal people will be able to grow rice from wet paddies, they said, instead of depending on wild mountain rice, and you can cultivate tomatoes, beans, coffee. They had brought bright packets of new seeds, glossy pamphlets explaining how to sow and when to harvest the new crops. Nothing good had come of it. Jamu and his neighbours had tried growing the new crops. Floods destroyed most of the tomatoes and beans. The coffee plants did well, but when the mountain farmers made the long trek down to the city markets to sell their harvest, the prices offered by the city vendors barely covered costs. Jamu hated the city: the traffic, noise, heat, and worst of all the turned-up noses. *The government*, thought Jamu as he deftly scored another pod, *can keep their projects.* He glanced up at the sky, the sun starting to slip behind the mountain. *I should start for home soon.* He would return in the following days to scrape the hardened opium from the pods' surfaces, to score the pods again and again, to wring out as much of the thick gum as possible.

By the time he reached his mountain village it was almost dark. Candles burned in most of the houses, a few oil lamps. A fire had been lit in the clearing between the houses, with a group of six or seven people sitting close to it, other people scattered at a slight distance. Nights were chill this high in the mountains, and close to freezing during the dry winter months.

As he drew nearer to the fire he could hear a mixture of Thai and farang voices – another trekking tour. Over the past year or two such tours had become a regular feature in the dry season.

"*Aow* Jamu, my old friend!" called the Thai guide. "How would you like to earn some pocket money tonight?"

The guide came from the city; he had his own agency there. The man had been alone when Jamu had met him the first time, wandering around the mountains with an old army map. Jamu had taken him to his village, inviting him to sleep in his house, share his meals. The guide had stayed for several days. Jamu drew a new map for him, a much better one, showing all the different routes across the mountains, the location of other tribal villages, waterfalls, rivers and streams. In return, the guide had promised to bring his farang treks through Jamu's village.

"When did you get here?" asked Jamu, laying down his bag. He crouched behind the guide, staring without expression at the farang.

"Just before sundown. What a job I had getting them over the last summit! See the fat one over there? He was puffing like an old buffalo. Took hours! They're ready for a rest, something relaxing – you know what I mean?"

"Huh." Jamu continued to study the farang. It was quite hard to tell them apart in the firelight – big clumsy limbs, ghostly pale skin, and strange coloured hair. They dressed the same,

41

they sounded the same, they even smelt the same: of sweat and insect repellent. And all so very rich. The guide had told him once how much they would pay for the trek, for an airplane ticket, how much it cost for a night in a hotel. If they had so much money, Jamu had asked, why do they want to come up here? The guide had explained that foreigners liked to walk, look at views, and see how the tribal people lived, high up in the mountains. Life up here, said the guide, is more *traditional* than where they come from.

Jamu had seen postcards in the Chinese merchant's shop down in the valley, pictures of villages like his, of men like him, of fields of brightly coloured poppies. The farang liked them. They bought homemade souvenirs from the village women: purses, bags, colourful hats. A few of Jamu's neighbours had even sold their old jackets, leggings, antique coins. The farang were willing to pay good prices for any old broken junk. In the beginning, when the treks were a new thing, the children had hidden behind door posts, staring at the white people, their shoes and clothes, frightened by their loud booming voices. But these days the bolder children ran after them, giggling, daring one another to tug at their clothes. Sometimes the farang gave the children money too.

"So what do you say, Jamu?" The guide nudged him.

Jamu nodded. It would be rude to refuse. Anyway, he would be paid for preparing the opium pipes. Twenty baht a pipe – ten for the guide, ten for himself. Jamu got to his feet, gesturing for the group to follow him, to take off their boots before climbing the wooden steps up to his house.

His wife was under the house stilts, pounding rice, operating the long handle of the low wooden pestle with her bare foot.

Pok! Pok! Pok! The guide said something and the farang all peered into the rough wooden bowl where the husked rice lay. Jamu's wife glanced up, spat out red betel nut juice, wiped her mouth, then continued to pound.

Jamu led the group inside and lit a few small candles, motioning for his guests to sit on a split bamboo mat in the centre of the room. He slung his bag over a nail in the wall and reached up to a shelf, taking down a tin plate on which lay a small wooden box, a long pipe, a metal spike, a spirit lamp and matches. Jamu listened quietly to the incomprehensible sounds of the Thai guide talking to his group. The farangs followed Jamu's movements closely, glancing over at the guide every so often, nodding seriously. Now and then one of them seemed to ask a question. Jamu handed the guide a small square pillow. The guide lay down on his side and rested his head on it, still talking, gesticulating with his hands. The farangs laughed loudly. Jamu knelt down beside the guide and lit the spirit lamp, handing over the pipe. He opened the box, taking out a round opium pill about the size of a pea, which he impaled on the metal spike, drying it quickly over the lamp flame before inserting it into the pipe's tiny bowl. With slightly shaking hands, the guide turned the bowl over the flame of the lamp until the pill melted and began to vaporize. Then he stopped talking, putting his lips over the pipe to inhale greedily, sucking through the tube in one long inhalation, holding the smoke in his lungs for nearly thirty seconds before breathing out. One of the farangs whistled. Another one reached for a camera. The guide grinned at them, handing the pipe back to Jamu.

Jamu reached into the wooden box for another pill. The guide was a seasoned smoker, would need six or seven pipes at least. Then a few of the farang would try – some of them would vomit after one pipe. Jamu didn't smoke, never had, but the money was welcome. His share might come to about one hundred and fifty baht – not bad for a few hours' work.

* * *

The Chief's wife had walked down to the main road. Her husband "wasn't available". She tried to breathe deeply, slowing down her steps. *Imagine*, she thought, *having to wait outside my husband's office like that, all those men staring at me, that fat idiot of a sergeant attempting to make conversation? What was it he asked? How was the weather when she left the city? Had she eaten lunch? Did she feel sick on the journey up? Did she want to try a banana fritter?* She grunted with anger. She could feel beads of sweat running down her back, knew that there would be stains under her arms. The silk suit would be ruined.

The fat sergeant had offered to accompany her, worried that she might get lost. *As if anyone could get lost in this tiny backwater*, she fumed, glancing round at the wooden houses, the shabby striped awnings, the shop fronts. *And what is that? A man – well, it looks like a man – slumped against a tree, his lap filled with rubbish, muttering to himself. Is he begging? Should I give him some money?* She hesitated. *Better not – he might be dangerous.* She looked the other way instead, speeding up until she passed him, trying not to hobble. *I should have worn different shoes!* Her toes were pinched, but the new shoes matched the pink silk so perfectly. *I made a special effort! Over an hour this morning just for my hair!* She hadn't dared lean

44

her head back in the car, although all the bends and curves made her feel so sleepy. *And then*, she seethed, *I have to sit and wait to see my own husband! Sitting outside his office like a disgraced constable!* She pressed her pink lips tightly together and dabbed a handkerchief to her brow. To her left there was a busy noodle stall, and behind that there was an area covered with a corrugated iron roof. *Is that*, she wondered, *the market?* She crossed the road, walking past the green papaya salad stall. She would have bought some if the vendor and her husband hadn't been arguing. She strained to listen. They were shouting about money, and the wife looked close to tears. *Is this*, thought the Chief's wife, watching the husband stride off, *how people behave up here?* She walked on, past the noodle soup stall, inhaling the delicious aroma. *If only*, she groaned, *I'd had some lunch!* She hadn't wanted to break her new diet, especially after putting on another kilo in the last month. Things had been so stressful. She had put on five kilos since her husband's transfer from the city last year: the scandal had taken its toll.

She entered the shade of the covered stalls. *At least it's cooler here. But there aren't many stalls still open this late in the day. Why do these country folk have to stare? What are they whispering about?* She raised her chin. *What will I buy? The guavas look nice, but wait a moment, aren't those mangosteens over there? Yes!* Mangosteens were the Chief's favourite fruit. She walked over to the stall and picked one up, pressing the thick purple skin.

"They're ripe, madam," said Mother Noi, "I'll cut one open for you to taste, if you like." She cut along the dark skin, pulling off the top half to reveal the plump white flesh. "There madam – have a bite of that!"

The Chief's wife took the fruit, delicately picking out a small segment of flesh. It was very sweet.

"I'll take three kilos," she said, sure her husband would appreciate the gesture.

"Right, madam." Mother Noi packed the mangosteens into a bag. "Something more?"

The Chief's wife shook her head and pulled a pink five hundred baht note from her purse.

Mother Noi fumbled through her apron pocket and frowned. "Just a minute madam, I'll ask Mother Suree for some change."

Mother Noi hurried over to the papaya salad stall, and pulled on Mother Suree's arm. Suree turned around to look crossly at the Chief's wife. The vendor's eyes were red from crying. She raked through her money belt and drew out a bundle of smaller notes and coins. Mother Noi hurried back, counting out the change.

"Here you are madam. Sorry about that." Mother Noi smiled, turning to another customer.

The Chief's wife turned to go, noticing, on her way out, a sweet stall. *Coconut cakes. No, I shouldn't have coconut cakes.* She slowed down. *But surely one or two can't do any harm? I've had no lunch, after all.* Drawing a deep breath, she pulled in her belly. *Isn't the suit just a tiny bit looser around my waist than it was last time I tried it on?*

"Twenty baht of those," she whispered to Grandmother Gaysuda, pointing to the mouth-watering coconut cakes.

"Madam! Madam!" bellowed a male voice.

It was the fat sergeant, lumbering at her through the stalls, waving his hand in the air. "Chief asked me to come and fetch you. Have you finished shopping yet? *Oh-ho*, coconut cakes! They're very good. Heh-heh! A village speciality!"

The Chief's wife pulled her finger back from the cakes, regarding him coldly.

"Yud! Yud!" hissed a voice behind her. She turned round to find a woman at her elbow, a fawning smile on her lips. The Chief's wife quickly registered her clothes.

"Madam, this is my wife, Mother Nong."

Mother Nong simpered, putting her palms together in a deep *wai*, to which the Chief's wife had little choice but to respond.

"Is there anything I can help you with?" asked Mother Nong, hands clasped eagerly in front of her, her head inclined to one side. "Are you looking for something in particular? I'm sure you must find the selection in our little market very poor. We go shopping in the city whenever we get the chance." Mother Nong leant over to whisper. "The department store, of course. Isn't that right, Sergeant?"

Sergeant Yud cleared his throat. "Oh yes."

"If you will excuse me," said the Chief's wife, cornered in the narrow aisle between the stalls, "I should be getting back to the station. My husband is waiting." She turned to go, breathing in to squeeze sideways past Sergeant Yud, hurrying back outside, catching the heel of her shoe in the rough wooden planks that covered the drains. She jerked her foot free. A strand of hair fell over her face with the sudden effort.

"Your cakes!" shouted Mother Nong.

"Don't worry," cried Sergeant Yud, grabbing the bag, puffing out his chest, "I'll make sure she gets her cakes!"

* * *

47

The Chief reached across the desk for the envelope, picking it up to look inside.

"It's all there." The man leant forwards, elbows on the desk. "You'll get the other half once we hear our stuff has safely arrived in the city."

The Chief nodded. "That's fine. Just let me know the dates."

"No searches at the checkpoints?"

The Chief smiled, raising his eyebrows.

"Good." The man stood up, putting on a green army cap.

The Chief moved towards the door, opening it to let his visitor pass through just as his wife appeared on the steps to the station balcony. The Chief noted her flushed face, the too-tight suit, the slightly dishevelled hair. He sighed as she walked up to his office.

"Who was that?" demanded his wife. "What could be more important than seeing your own wife after she's travelled all the way up to this… this *place*?"

The Chief sat back down, lit a cigarette, leaning back in his chair. "Shall I turn up the air conditioner, my love? You look a little hot and bothered."

She felt his eyes travelling up and down her body. Reaching to push the stray hairs off her face, she remembered the sweat stains on her armpits and pulled her arms down quickly. *Too late*, she thought, *he's noticed. This is going all wrong! If only I'd worn something different! The dark blue, or the black dress, but he prefers bright colours, doesn't he? Why is he staring at me? I won't be beaten down!*

"You haven't answered my question," she said, "I hope you're not getting mixed up with *gangsters* again. I couldn't bear any more scandal!"

The Chief smiled, turning the cigarette between his fingers. "Scandal? Is that what you call it?" He put his head on one side. "I think it's worked out rather well for us. Haven't I increased your allowance? And now, at least, we don't have to live together any more!" He glared at her bitterly.

"Do you think our marriage brings me any pleasure? If I could have refused my father's wishes, I would never have married you in the first place!"

"Oh, is that right? Who else was going to marry you? Who, do you think, would have cleared all your father's debts for him? It took me long enough, I can tell you, to deal with that queue of creditors!"

The Chief's wife battled against the tears welling up in her eyes. "You needed his influence, you needed his contacts to help you get on, get promoted! Don't pretend you didn't!"

"Keep your voice down!" he spat.

Too late, she remembered the bag of mangosteens in her lap.

"I bought you some fruit," she whispered, holding it up, "your favourite…"

The Chief sat in silence, ignoring the proffered fruit. Smoke curled up from his cigarette to the ceiling. She lowered the bag to the desk.

"You said on the phone you had something important to discuss." He stubbed out the cigarette wearily.

"I do. But can't we spend some time together first? Go for dinner, for a drive? Isn't there supposed to be a lovely waterfall nearby? What about the guest house you told me about? I'd like to see how the building work is progressing. I can stay as long as you like. I've no engagements, really, until next week."

The Chief examined her curiously. "You may have nothing to do, but I have to work. This is a very busy time for me. But you wouldn't understand that, would you?" He got up to open the door. "I'll arrange for the driver to take you back in the morning. One of the men will take you to my quarters – you should shower and change." The Chief opened the door wide and clicked his fingers. "Yud! Over here! Then," he said, "you can tell me what this important business is all about."

The sergeant appeared, red-faced. "Your wife!" he panted, "left these in the market!" He handed over the coconut cakes.

"Yours, I believe," said the Chief, turning to his wife, holding the bag up to her face. "Yud, take my wife over to my rooms, make sure she's comfortable. Oh, and better get someone to change the bed sheets – she insists she's staying the night."

"Leave it to me, sir," said Yud, winking.

The chief watched them disappear down the steps. He looked around the empty station, checking his watch. *Twenty-five past seven – where are all the men? They're supposed to be jogging round the village in five minutes!* He shook his head and returned to the office, banging the door behind him. *I'll make them run,* he decided with a grin, *at midday tomorrow instead.* He fingered the fat envelope on the desk, slipped it into the inside pocket of his jacket. Opening the desk drawer, he took out a small folding knife, leaning across to pluck a mangosteen from the bag on the desk. He cut it open, biting with solitary pleasure into the sweet, sticky flesh.

* * *

Jamu woke before dawn. He had agreed to accompany the guide and his group back down to the valley. The guide's porter had fallen sick – too many pipes – and someone was needed to help carry the farangs' luggage and provisions back down the mountain. Jamu didn't mind. He had money now to buy things from the village: salt, matches, thread for his wife, some dried fish. His wife would go up to the opium field after tending to the animals, to collect the opium from the previous day and to carry on scoring the pods.

Jamu prodded the guide, who had fallen asleep on the mat in his house, and went outside to rake through the fire's embers, piling on new twigs to relight it, ready for boiling water in a large blackened kettle. He crouched by the fire. It would take at least an hour for the farangs to get up, wash, dress and eat breakfast. He unpacked the supplies: coffee, sugar, condensed milk, bread, jam, eggs. Easing off the kettle lid with a twig and gently dropping a dozen eggs into the water, he sat back on his heels and waited. A mist hung over the mountains, the air damp and cold. The sun would not break through until late morning. He watched the tourists emerge from the houses, rubbing their eyes, blankets wrapped around their shoulders, standing on one leg to put on their heavy leather boots. The guide appeared, calling out to his group as he came to sit next to Jamu, slapping him on the back. The tourists pulled out their cameras. They started to wander around, posing for one another, pointing and laughing at the piglets under the houses.

"It's their last chance," explained the guide, warming his hands at the fire, "to get some photos from a tribal village."

It took four hours to reach the valley, the guide in front, leading his stumbling group down the mountain trails, Jamu bringing up the rear with the heavy basket on his back. The sun was through, warming their backs as they walked. A mile or two outside the town, they stopped at the waterfall: the farangs wanted to bathe. The men were ready first, stripped down to their underwear, roaring as they plunged into the freezing water. The guide nudged the tribesman as the women emerged from behind some bushes, dressed only in bikinis. Jamu couldn't help but stare at the pale flesh, soft bellies, and large breasts as the women tiptoed, squealing, into the water. As he and the guide unpacked lunch, the farangs draped themselves over the warm rocks to dry.

A pick-up truck was already waiting for the guide and his trekkers in the town, parked across from the police station. The tourists climbed into the back, arranging themselves under the canopy. The guide sat in the front. As the driver started up the engine, the guide pulled a fifty baht note from his pocket, handing it through the open window to Jamu.

"Thanks, my friend. I'll be back soon with another load!"

Jamu nodded, watching the truck pull away, waving at the farangs in the back. He crouched by the roadside, deciding where he would go first. *Market or the Chinese merchant's shop?* The old Chinese man always tried to trick him into buying something he didn't want. *I should go there last*, he resolved, *when my money is almost spent.* He stood up, stretching his back. A motorbike slowed down on the opposite side of the road, the driver staring at Jamu from under a green army cap. Jamu stared back. It was the trader. For the past four or five years Jamu had sold his opium crop to him. He came from across the border, from the Shan State. Late at night, Jamu had listened to the trader's stories, his descriptions of life across the purple mountains, of villages burnt by Burmese troops, of a people determined not to surrender their land, their language and culture to an evil regime. The trader talked about how Khun Sa, the leader of the resistance, knew that drugs destroyed lives, but how else could they raise funds to fight? Jamu lifted his hand to wave at him. The trader smiled, saluting back. They would see one another again soon. Jamu picked up his bag and started to walk slowly along the road to the market.

From the balcony of the police station, the Chief's wife was gazing disconsolately at the village. She narrowed her eyes. *Isn't that a tribal man going past?* She could tell from his baggy trousers, the short jacket, the bag. *Didn't I hear someone saying they'd taken on a hill tribe maid who was very hard-working… I could speak to my husband about that. A new gardener maybe?* Over the years she had donated a great deal of money to organizations working to help the tribal peoples, building schools to teach them proper Thai, showing the women how to make handicrafts to sell, encouraging the farmers to give up their opium and move into other crops instead. Charity was her *raison d'être.* Her name was on dozens of plaques across the country, engraved in big letters next to the amount of money she had donated. She was known in the city for her generosity, invited to all the major charity receptions. *Why can't my husband understand that? Why do I have to beg for money each time? Doesn't he want to help the poor, the needy? Doesn't he want to improve his store of merit? I'm doing it for both of us!*

"Car's ready, Madam."

She leant back from the balcony, taking her weight on her feet, wincing at the blisters caused by the new shoes. She hobbled down the steps after the fat sergeant.

"My husband?"

"He… em… said to wish you a safe journey. He's very busy at the moment… and, heh heh… can't come out…"

The Chief's wife looked up at the station one last time before getting into the car. She rested her head against the leather seat and sighed. *I'll need another hair appointment as soon as I get back – I look a fright. And my pink suit is quite spoilt. Maybe a blue one would have been better after all; I'll speak to my dressmaker tomorrow. A dress and jacket maybe, with a bow at the back of the dress… yes, a bow.*

As the car swung out of the gates she saw two girls lolling against some railings – long hair, short skirts, slim legs. As the car passed they peeled themselves away from the railings, giggling, holding hands as they sauntered towards the station, swinging narrow hips. One of them seemed to lead the way, tip-tapping confidently ahead of the other in a pair of dainty red shoes.

The Widow Ghost

I'll make it th' last glass of moonshine, one for th' road. Lov'ly. S'quiet at the bar tonight. Where'd they go? Daeng 'n' Yud 'n' all th' rest? Scared of their wives or something? Here a moment ago. Then – whumf – gone. Jus' like moonshine, ha ha ha. Down in one gulp: tha's th' way. P'rfect. Nobody around to nag *me*, Uncle Nun had boasted earlier to his cronies, pointing to his chest with his thumb. Wife won't be back for another two months. Until then I can please myself. Ha ha!

"Another shot?" Lai leant over his bamboo bar, rubbing the glasses with an old cloth.

"Nah, Lai. S'time for bed. Where's everyone gone tonight 'nyway?" Uncle Nun swung his arm out at the village behind him, almost toppling his stool.

"Oh, those poor men with wives at home, Uncle Nun." Lai yawned dryly.

"Poor men. Guess I'll be off home too, Lai. Be seein' you tomorrow."

"Sweet dreams, Uncle Nun. And watch out for ghosts on the way home – remember, it's only been a few weeks since that girl's funeral…"

Uncle Nun grunted, climbing down carefully from the stool, which felt higher than usual. Immune to the cool air, he walked unsteadily along the road, empty now except for a few dogs curled up on the tarmac, lifting their snouts and growling as he staggered past. Most of the houses were in darkness, just the odd light still on. His place was at the end of the street, the last house in the village before the rice fields. *There we go*, he giggled to himself as he climbed the steps, *one, two, three!* He opened the front door, switching on the light. *Tho-oei!* He blinked. Two shiny cockroaches scattered in opposite directions across the dirty floor; one disappeared under the fridge, the other between the wooden boards. Uncle Nun guffawed. He opened the fridge for some water, wrinkling his nose at the smell as if it was someone else's fault. The shelves were empty except for a few bottles of water, a shrivelled half lime and a nub of galangal that was furry and blue round the edges. These days it was easiest to buy cooked food from the market. Rice and curry for breakfast, noodles at twelve from Aunty Wassana's stall, fried chicken with chilli paste and sticky rice most nights. And a few glasses of moonshine. *What more could a man ask for?* Uncle Nun shrugged. It's not as though he couldn't cook. His jungle stew was legendary. He made it every year on his birthday. Legendary was the word, his wife Mother Pensri said – a legendary mess in the kitchen to clean up. *Aow. What does she know?*

The only problem with market food was indigestion. The doctor had told him to avoid anything too spicy. Because of his ulcer or something. He belched and rubbed his stomach with one hand, rustling about with the other on the top of the fridge. *Where'd she put the Chinese medicine? Why're women always hidin' things? Tho-oei, might s'well go t' bed. Look for't in th' mornin'.* He stumbled into the bedroom and swayed. The bed sheets were crumpled. The mosquito net had been lying open all day. He pulled his shirt over his head without undoing the buttons, let it fall, and sank down, tucking the net around the bed, sighing. Now that he was on his own, there was lots of space to stretch out in. He rolled over to his wife's side, sniffing her pillow, the faint smell of talcum powder and face cream. He turned over on to his back, feeling the familiar acid rise in his throat. He belched and closed his eyes. A mosquito buzzed, biting his leg. Uncle Nun slapped at it, yawned noisily, and fell into another night of fitful sleep.

He had gone to sleep on his back, snoring, and dreamt that his wife was poking his ribs to make him turn over and shut up. Uncle Nun rubbed his eyes and looked over at the bedroom window, the shutters open to let the night breeze blow cool. He blinked. A white shape seemed to shine in the darkness outside. *Must be the moon*, he thought. His eyes opened wider. *It's not the moon.* The shape grew larger, became more distinct. *What is it? It looks like... yes...* Uncle Nun swallowed, propping himself up on his elbows. It was a young woman, moving in the night air towards the window. Suddenly she was shimmering inside, tiny feet barely resting on the wooden floor. She gazed at him from the corner of the room for a moment, her beautiful head on one side, then drifted over to his bed, pulling back the mosquito net. Uncle Nun watched her, transfixed. She knelt down and reached inside, stroking the side of his head with her pale, cool fingertips. A delicious heaviness overwhelmed his limbs. He sank back, pinned to the sheets. The woman's slim body was barely covered by a thin nightdress. Her long black hair brushed his naked chest as she leant over him. He could smell frangipani blossoms. She smiled with full red lips, showing perfectly formed little teeth, and whispered tender words in Uncle Nun's ear, words long forgotten, words his mother had soothed him to sleep with, uttered in the same velvet accents he had once used with his wife when they were young. Stirred into a deep yearning by his memories, he gripped her smooth arm and looked into her eyes. He saw naked, grinning lust. She hitched up her thin nightdress, moved her pale thighs apart and made to straddle him – *straddle him*, mind you – and only then did Uncle Nun come to his senses. He pushed the unnatural female aside, jumped up, fumbled his way out from the mosquito net and ran out of the house and into the breaking dawn, covered in sweat, in bare feet and old trousers.

"A widow ghost!" he cried out to the startled villagers on their way to the morning market. "A widow ghost has tried to steal my soul."

* * *

Since the morning of Uncle Nun's announcement, the village had been in turmoil. Rumours abounded. At first the ghost was seen once a week, then every night. It came from a darkly evil place somewhere beyond the valley, behind the mountains, far from the village. Some people guessed it was the ghost of the girl who had died in Bangkok, whilst the older villagers insisted it was the ghost of poor Gop's mother, the long dead Mali Foi Thong. It flew in high over rice fields, low through the village streets, in and out of the deserted stalls in the morning market. Uncle Daeng claimed to have heard it whooping over the field behind his house, then stealing across the backyards. Mother Nong whispered to her neighbours how she had found its bloody fingertips on her husband's laundry, left out on the washing line. It had upturned Mother Suree's vegetable baskets, and scattered children's toys. The widow ghost, said Mother Pon, the Chinese grocer's wife, had withered the tiny chillies on the bushes in her garden. And Sergeant Yud, after a night duty, told everyone how he had been forced to cover his ears and huddle with the prisoners in their cell to escape the hideous gulping noises of the ghost as it drank the blood of the old dog that slept behind the police station. The dog had been found dead in the morning, eyes glassy, fur rigid with fear. Mosquitoes got under tightly closed nets, glasses and plates were inexplicably dropped and smashed, rice and curry were spilt on floors, attracting armies of ants, and the noon breeze blew hotter than ever before. It was all the fault of the widow ghost. Children screamed, mothers wept and farmers furrowed their brows. *Something*, thought the Abbot, *has to be done*. He sat in the temple, cross-legged in the main hall, hands upturned in his lap, trying to make sense of it all.

The single men in the village were the most afraid. They knew the widow ghost had come for them. But it seemed there was little the Abbot could do to help them. Uncle Nun, whose wife was four hours' drive away in the city, had been the first to visit, kneeling in front of him with an uncommonly large offering of mangoes, lychees, lotus buds and an envelope of money, pleading for an incantation, a prayer, a piece of magic cotton to wear around his wrist to ward off the wicked ghost and her desire. The Abbot had responded with a standard Pali text, a sprinkling of holy water over Uncle Nun's head, and a piece of white cotton more sacred than magic. The Abbot didn't do magic. Magic was not his business, and it had never before been part of his religious duties to deal with widow ghosts.

He had been over the texts again and again and there was no mention of ghosts. And yet, with each day that passed, the line of men queuing to see him grew longer and longer; he saw the young and old, the divorced and widowed, the available and the abandoned. All of them were seeking powerful protection from the ghost. He could only offer them advice and a blessing.

"Adhere to the Five Precepts. Make some merit. Keep your feet firmly on the Middle Path. Fill your head with righteous thoughts and your heart with compassion. *Saddhu, saddhu, saddhu!*"

The men nodded, performing respectful *wais* in front of the Abbot. As soon as they were outside the temple, they shook their heads and bit their lips, exchanging worried glances. Prayers were not enough. Frenzy about the ghost increased. There was more than one ghost, some said – a band of widow ghosts was roaming the countryside looking for men to seduce, take as husbands and kill. An old man chanced to die in his sleep. Was he the ghosts' latest victim? The men turned from religion to the Shan Fortune Teller. On his advice, wooden phalluses were hastily carved, and hung from the village gateposts and in almost every doorway to distract the ghosts. One farmer even complemented his wooden phallus with a pair of testicles made out of coconut shells, and wove an impressive thatch of pubic hair from an old fishing net. The authenticity of his phallus made him the envy of every man in the village. By now many of those who considered themselves to be most at risk were wearing red nail polish to fool the widow ghosts into thinking they were women. Uncle Nun was seen wearing an old blouse that Mother Pensri had left behind when she went to work in the city. Uncle Moon, now drinking two bottles of whisky a day instead of his usual one, had taken to wearing a sarong instead of trousers and had attached at least half a dozen carved penises to the village dustcart.

The drunken games of poker started to last all night, ensuring the men were kept awake, together, safe from attack. Business at Lai's moonshine stall was particularly brisk. Even the most confirmed bachelors were looking for women to whom they might propose. But to whom? There had been a shortage of women in the village since Sia Heng, the local Chinese businessman, had invited his rich cousin to visit. The cousin had used the opportunity to recruit female workers for his fruit processing factory in the city. Apart from the managers, his workforce was all women; he could pay them less and trust them more. Even some married women had joined the recruitment drive, eager for a regular wage and a chance to experience city life, a bit of independence. Fathers, brothers, husbands were left to fend for themselves. The Abbot in his temple shook his head sadly. It wasn't right. The natural order of things had been upturned. He couldn't deal with this on his own. He sighed, deciding that the only way forwards was to speak to the village Headman, and call a meeting of the elders.

* * *

The meeting was held in the temple's main hall. A semicircle of elders faced the Abbot, whose superior status allowed him to sit with his back to the Buddha statue. Portraits of the great Thai kings adorned one wall: Taksin, Mongkut, Chulalongkorn and Bhumibol, whilst a colourful mural of the Buddha's ten incarnations filled the length of the other. Electric fans on either side blew the mosquitoes off course. The evening was warm and sticky. Nature was slipping into the hot season, when tempers would run notoriously short. The Abbot cleared his throat and began.

"Well, all of you know why we are here tonight. I am disturbed by these attacks," the Abbot waved his wand absently, "these so-called attacks on the village by... hmm... ghosts."

"Not just any old ghosts," said the District Officer. He had read a great many books on the subject. "*Widow* ghosts."

"Not necessarily," interrupted the Headman, "it *could* be the ghost of a woman who died in—"

"*Tho-oei!*" exclaimed the Schoolmaster. "There's no such thing as ghosts, widowed or otherwise. Who's actually seen these ghosts, apart from Uncle Nun? Uncle Nun! Drunk every day on moonshine? Ghosts? Hallucinations, more like."

"The question is," said the Abbot, hoping to prevent the meeting from collapsing into the usual bickering, "how to allay everyone's fears about the ghost, real or imagined."

The Headman cleared his throat and took a deep breath. The other men cast their eyes heavenward, waiting for the usual boring speech to begin.

"The problem of the widow ghost," he began, "reminds me of a problem I encountered in the year 2522,[1] in the month of June. Or was it July? It may have been July. Hmmm. At that time a similar excitement had taken hold of the village. Yes, a similar excitement. There was this old woman who made sweets and desserts. Now, what was her name? Let me see... yes, Grandmother Rung... Grandmother Rung was very old, perhaps eighty at the time – a very fine age to live to, if you

1. The Thai calendar counts from the birth of the Buddha, which supposedly took place 543 years before the birth of Christ.

ask me." The Headman paused to nod wisely, wagging his forefinger at the rest of the group. "She was a healthy woman. Two boiled eggs every morning for breakfast. I remember her telling me. Two boiled eggs. That was her secret. Grandmother Rung never suffered a day's illness in her—"

"Could we get to the point?" the Schoolmaster interrupted.

"I was just getting to it," huffed the Headman. He was older than the Schoolmaster and didn't take kindly to such disregard for his age and position. "Grandmother Rung had a young apprentice. Mali was her name, Mali Foi Thong. Hmmm." He sighed, shaking his head. "Both Mali *and* her mother died in childbirth. Tragic. Well, it wasn't long before Grandmother Rung was telling everyone that the ghost of her young apprentice had visited her in the night. The villagers were in a state of terror! That's when we decided to hold a merit-making ceremony. I mean, think about it! The ghost of a woman who dies in childbirth?" The Headman shuddered. "We held a big ceremony. A *suepchada* ceremony. It worked. The ghost of Mali never appeared… until, that is…" The Headman cleared his throat. "Anyway, I propose we do the same now."

"*How ingenious*," said the Schoolmaster sarcastically. "What do you think, Abbot?"

"Well, a merit-making ceremony can never be a bad thing. Brings the people together as a community, encourages them along the right path."

"But aren't we going too far?" asked the Schoolmaster. "By arranging a ceremony, aren't we vindicating belief in the ghost's existence? Is that wise? Does it not merely set a precedent for more scares, hauntings, strange sightings, and who knows what?"

The Headman and the District Officer winked at each other. They weren't entirely sure what the words "vindicating" and "precedent" meant, but such words were typical of the Schoolmaster, who was from Bangkok. Even though he had lived in the village for twenty years, he still stuck to his central dialect and his highfalutin nonsense.

"Well, what's your suggestion then?" asked the District Officer.

"We should calmly examine the reasons behind such frenzy. *Aow*, grown men – carving penises out of wood, wearing wigs and nail polish! All because one drunken fool had a bad dream?"

The District Officer coughed. A few weeks ago his wife had gone to visit her mother, who lived in another village, and was yet to return. He felt that her absence left him vulnerable to attack. Rather than take any chances, he had been going to bed at night wearing his wife's nightgown, with a huge wooden phallus hanging above the front door.

"What are these reasons?" asked Sia Heng.

None of the men were sure that Sia Heng should be at the meeting. When had he become a village elder? Someone had invited him along just because he was rich and successful. The men looked around, each suspecting the other of inviting Sia Heng.

"Well," said the Abbot, "could the fact that so many of our women are absent have something to do with it?"

"And we've got Sia Heng to thank for that!" shouted the District Officer, excited at finding a scapegoat. "If you hadn't invited that cousin of yours to visit, the one with the fancy fruit-processing factory, there wouldn't be so many men without wives."

"That's right," chipped in the village Headman, "it's hardly natural!"

"No wonder we are being attacked by widow ghosts – the ghosts are drawn to our village because so many men are on their own now!" concluded the District Officer.

"Gentlemen, gentlemen, calm down." The Abbot raised his hands, shaking his head sadly from side to side. It was always like this. He should have found a way to solve the problem by himself.

"Is it my fault if the village women want to leave and work in a factory?" asked Sia Heng. "Surely the extra money they bring home can only improve the village economy? Since when was it wrong for people to contribute to the family purse by working away from home?"

"Women though? It's not right," said the Headman. "In the old days they stayed at home and we knew where they were, what they were doing. Women off alone in the city isn't right. Coming back home with ideas. I should know. Look at my granddaughter. Two years working in Bangkok and she won't listen to anyone now. Doesn't want to get married, even though she's twenty-three. Drinks beer and smokes cigarettes. Spends half her money on clothes and going to the cinema."

"And it's anyone's guess what these girls get up to with young men in the city," said the District Officer, fanning his red face with a folded newspaper.

"What if they do?" shouted the Schoolmaster. "This is supposed to be the modern age, isn't it?"

"*Modern*?" sneered the District Officer. "Is that what you *city* people call staying out all night and sleeping around?"

At that the Schoolmaster made to get up, reminding himself just in time to bow three times to the Buddha statue before leaving. "Oh, do whatever you like," he told them wearily. "Have your *suepchada* ceremony if it makes you feel any better."

"It's all very well for him," said the District Officer, watching him go. "He's got a wife for protection. What about the rest of us? It's our civic duty to protect those most at risk!"

"I second the idea of a merit-making ceremony, and I'm willing to meet most of the costs," said Sia Heng, knowing his generosity would go a long way to repairing his standing in the village.

"That's kind of you, Sia," said the Headman. "And we haven't forgotten it was you who paid for the new temple roof."

"Yes, very generous," said the Abbot, eager to bring the matter to some sort of close. "We all agree then, a merit-making ceremony is the best way forwards?"

The District Officer nodded, happy that Sia Heng would be paying for it. It would be an excuse for a big party. The women working away in the fruit processing factory might even be able to come home for it, said the Headman, and Sia Heng promised to speak to his cousin about it. The women would certainly be needed anyway, added the Abbot, to prepare the food. He found it comforting to think that many of his regular alms-givers would be back for a few days – maybe the monks and novices could look forward to something more substantial than the instant noodles they had been relying on recently.

* * *

"Hey Lai, set me up another round!" said Sergeant Yud, red-faced.

"Eleven Tigers or Widow Ghost?" asked Lai, pointing to the different coloured bell jars behind him.

"Make it a Widow Ghost. And wait till you hear what Sergeant Pan dreamt the other night after a few glasses of your new blend."

Lai laughed. The mixture had become a great favourite.

"Still no sign of Uncle Nun then?" asked the Sergeant, peering down the road.

"Not since—"

"His hilarious sword dance!" concluded Yud, guffawing.

Apart from Uncle Nun's sword dance, the ceremony had been a success. Sia Heng had not only bought in a generous amount of whisky, but had also hired a karaoke machine. Singing lasted well into the night. The Schoolmaster had remarked to the Headman that if the cacophony didn't scare away the supposed ghosts then nothing would. The Headman had nodded sagely, not knowing what cacophony meant. The District Officer felt much more comfortable now that his wife was home again, and the Abbot was happy the village had shored up on its store of merit. The farmers were even convinced it would help the rains start a little earlier, and so were looking forward to a bumper rice crop. When Mother Pensri and the other women who had gone to work in the city found out what their menfolk had been up to – wearing women's clothes, painting their finger nails and staying up all night to drink and gamble, most of them decided to give up their jobs and come back home. The days of widow ghosts, it would seem, had passed.

Only Uncle Moon was unconvinced. He refused to unfasten the phalluses from the dustcart. Sergeant Yud took them off one afternoon while Uncle Moon, blind drunk, was snoring in the *sala* next to Gop. At dawn the next day, when Uncle Moon realized his loss, he abandoned the dustcart and walked up to the old Fortune Teller's cave. He emerged at nightfall, exhausted, wearing around his neck one of two small penis amulets that the Fortune Teller had sacralized in a ceremony lasting several hours. The other amulet hung around the Fortune Teller's neck. It wasn't just that they were single men and thus more susceptible to attack. Both Uncle Moon and the Fortune Teller had their own reason to dread the tragic spirit of a young woman called Mali Foi Thong.

The Sword

It was not as though Mother Pensri had never seen foreigners; she saw them every Saturday night on Channel 7. But the American films that Uncle Nun, her husband, loved to watch were all dubbed into Thai, so the actors' mouths moved uncomfortably out of synch with the words. She had the vague feeling there was something suspicious about the foreign actors – it was as though they didn't mean what they seemed to be saying. Too much running around and shouting, waving guns, undressing and kissing, for her liking. But the actors were certainly better looking than most of the real farangs she had seen in Chiang Mai. They came up from Bangkok and the south to visit the famous northern capital, to buy silks and souvenirs at the night bazaar, to wonder at the ancient temples, to smack their lips at the excellent food. Their bare white arms, fleshy shoulders and plump legs enthralled her, as did the way they strode around in the hot sunshine even though they could, she presumed, so easily afford to hire a taxi or a *tuk tuk*.

Over the last year or so, farangs had even started to venture as far as the village, especially in the winter months when the weather was dry and cool. They took pictures of the rice fields, of farmers posing stiffly beside their buffaloes, of smiling women frozen over their wares in the marketplace; they climbed mountains and admired views. The way of life in the remote hill tribe villages scattered across the mountains was of particular interest to them: the colourful costumes, opium pipes and strong marijuana. Mother Pensri couldn't understand it. There was no electricity in many of the mountain villages and she knew for a fact there was no sanitation. But it didn't put off the farangs. They bought homemade knick-knacks from the Lesu people to take back home: cheap cotton wristbands, pom-pom hats and shoulder bags. One old man had so fallen in love with the simple lifestyle that he had married a young Lesu girl. A great deal of money had exchanged hands, Mother Pensri had heard.

Once, on the bus coming back home the city, she had sat next to a young farang. He had struggled onto the crowded bus with a huge rucksack. The driver had made it clear the rucksack should go on top of the bus with the rest of the luggage – the battered suitcases, sacks of crispy pork skins and boxes of newly harvested *lamyai* – but the young man was resolute in his refusal. He squeezed in next to Mother Pensri, his giant knees wedged painfully against the seat in front, hugging the rucksack on his lap during the three-and-a-half-hour journey. Mother Pensri had watched him out of the corner of her eye, wrinkling her fat little nose. He was red and hairy. His arms were especially hairy, and freckled too, which was doubly unfortunate.

Halfway into the journey she had caught his eye and smiled, nodding her head, giggling, racking her brain for the few English words she had learnt at school. Where you go? she had asked. The young man had answered with a long sentence. *At least his mouth matches the words*, she had thought, nodding. He had reached into his rucksack, pulling out a dog-eared book, which he opened at a page featuring a map of north Thailand. The young man had pointed at a dot on the map and

Mother Pensri had nodded again, pointing at the road winding upwards in front of them, at her chest, then back at the dot on the map. He repeated her gestures and they had both smiled. She had offered him some fried banana, urging him to eat the whole bag. They had looked through the book together, at the pictures of markets, tropical fish, southern sunsets, temples, traditional costumes, festivals, mountain mists and pretty girls, at the old men with wrinkled faces peering humorously at the camera. She tried to teach him a few Thai words, pointing at the photographs, laughing at his mispronunciations. Mother Pensri especially liked the images of Bangkok. She had never been as far as the great city, but she had a beautiful poster of the glittering tiled roofs and golden spires of the Grand Palace on her wall at home. She had saved it from an old calendar.

* * *

A few days later she saw the young man in the marketplace, sitting with a group of farangs at Aunty Wassana's noodle soup stall. She went over to chat to Aunty Wassana, smiling and waving at the man.

"So, even farangs can eat your noodle soup then, Wassana."

"You wouldn't believe it, Mother Pensri! I'm busier than ever. I've been up all night making pots of stock. The only problem with the farangs is they sit for hours on the stools after their soup is finished. Some of my regulars have to take their soup home and eat it there."

Trust her to complain, thought Mother Pensri, determined not to give the new gold bracelet on Aunty Wassana's wrist a second glance.

"Still selling lottery tickets, Mother Pensri?"

"Oh, when I've got time." Mother Pensri fumbled in her pocket for her notebook. "Any numbers for next week, Wassana? Looks like you might be in the middle of a lucky streak right now."

"I've no time for *gambling* these days, Mother Pensri. I've got a business to run."

Mother Pensri turned away, bristling. *What's wrong with selling lottery tickets?* It was all very well for Wassana, who had a husband working abroad in Saudi Arabia. *Anyway, whom does Wassana think she's kidding?* Mother Pensri had seen her at that poor girl's funeral last month, sitting with all the other poker players and fleecing them bare. *No time for gambling indeed!*

Mother Pensri trudged between the market stalls. *Doesn't Wassana realize I have to earn a living somehow? What else am I supposed to do?* She pursed her lips. *If only that job in the fruit-processing factory had worked out.* But when she had gone away to work in the city with her daughter and the other village women, her husband had done nothing but drink, making his ulcer play up so badly that he started having nightmares about ghosts.

"*Aow!* Mother Pensri."

It was the Schoolmaster, hurrying over to one of the vegetable stalls where she was staring angrily at a mound of aubergines.

"Yes, Schoolmaster? Are you after a lottery ticket?"

"No, no, nothing like that. I wanted to ask you a question."

"A question? About what?"

"Well, I heard from the District Officer's wife that you have a very rare old Shan sword in your house. Is that true?"

"Yes. It belonged to my husband's great grandfather. Would you like to see it?" Mother Pensri looked up at him, shielding her eyes from the hot afternoon sun. "Are you preparing a lesson about swords, Schoolmaster?"

"I have a visitor – a foreign visitor – who would be most interested in seeing the sword."

"A farang?"

The Schoolmaster cleared his throat, reluctant to use the vaguely insulting word, yet anxious not to offend Mother Pensri.

"Yes, a... farang. An anthropologist."

"A what?"

"An anthropologist, Mother Pensri," repeated the School-master in the tone of voice he found worked best with his pupils. "An *an-thro-pol-o-gist.*"

* * *

On the evening of the following day, Mother Pensri was at home waiting nervously for the anthropologist and the Schoolmaster. Entertaining a farang inside her house was quite another prospect from sitting next to one on the bus. She had been awake all night worrying about what to offer him. *Fruit? Watermelon or pineapple? Maybe he'd like some green papaya salad? Or something cooked? Did the occasion merit some* gaeng hang ley? *But would the anthropologist like chilli, and be able to eat rice? Didn't farangs only eat potatoes and bread? And yet,* she had reasoned, *hadn't she seen some of them enjoying Aunty Wassana's soup?* Mother Pensri swept the floor one last time. She wondered if the Schoolmaster would bring the anthropologist along past the marketplace, in front of Aunty Wassana's noodle stall. She thought with satisfaction of the expression that would appear on Wassana's face when she saw the Schoolmaster lead the foreigner up the steps of Mother Pensri's house. She went over to look out the window. *But where*, she wondered, *has Nun disappeared to? Has he gone to Lai's whisky stall?* She hadn't told him about the visit.

Isn't that them now, coming along the road? It must be! Mother Pensri hid the broom and looked in the mirror one last time, smoothing back her hair, examining her teeth for specks of food, grinning sideways at her reflection.

It amazed Mother Pensri, as she invited her guests inside: the farang was a – was she? *No.* Mother Pensri peered closer. *Yes!* The farang was a woman. And fifty-one, the same age as herself – this was one of the first questions she asked the Schoolmaster to translate. *The same age!* Mother Pensri would never have guessed. The woman's casual dress and easy manner made her seem so much younger. She was thin for a farang, and tall, with pointed elbows and a sharp nose. She wore her hair very short and made no attempt to cover the grey. *Yes*, thought Mother Pensri, *she looks a bit like a man.* She had small square glasses that rested halfway down her long nose, and two deep furrows ran across her big forehead. *Too much thinking*, Mother Pensri reflected, *isn't good for you.* She stared at the skin on the woman's neck and hands – it was all loose, lined and freckled. *And she's not so white. Quite sunburnt actually. Her nose is peeling. Doesn't she wear a hat when she goes out in the sun?* She wore no jewellery except for a tiny silver cross on a chain around her neck. *She must be a Christian*, decided Mother Pensri with a sniff. *They all are.* The first farang Mother Pensri had ever seen was a Christian missionary. She was a little girl then. She had gathered with her friends to stare at him and his big black bag full of Bibles. He had disappeared into the mountains to stay in a hill tribe village. It had taken him years to convert them.

The anthropologist's bag was full of cameras and lenses, tripods, books. Mother Pensri smoothed back her hair again and whispered to the Schoolmaster to ask the woman how many children she had, glancing over at the photograph of her own daughter Kwan. *It's a pity*, she thought, *Kwan isn't here. She's clever at English. She'd know what to say. What was that? No children? No husband either?* Mother Pensri clicked her tongue against her teeth and felt sorry for the woman. *Who*, she asked herself, *is going to look after her when she's old?*

"Our visitor," said the Schoolmaster, anxious not to waste any more time, "is carrying out a field study of old Burmese and Shan swords and daggers."

"Oh, you won't find many old swords in the fields," answered Mother Pensri blithely. "Most of them are kept indoors these days, Schoolmaster."

"Ahem. Yes, Mother Pensri. What I meant was that this lady is *collecting information* about swords. For a big *museum*. A big museum in *London* in *England*."

"I see," said Mother Pensri, smiling brightly and nodding.

"So it would be useful, Mother Pensri, if we could *see* the sword."

"Of course, Schoolmaster. I'll just go and fetch it."

Uncle Nun kept the sword in the glass-fronted cabinet with all the other family treasures: Mother Pensri's wedding silk, the Burmese lacquerware box, her grandfather's Pali manuscripts, some faded photographs, a pile of magazines, and her daughter's old teddy bears, frayed noses pressed against the glass. Mother Pensri padded over to the cabinet, unlocking the door with a tiny key she always wore around her neck. The sword lay on the bottom shelf, wrapped in newspaper. She lifted it out carefully and brought it over, laying it in front of her two guests. To be honest, Mother Pensri didn't care for the sword. Uncle Nun's father had passed it down to him as part of the dowry which had included a buffalo, a gold necklace with a ruby pendant and two thousand baht – quite a lot of money in those days. The buffalo had been sold a long time since, and Mother Pensri planned to give the necklace to her daughter on her wedding day. With any luck, her daughter would find a good man. But the sword, though rare and beautiful, left Mother Pensri cold. It reminded her of her wedding ceremony, of her mother's fluttering hands and her father's grimly determined face, of a younger Nun dancing in front of their guests in a drunken imitation of a ceremonial sword dance – a distant memory she tried to shake off as she watched the Schoolmaster unwrap the newspaper.

The anthropologist picked up and admired the scabbard for a very long time, scrutinizing its silver chape, then slowly pulled the sword out and ran her fingers across the decorative hilt and along the thick, still sharp blade. Mother Pensri shuddered and went into the kitchen to fetch a tray piled with fruit, sticky cassava sweets and a pot of steaming jasmine tea.

As she poured the tea the Schoolmaster and the anthropologist were deep in conversation. A glossy book lay open at a page with pictures of similar swords. Mother Pensri pushed the plate of cassava sweets in the direction of her guest, smiling and nodding with raised eyebrows to encourage the woman to taste the sweets, which had taken several hours to make.

"The anthropologist would like to know," said the Schoolmaster, helping himself to the sweets, "how old you think the sword is."

"Hmm... Uncle Nun's great-grandfather..." Mother Pensri calculated rapidly, an expert with numbers. "Maybe one hundred and fifty years?"

The Schoolmaster and the anthropologist talked together in low, urgent voices, flicking though the pages of the book and examining the sword's hilt with a magnifying glass. The anthropologist still hadn't touched her tea or tasted the sweets.

"This sword," said the Schoolmaster at last, brushing crumbs from his shirt front, "is most valuable, Mother Pensri. It dates back to the nineteenth-century wars between the Shans and the northern Thais. It's a near-perfect example of its kind. A rarity. A one-off. An *antique*. Think of it, Mother Pensri: your forefathers probably used this very sword in battle, defending the village." He leant over her, his voice low. "It might even have been used to fight off the foreign invaders, to keep the colonialists at bay. The only country in the region not to be colonized, just think about that." He leant back again and folded his arms triumphantly. "Have you any idea, Mother Pensri, just *how* valuable this is?"

Mother Pensri gazed at the sword with a new respect. *What,* she pondered, *is the Schoolmaster suggesting? Is the sword worth a lot of money?* She cleared her throat.

"*Aow!* Of course I know it's valuable. It's an antique. One hundred and fifty years old, at least. Maybe older." Mother

Pensri could feel the eyes of the anthropologist and the Schoolmaster upon her, and felt that further information was expected from her. "My husband Uncle Nun," she tried, "is a fine sword dancer. Did you see him at the *suepchada* ceremony last week? He never misses an opportunity to dance with the sword."

The Schoolmaster and the anthropologist leant together and conferred for several minutes. The anthropologist produced a calculator from the bag. The Schoolmaster shook his head and the anthropologist shrugged, glancing up at Mother Pensri.

"Mother Pensri," he began, the tips of his long fingers placed together in a pyramid, "the anthropologist is interested in your sword. So interested, in fact, that she is willing to *buy* it, take it back to London *in England* and hang it up in the museum. To give it pride of place in an exhibition. For *posterity*."

Mother Pensri stared at the Schoolmaster, the tips of his fingers, her mind racing, wishing she knew what posterity was. *What will Nun say if I sell his sword?*

"How much?"

"Fifteen thousand baht, Mother Pensri."

Mother Pensri patted her hair and looked through the doorway, outside the house, to where dusk was falling on the village. Men and children were making their way home to bathe, to rest after work and school, to eat. She didn't have much time. *Tho-oei! No time at all*, she panicked, hearing heavy bare feet sound on the steps up to the house. Mother Pensri felt the familiar sinking of her heart that occurred whenever her husband came home. She glanced from the door to her guests and back again. But instead of the husband she expected, Sergeant Yud appeared in the doorway, breathing heavily, weaving slightly, bemused at the scene before him. Tripping over the tray and upsetting the cassava sweets, he sank, like a circus elephant, to his knees, and brought his palms together in front of his nose, bowing elaborately first to the Schoolmaster and then to the farang. His sense of propriety satisfied, he leant back, turning to Mother Pensri with raised hands.

"Moth'r Pensri," he slurred, "your husband's at th'whisky stall. Sleepin'. Fell off th'stool." Sergeant Yud giggled. "Cel'brations." He jabbed his thumb proudly at his fat chest, grinning around the room. "Won at th'cock fight."

Mother Pensri stared at the sergeant, momentarily lost for words, then began picking up the cassava sweets. Some of the sweets had landed on the anthropologist's book, sticking to the open page. The Schoolmaster sniffed loudly and examined his watch.

"Won at th'cock fight," repeated Yud.

"Oh, well done!" said Mother Pensri through gritted teeth. "Now, hadn't you better go back to the whisky stall? I'll be along to fetch Nun home just as soon as I can." She glared at Yud, tilting her chin to her guests meaningfully. After a few seconds Sergeant Yud wagged his big head up and down, then backed obediently out of the room on all fours, turning at the door to negotiate the steps. Mother Pensri waited until he'd gone, cleared her throat and held her head high.

"Thirty thousand."

The Schoolmaster turned to the anthropologist, whispering.

"Twenty-two," he said at last.

"Twenty-eight," said Mother Pensri, ignoring the Schoolmaster, holding up eight fingers to the anthropologist. The thin woman nodded, smiling over the tops of her glasses at Mother

Pensri, as though the two women had known one another for a long, long time.

* * *

"Well, Mother Pensri, I see you had some important guests last night," Aunty Wassana said.

"Important guests? I suppose you could say that, yes. The Schoolmaster brought a farang to look at Uncle Nun's old Shan sword. She took many photographs. For an exhibition." Mother Pensri cleared her throat. "In a *museum*. In *London*. In *England*."

Mother Pensri didn't give Aunty Wassana time for any more questions, moving past the noodle stall quickly. The sale of the antique was her business. The transaction had been swift; tissue paper was produced from the anthropologist's bag to wrap up the sword, and the money had been passed over before she could even think to change her mind. After the Schoolmaster and the farang had left, Mother Pensri had rolled the money up into a tight bundle and hidden it amongst her underwear. Then, before going to the whisky stall to collect Uncle Nun, she had gone into the backyard with his long knife and chopped down a length of bamboo. She had wrapped the bamboo up in the old newspaper, laying it in the wooden cabinet, next to the faded wedding pictures. Her dowry. It would be months before her husband would find out. The Schoolmaster wouldn't say anything; she had his word. He wouldn't want Uncle Nun on his tail anyway. Nun wouldn't look for it until the end of Lent celebrations. *No more embarrassing ceremonial sword dances*, she thought victoriously.

Mother Pensri made her way quickly from stall to stall. Dawn was often the best time to catch the vendors. Some of them might have had dreams that could be interpreted as particular numbers to buy in next week's underground lottery.

The early morning bus back to the city was just leaving, pulling out on to the road from the bus station beside the market. Everyone glanced up to see who was on the bus, as everyone always did. *Isn't that Mother Suree's husband at the back, sitting next to a young girl? Yes*, thought Mother Pensri, *it is! So maybe the rumours about him having taken a minor wife are true after all...* Mother Pensri's gaze moved along the rest of the bus. The anthropologist was sitting near the front, squashed against the window, a huge rucksack wedged on her knees, glasses pushed up on top of her grey hair. She looked even younger without her glasses on. *She's brave*, thought Mother Pensri, *brave to be travelling alone in a foreign country with no man to protect her. And carrying all that money on her, too: anything could happen.*

The farang smiled, waving at Mother Pensri as the driver changed gears and the bus trundled along the village main street, gathering speed.

The Relic

If I make a noise will they give me another cigarette? Then it won't be so bad: the voices grow quieter, softer when he is smoking. Sergeant Yud posted one through the prison bars earlier, though not without some teasing. Oi Gop-Guu, the policeman had shouted, want a smoke? But when Gop shuffled over to get the cigarette, Sergeant Yud withdrew his hand, laughing. "Say 'please' Gop," he had said, "where are your manners?"

In the cell he has no stuff, it was confiscated early that morning when he was locked up. Now he has nothing to do with his trembling hands; his old papers, his plastic bags, his left over bamboo strips, and all the many cigarette butts he had collected have been thrown away in a green plastic bin. He rocks back and forth inside the cell, moaning gently, glancing at the policeman. *Some good stuff in that pile*, Gop senses, *which I didn't have time to sift properly.* He likes to sort it in the evening, under the shelter of the little *sala*, at the edge of the village. He watches the lights in the houses going out, one by one, and falls asleep, his stuff arranged into careful piles at his side. The voices demand this of him. Then the old dustcart comes to waken him, rattling and chugging past in the early morning, Uncle Moon at the helm. Uncle Moon stops at the *sala* and gets down, shaking his head, threatening to sweep Gop away in the cart with the rest of the rubbish. But he never does. Instead he takes one hand out of its big dirty glove and unscrews the cap from the half bottle of whisky kept in his back pocket. After taking a swig, Uncle Moon looks at the bottle, holding it at arm's length as though reading the label for the first time, smacking his lips before screwing the lid back on, putting it away. He stands with his hands on hips, looking at Gop. What should I do with you, eh, you and all your rubbish? That's when Gop always laughs. Moon puts his glove back on, fetching his brush and shovel from the cart to sweep away the stuff. It's the same every day. Gop will get up and go back out to collect more rubbish. There is always more rubbish.

One day last week Gop found something on the hill behind the village, at the old ruined shrine. He goes up there quite often to sit under the shade of the big old jackfruit tree that casts its shadow over the shrine. There is always plenty stuff lying around too: wrinkled garlands, burnt-out incense, tiny scraps of food from leftover offerings. Gop likes to lean back against the cool lingam during the hot hours of early afternoon, unpicking jasmine blossoms, nibbling at dried up rice, scratching away at the itches underneath his filthy clothes. There are no dogs or people up here to bother him. That day he'd noticed a dull metal object poking up through the earth between the huge slabs of stone. He pulled at it. Sniffed it. Gave it a lick. It wasn't for eating then. But the object lay comfortably in his palm – round, smooth, heavy, pleasing. Gop peered at the writing on one side, turning it over to look at the picture on the other. The feel of it was good. The voices in his head were quiet, gave no instruction, so he decided to keep it, fingers closed around it tightly. Before long he fell into a deep sleep, waking hours later feeling strangely refreshed and free from itches.

It wasn't until wandering around the market the same evening that he remembered the metal object, reaching into his pocket to pull it out. Aunty Wassana noticed first. He was near her stall, stuffing cabbage leaves up his shirt.

"*Oh-ho* Gop, what have you got there? Lai, quickly, Gop has found something!"

"Come on Gop; let's have a look! *Aow*, Gop, don't run away, I'm not going to hurt you!"

"Quickly Lai, don't let him get away! It looks like an old medal or coin or something – quick!"

But Gop had started running, dropping a trail of litter from the bundle stuffed up his shirt. Dogs leapt up from where they were sleeping to give chase, barking and snapping at his legs. Gop didn't stop running until he reached the *sala*, heart thumping, the voices clamouring in his ears. He sat down, spreading the remainder of his stuff around him in a circle, gripping the object tightly in his hand. It wasn't long before a crowd of people came up the road, talking in loud voices, standing around him, waving their arms and pointing. *Too many people*, he panicked. He didn't even like being close to his best friend Uncle Moon, who would catch hold of him every so often, enticing him with fried chicken, then drag him into his house for a scrub, a change of clothes. *What if the big crowd catches me*, he thought, *and makes me wash?* But they had fallen silent, smiling, their heads tilted on one side, and Lai came forwards to offer him a Burmese cigar. When he got up to take the cigar, Uncle Daeng went behind his back and sifted through his stuff, messing it all up. Then Sergeant Yud grabbed him from behind and Lai searched his pockets. Gop howled; the voices in his head shrieked. Yud and Lai unfurled his hand and stole the metal object. They went back down the road much quicker than they had come, leaving him alone again. It took hours to calm down, and the voices were very bad that night and for days after. And now, today, Sergeant Pan and Sergeant Yud have rounded him up and stuck him in the cell.

Outside the police station, the village is fraught with excitement. A procession will take place that afternoon along the main street. People are running in and out of each other's houses, borrowing clothes, putting the finishing touches to costumes and make-up, sweeping balconies and front yards. There was no market this morning; the women vendors are too busy helping to prepare the feast. Mother Pensri and Aunty Wassana are in charge of the food arrangements, quarrelling about whether the *gaeng hang ley* needs more fish sauce. Gimsia, the Chinese grocer, has changed out of pyjamas into proper clothes but refuses to close his shop, protesting that someone might need to buy something at the last minute. Lai has closed his moonshine stall and is helping Daeng and Uncle Nun to hang up red, white and blue bunting across the street from tree to tree. Sia Heng, who donated the bunting, shouts orders from the foot of the ladders.

"A little bit to the left – that's it!" He dashes up and down the street, rubbing his hands, craning his neck, gazing down the road for any sign of the guest of honour.

"Just look at him," whispers Uncle Nun to Lai, "anyone would think it was his birthday!"

"*Tho-oei*! And have you seen Gimsia?" Lai answers, tilting his chin to the old man's shop. "He's actually trying to sell those rotten bananas at cut price!"

* * *

The Relic Committee, formed almost immediately after the metal object was so fortuitously rescued from Gop, had argued for days before coming to a decision on who should go first in the parade. The Schoolmaster won, claiming that the village youth represented the future of the Thai nation and should therefore be given pride of place, led of course by the school brass band. The Housewives Group were to bring up the rear as usual, but the District Officer and the Police Chief both insisted on second place. A vote was taken and the District Officer, a local man, won by a narrow margin. But the committee were eager not to get on the wrong side of the Chief, so they asked him to make a speech on behalf of the village dignitaries. The Chief had shrugged his shoulders at the suggestion, but didn't turn it down. "*Speech,*" he had said, as though it were an insect in need of swatting, "I suppose I can make a *speech.*" Then he had turned on his heel and marched out of the meeting, back to the police station. He strode into his office and banged the door, turning the air conditioner up full blast. It was the only air conditioner in the village. *March behind the government workers? Might as well march behind the housewives' group*, he fumed. *What do the committee think they're playing at?* He had drummed his fingers on his desk, glancing over at the safe in the corner of the office.

During the first committee meeting, the Police Chief had proposed that the relic should be kept in the station safe; it was the best place, everyone had agreed. It was worth a great deal of money, after all. The Police Chief went over to the safe and unlocked it, withdrawing the relic. Returning to his desk, he reached into a drawer for his magnifying glass. *Such beautiful markings! And perfect condition! Any man*, he thought, *would swap his wife – no, even his mistress – for something this good!* Those rich enough, he knew, would pay a high price to have it hanging round their neck, encased in gold, warding off enemies and ill fortune.

The Chief was a regular subscriber to magazines about charms and amulets: Buddhas, Shivas, lingams, the Chinese deities, anything that purported to offer protection. Protection was one of the Chief's hobbies. Charms were much sought after in his line of work: insurance against stray bullets. He'd read countless tales of men whose lives had been saved by some apparent miracle: men who were the only survivor in a fire, a shoot-out, a shipwreck, a crash. It turned out that they all wore charms of one sort or another, and the more ancient the charm, the more potent the protection. The Chief sat brooding for a while, ignoring the knocks on his door, turning the relic over in his hand. He peered at the Pali inscriptions (the Schoolteacher had told him what they meant but he had forgotten), the engraving of the Enlightened One under the sacred banyan tree. He had thought about the matter long enough. It was time to pick up the phone and call some old friends.

* * *

All those not involved in the procession are lining the roadside, getting ready to cheer, holding flags. A makeshift platform has been built on the lawns outside the new district office, on which will sit the Abbot, the Headman, the Police Chief and their guest of honour – the Provincial Governor. Sia Heng has paid for an enormous poster of the King, ordered specially from the city, to be hung behind the platform. The procession will follow the governor's car along the main street, filing behind it into the grounds to take up carefully designated positions on the grass. Some of the school children are going to perform boisterous Shan-style dances while dressed up in the costumes of mythical creatures. The housewives have volunteered to put on a show of traditional Thai dance, and are looking almost unrecognizable in their elaborate hairstyles, tight sarongs and long fake fingernails. Uncle Nun has pulled out of his ceremonial sword routine at short notice, to everyone's amazement and secret relief. The performances will be rounded off by the school band's rendition of the national anthem, when the police officers, dressed in their white suits and ceremonial swords, will step forwards and draw their resplendent blades, holding the swords upright in front of their noses as they go down on one knee in front of the poster of the King.

Sergeant Yud and Sergeant Pan have been assigned to stay behind and man the police station, guarding the prisoners, just in case. There is only Gop and an old opium addict from the mountains, who was caught selling marijuana to a couple of young farangs. Not exactly a dangerous gang of outlaws, but someone must stay behind, and Sergeant Pan has a terrible hangover and can't be exhibited in front of the distinguished guests, whilst Sergeant Yud has been barred because his uniform won't fasten up. The two men hang over the station balcony railings, watching the preparations. Out on the lawn the officers are pulling at each other's waists, rearranging their swords coquettishly.

"Who's that?" asks Sergeant Pan, indicating a tall, well-dressed man leaning against a truck, lazily smoking a cigarette.

"He's not from round here. But he looks familiar."

"He's definitely not from round here! Just look at his fancy boots!"

"Isn't he a friend of the Chief? I think I saw them together a few months ago. He's probably up visiting from the city. Maybe the Chief told him about our relic and he's come to see the procession."

"Or maybe," says Sergeant Pan, turning enthusiastically to Sergeant Yud, "he's a news reporter from Channel 7!"

"Or one of the Provincial Governor's bodyguards!"

"Does he have bodyguards?" asked Sergeant Pan.

"Who?"

"The Provincial Governor, of course! What's-his-name."

"What *is* his name?"

"*Aow*... nearly had it. No, it's gone. Can't remember."

"Funny that, isn't it?"

"What's funny?"

"Well, everyone knows Gop's name, don't they, but I bet few people can remember the name of the Provincial Governor!"

Sergeant Pan and Sergeant Yud snigger, turning round to look at Gop, who has fallen into an open-mouthed doze, sitting cross-legged, hands resting upturned on his lap, shaggy head against the bars of the cell. They will let him go later, once the guest of honour has gone. The Provincial Governor doesn't want to see Gop and all his rubbish.

* * *

By two o'clock in the afternoon the sun is high and hot, and the Chief is in the middle of his speech. The schoolchildren are flagging, beginning to slouch forwards where they sit on the grass. The velvet body of the mythical yak costume lies crumpled on the grass, the head tossed to one side, its mechanical eyelids wide open, frozen in an attitude of bewilderment. The government officers discreetly fan their faces with pieces of paper, whilst the police officers, who at least have the advantage of hats, are shifting their weight from one leg to the other, swords slapping irritatingly along their thighs, necks itchy under stiff collars. *How much longer*, they think, *is the Police Chief going to speak? It's almost as if he relishes our suffering!* The only one who seems to have any energy left is Sia Heng, who bobs up and down in front of the stage, nodding enthusiastically at every word the Chief utters.

"...once again, how *honoured* we all are today to welcome the Provincial Governor to our little village. I would shortly like to ask the Headman to present the governor with our *precious* antique relic, to hand it over into his *safekeeping*. We are, I am sure, all proud to think of it being displayed in the museum in the provincial capital. Such a discovery is a credit to our village, our district, our province, our *nation*; a discovery that proves beyond doubt – not that there ever was any doubt – our forefathers were just as devout Buddhists as we all are today."

From his chair on the stage, which is perceptibly higher than the others, the Abbot sighs. This is the kind of rhetoric he most hates. Against the committee negotiations from the start, he feels it is a mistake to turn the relic over to the provincial office; and all for the sake of a business grant. It is a *religious* relic, after all! But Sia Heng has been in league with the District Officer and the Headman about using the grant to "improve the local economy". There had been talk of "unique opportunities", "progress" and "moving with the times". *Why*, the Abbot thinks, *before they know it, the villagers will be laying down their farm tools to work in factories making imitation relics, sold as pendants! Tourists trooping through the village in search of a "spirituality" they can buy and hang around their necks!* He shook his head. *It's wrong: the relic should be housed in the temple's main hall. If, as the Schoolmaster claims, it's historical evidence of the conversion to Buddhism that occurred in the area over two thousand years ago, then it belongs next to the Buddha statue, where the devout can pay homage to it, free of charge. They can always make an offering to the temple to improve their merit, if they so wish.* The Abbot pulls at a loose thread on his robe. *Why should the relic be turned over, be as good as sold, to the governor to hang in the museum of the provincial capital? If the Schoolmaster wasn't so obsessed with reading up on ancient history*, thinks the Abbot grimly, *none of this would have happened.* He shifts uncomfortably in his seat and looks over to the awning where Mother Pensri and Aunty Wassana are laying out the food. The cooking smells are tantalizing but his vows prevent him from eating after twelve o'clock.

"It's going sour; I told you not to turn up the heat," whispers Mother Pensri, mopping her brow with a small towel.

"If you hadn't insisted on starting to cook it so early, it would be fine!" hisses Aunty Wassana.

The older villagers are sitting on folding chairs at tables set up under the awning, and many of them have fallen asleep in the heat. The Shan Fortune Teller sits at one of the tables near the back, smoking a pipe, frowning at the platform and the steadily wilting audience. *What fools they all are! Don't they realize the value of what they relinquish? Why, a relic as old as this has unimaginably powerful forces attached to it! If I could only lay my hands on it,* thinks the Fortune Teller, *I could harness its powers to tackle any evil that dared to attack the village. Take those widow ghosts, for example. Just one incantation, spoken over the relic on the right day at the most auspicious time, would have sent them packing! And if they only let me use the relic to its fullest potential, they would never have to worry about bad harvests again!* He stuffs more tobacco into the bowl of his pipe. *But who will listen to an old Shan man who lives with a bunch of cats? Until they need me, of course; then they come pleading for help. Fools!*

The chief is winding up his speech at last. People's eyelids flicker back into life as they realize the ordeal is over.

"...would like to ask the Headman to present our precious relic to the Provincial Governor."

The Headman stands up and walks over to a small table on the platform, picking up the wooden box in which the relic has been kept for the past week. The Police Chief and the Governor exchange a glance – later that night, tossing and turning on his pallet in the temple, dreaming of the day's events, the Abbot half remembers that glance. The Headman, slightly nervous, has opened the box and is ready to deliver the treasure. The Headman glances down at the relic, nestling safely inside the box. It seems shinier than before. *Someone has been polishing it,* he thinks proudly, as he hands it over into the safekeeping of the Provincial Governor, amidst a round of grateful applause.

Skin Deep

The makeshift platform erected in the district office grounds for the relic presentation ceremony did not go to waste. Nor did the Relic Committee, which transformed itself into the Buddhist New Year Committee. The village, thought the committee members, was in need of a more spectacular Songkran festival now that it had a reputation as a historical site. The Headman suggested the platform would provide a perfect venue for the *Songkran* dancing and singing performances. "Not only that," Sia Heng piped up, "it's ideal for a proper beauty contest, instead of the usual temple fair angel competition!" Much more progressive, the other men agreed, nodding at one another with raised eyebrows; the village beauty queen could enter the district contest, then the provincial and then who knows – she might end up winning the national competition! It was yet another way to put the village on the map. And such perfect timing, declared the District Officer, what with all the media interest over the relic: after winning fame for history and culture, the village could become known for its feminine beauty too. "Yes, it's an investment," concurred Sia Heng, striking his fist into the palm of his hand, already dreaming of a glossy poster featuring the beauty queen in traditional costume, hard at work on handicrafts and homemade sweets, bending gracefully to plant a rice seedling, perhaps even biting into a local fruit or delicacy with her little white teeth. And just think of all the tourists, said the Police Chief, leaning back in his chair as he lit a cigarette.

* * *

Preparations for the April Songkran festival had already begun. School was over for the long, hot holiday and children were preparing water pistols and hoses for the three days of soaking neighbours and friends in a frenzy of celebratory water play. The paddy lay fallow around the village, buffaloes nibbling disconsolately on the frazzled stubble of the winter rice harvest. Fires were raging on the slopes flanking the valley, adding to the terrible heat, as tribal people slashed and burned, swiddening the mountain jungle for fresh planting. Dogs panted under bare trees. The market women chewed on pickled tobacco leaves and raw ginger, swapping recipes for spicy dishes and pastes: anything to combat the torpor that descended when the sun reached its highest point, glaring down on the trapped villagers in the wide valley, melting the tarmac on the main street, baking the moist red earth into a hard clay. A hot wind whipped up dust, stinging eyes and throats. Scorpions scuttled out from the ground to hide in shoes, snakes hissed at the bottom of bone-dry wells, and tiny, almost invisible mosquitoes hatched and hovered, hungry for blood. The villagers slapped, fanned, showered, cursed and quarrelled, squinting hopelessly at the sky, desperate for cloud.

Mother Pensri hated the hot season more than anyone. Sweat trickled down her face and her clothes stuck to her back. She snapped at Uncle Nun without reason. He bought her a wide-brimmed straw hat to wear when she went about on her bicycle.

He even bought her a bag of ice every evening, to cool the water in the basin before she bathed, but within five minutes she was sweating again. She sat on her balcony, fanning her face with a lottery magazine, too hot even to smoke. Craning her neck, she listened for the bus. It was due any minute. Her daughter Kwan was coming home. She had five days' holiday from the fruit-processing factory to celebrate the New Year. Mother Pensri glanced inside: a white cotton blouse and a pink silk sarong were hanging by the door, washed, dried and ironed that morning. Mother Pensri's wedding outfit. Strings of fresh jasmine blossom hung around it. It would fit: Kwan boasted the same perfect proportions that Mother Pensri had gloried in as a young woman: 33, 22, 35. But when Mother Pensri was young there was no real beauty contest, just the selection of the Temple Fair Angel, the girl who would lead the communal dancing at the start of the Songkran celebrations. Mother Pensri was lead dancer four years running. She smoothed back the hair from her damp brow and sighed, holding out her hands. She bent her fingers back. The flexibility necessary for that difficult, slow dance had long gone. She examined her arms, the loose brown skin, the freckles, running a finger over the welt near one elbow – she'd been frying a fish last week when the hot oil spat at her. But she'd been a beauty in those days, everyone said so. She had turned heads, caught the eyes of strangers, and could have had her pick of any man.

Mother Pensri rubbed her plump knees and frowned. Only one man had ever caught her fancy. A man from the south, from Yala province, tall, swarthy and handsome: a government worker in a neat, light-coloured uniform. They'd sat together on the street corner in the cool of evening. He told her stories of curly-haired men who sailed the seas on homemade rafts, of the giant octopus and sharks they caught, of the coconut plantations she would be mistress of. But her father was outraged. Move south? Marry a Muslim? Southerners were scoundrels, villains. No daughter of his would marry a southerner. Her marriage to Uncle Nun was quickly arranged.

Well, it's Kwan's turn now, she thought, *and times are changing: opportunities for women are much better than in my day. Why, this new contest is just the beginning.* Mother Pensri had heard a rumour that the Chief was offering a sewing machine as first prize. *A sewing machine! A clever girl like Kwan could turn a sewing machine into money, a career.* But it was more than the lure of first prize. Mother Pensri thought of all the female stars on Channel 7. Many of them started out as beauty queens, and once they became famous, their faces were everywhere: on billboards and calendars, face cream jars, shampoo bottles and soap powder boxes. *If Kwan wins the village contest there will be no stopping her*, thought Mother Pensri. *She's special, set apart from the other village girls by her unusually straight nose and wide brown eyes. Her pale, flawless skin.* Mother Pensri cleared her throat. She had taken great pains with Kwan's skin. It was a northern girl's greatest asset and Mother Pensri was proud to show just how *northern* Kwan really was. All through the pregnancy she had eaten greasy, pungent durian to ensure a pale-skinned child. She had never lost the weight after the birth but Kwan's complexion was more than worth the sacrifice of her perfect figure. *So what if Kwan is an up-country girl from a poor family? With her good looks and soft voice*, she thought fiercely, *Kwan could pass for a princess.* Mother Pensri stood up and went inside for ice cubes, stopping in front of the costume to flick imaginary dust from the blouse's delicately embroidered collar.

* * *

Sergeant Yud mopped his brow, gazing miserably at the construction site. *Why do I get all the worst jobs: cutting the grass outside the police station, washing the Chief's car, and now this – supervising these lazy workers building the Chief's guest house?* He sat outside one of the half-finished bungalows, boots up on the balcony railing, staring out from the shade at the construction workers labouring in the sun: they were mixing mortar, lugging bricks, building a low wall round the garden restaurant. Hot, thirsty work. The Sergeant cleared his throat and called one of the workers. He needed a bottle of beer.

"Jai Kham! Over here! Now!"

No response. Jai Kham hadn't heard: he was too busy larking about again. *Bloody Dai Nok migrants*, Yud fumed. The whole district was crawling with them since all the trouble began in Burma. Everyone could spot them a mile off: on construction sites, in restaurants and bars, in the fields. Their appearance gave them away even before they opened their mouths. The men wore long sleeved shirts to hide their tattoos, and the women had really long hair. Not that there weren't one or two very pretty ones up at the brothel – young and shy, just as Sergeant Yud liked them. *All in all*, he reflected, *life is easier with them around – twice the work for half the money*. But everyone knew the migrants had to be watched closely – they could be flighty and unreliable all the same. Sergeant Yud sighed and struggled to his feet. Putting on his hat, he strolled out into the hot sun, over to where Jai Kham was supposed to be slapping mortar on to the wall. *There he is – look at him laughing, joking, distracting the other workers with his chit chat!* Sergeant Yud put his hands on his hips and prepared to shout. But just then, without warning, Jai Kham's left hand flicked up, his head tilted, his back straightened and he jumped from his left foot to his right like a cat. He threw down his trowel and began to prance, feet twisting and stamping along the dusty ground, fists on hips, chin held high. The other workers were quickly standing in a circle around him, clapping furiously. One of them started beating the palms of his hands on an upturned pail. Another was crashing two paint pot lids together in a steady beat. None of them had noticed the Sergeant approaching.

"*Tho-oei*, you lot! What do you think this is? Stop fooling around and get back to work!" cried Sergeant Yud, waving his toothpick in the air.

Jai Kham bent down to pick up his trowel.

"Sorry Sergeant Yud."

"Jai Kham was just showing us his dancing, Sergeant," said Lek, one of the other boys. "He's a champion dancer up in the Shan State. Nobody dances like Jai Kham. He's won all the national competitions."

"Well, you're not in the Shan State now, are you," snapped Yud, fumbling in his trouser pocket for some money. "Away and buy me a bottle of Singha beer, the coldest one in the shop. And hurry back with it: I want to drink it while it's still cold!"

Jai Kham nodded, pocketing the money. Yud watched him trotting up to the main road, a small creature in shabby, baggy clothes. He scratched his chin thoughtfully. *Champion dancer, eh? Champion dancer...*

Sergeant Yud strolled back into the shade, deep in thought. It had been all change at the police station, what with the

Chief's insistence on full uniform at all times, promptness, physical fitness, cutbacks, paperwork. Endless paperwork. And yesterday, to cap it all, the Chief had announced that they were all to get involved in making this year's Songkran celebrations really special because he'd invited some bigwig from the tourist board. Some of the younger officers were organizing volleyball and *takraw* games. Sergeant Pan was planning a homemade fireworks competition. Sergeant Yud chuckled.

* * *

The district office grounds were packed as dusk fell over the valley on the first day of Songkran. People had heard about the festivities, arriving throughout the day from other villages across the hills to enjoy the dancing, singing and competitions. The revellers wandered around in wet clothes, talcum powder smeared all over their faces by enthusiastic neighbours. The steady, distant beat of a long Shan drum filled the air, growing ever closer to the grounds. Tempers had cooled, and voices were raised only in mirth and celebration. It was a new year, a fresh start. Earlier on in the day the main Buddha statue had been paraded through the village, allowing everyone to pour water over it in blessing. The grounds were filled with stalls and vendors. Aunty Wassana had made two pots of stock instead of her usual one, and Mother Noi's huge mound of fried pumpkin was almost finished. Mother Suree, looking even more tearful and bedraggled than usual, couldn't keep up with demands for her papaya salad. A hectic crowd of men clustered around Lai's moonshine stall. Only Mother Pensri's cold drinks stall was missing. She usually earned extra money each Songkran selling iced tea and coffee, but this year she was far too busy keeping her eye on Kwan. It had taken her long enough to convince Kwan to enter the competition; she wasn't letting her out of her sight at this late stage. Mother Pensri couldn't understand her daughter's reluctance – at first, not even the lure of the sewing machine had been enough to persuade Kwan to enter! Mother Pensri had been forced to resort to blackmail: "Even if you don't want the machine," she had argued, "is it any reason to deny me the chance of getting it? Is it too much to ask, after all the sacrifices I've made?..."

Mother Pensri peered out from behind the platform. A group of schoolchildren had just sung a tune famously composed by the King and were scurrying off the stage. The Headman mumbled into a microphone. Mother Pensri put her hands over her ears as the microphone screeched feedback over the audience. Next up, shouted the Headman, was a show of traditional Shan dancing! Mother Pensri glanced over at the side of the stage towards the judges' chairs, set behind a long table. The Police Chief sat between the Forestry Officer and a man from the tourist board, all three smartly dressed in silk mandarin collar shirts, guffawing at a shared joke. They seemed to have escaped the water play – who would dare? The District Officer, on the other hand, looked damp, dishevelled, perhaps even a little drunk? He and Sia Heng sat slumped back in their chairs, gazing open-mouthed at a group of teenage girls throwing water over one another.

Mother Pensri retreated behind the stage, where the beauty contestants were pulling anxiously at their shoe straps, unfolding and folding their sarongs ever more tightly around their waists, rearranging silver belts. Mother Pensri sniffed. Not much competition. She had been worried that Maew, Mother Nong's daughter, or Tuptim, Mother Noi's daughter might enter. Tuptim, especially, was turning into a real beauty. But Tuptim was too busy helping Mother Noi sell fried pumpkin, whilst Maew was engaged now and spending Songkran with her prospective in-laws on one of the islands in the south. Out of the other contestants, one girl was plump, another had dark skin. One wore a cheap nylon blouse with a frill down the front. Another had protruding front teeth – *what*, thought Mother Pensri, *was her mother thinking of?* There were two or three pretty faces, but one of them was emitting a rough, braying voice. Beauty wasn't just face and figure. Deportment and speech were important too. Mother Pensri looked anxiously at Kwan, who was dressed so simply and elegantly: the perfect flower for a bee to suck honey from. Kwan had it all. But so, unfortunately, did one of the other contestants. Mother Pensri recognized her, had seen her sometimes in the morning market, selling plump yellow bananas, handling the bunches deftly with elegant fingers. *She must be from a neighbouring village*, Mother Pensri decided, *but wasn't there… didn't I hear some kind of rumour?* Mother Pensri wrinkled her nose, trying to remember. The girl's sarong and blouse were very tight, nipped in beautifully at the waist, and she sported with ease a pair of extremely high-heeled, red shoes. Her hair was sleek, piled high, fixed in place with a diamanté comb. Mother Pensri stared at her, trying to convince herself the effect was more common than glamorous.

"Quick, you're going to miss the start of the dancing!" Mother Nong appeared at Mother Pensri's side to pull her arm, dragging her round to the front of the stage.

The sound of the long Shan drum was loud and insistent, beating out an irresistible rhythm. Children and adults began clapping their hands, and stood aside to let the troupe of dancers and musicians pass through the grounds to the platform. Sergeant Yud appeared behind the Chief, whispering in his ear. The Chief stood up to get a better view. Jai Kham walked confidently at the head of the troupe, dressed in a peacock-green costume covered with glittering sliver sequins, an elaborate headdress, sequined shoes. Held behind his back for safe passage through the noisy mob was a pair of folded wings.

"What's he going to dance?" asked Mother Pensri.

"*Fon nok*, of course," hissed Mother Nong.

The musicians followed Jai Kham; Lek carried the long drum over his shoulder, beating a deep, quick rhythm to accompany the steady clatter of gongs and cymbals. The audience quickly gathered, settling down cross-legged on the grass in front of the platform. The Headman had stopped mumbling into the microphone and was clapping along to the drum. Sergeant Yud appeared on the stage at his side, dressed in Shan peasant traditional dress: light brown trousers and jacket, an unwise pink sash drawing attention to his huge waist. Face glistening, he was looking anxiously down to make sure the Chief was still watching. Sure enough, the Chief was looking on with interest, camera in hand, a faint smile playing over his lips. The whole occasion was very quaint. Sergeant Yud took the microphone from the Headman.

"Ladies and gentlemen, honoured guests, allow me to introduce Jai Kham and his friends, our brothers from the Shan State. Jai Kham is going to perform a *fon nok*: the dance of the mythological *ginara* – a creature half bird, half human!"

Yud stood aside, arm outstretched.

"Aren't they the *Dai Nok* boys who work for the Chief?" said Mother Pensri, nudging Mother Nong

"Hard to believe, isn't it? Yud organized the whole thing. Borrowed all the costumes and musical instruments from the school." Mother Nong sniffed, folding her arms over her chest.

Jai Kham moved with his entourage into the middle of the stage, untying his wings. He nodded to the musicians and they began to play, closing their eyes and remembering other years, distant temples. Jai Kham knelt on the floor and bowed to the town dignitaries, his exquisite sequined wings fanning out behind his back – and began to move his hands and head in time to the drumbeat. As the musicians played and Jai Kham danced, the atmosphere in the village grew heavy, the audience spellbound at the way Jai Kham twisted his hands and feet with such dexterity, head held high, his wings trembling magnificently.

"Wonderful!" exclaimed Mother Pensri, peering up at the stage. "Why, he dances like... like a butterfly! It's years since I've seen anyone dance the old dances like that."

Mother Nong nodded, open-mouthed, gazing with loving pride at Sergeant Yud, who was standing behind the Chief again, winking over at her.

"Who was that young man?" asked the Police Chief, once the dance was over.

"Why, he's one of your workers," boomed the Sergeant, "he's almost like a son to me!"

"Thank you, Yud," said the Chief, getting to his feet. He grinned at the others. "Time to get down to the real business."

He rubbed his hands together and winked. "Bring out the beauty queens!" he called to the Headman.

* * *

Mother Pensri had searched everywhere. She had taken her eyes off Kwan for only a few minutes, to watch the traditional dancing. Next thing she knew, Kwan had disappeared from behind the stage. No one had seen her go. Mother Pensri looked all over the grounds, in and out of the crowds, asking everyone she knew. She'd gone the length of the main street twice, had looked at home three times, and had even looked in at the empty stalls in the deserted morning market. She'd gone through the temple grounds, but found only Gop, asleep under the old banyan tree. There was nowhere else. She wandered around the village, feeling upset, reluctant now to return to the noisy festivities, until she found herself down at the new guest house where the air, at least, was cool, watching the moon reflected in the river, listening to the boom of distant music. She sat on a half-built wall and lit a cigarette, too absorbed in melancholy to hear the soft footsteps behind her. A hand came to rest on her shoulder.

"Sorry, Mama."

Mother Pensri nodded, taking a long drag on her cigarette.

"I'm sorry I disappointed you."

Mother Pensri patted the wall, and her daughter sat down beside her. "But why Kwan? You could have won so easily!"

Kwan had already changed her elaborate beauty-queen outfit for long shorts, a simple shirt, hair twisted into a clip at the back of her head. "Oh, I don't know... I just don't want to be

a beauty queen if... not if it means those *men* staring at me..."
Kwan took her mother's hand. "I'm not like that. I want my life
to be... *different*."

"Different? What do you mean by different? How can it be
different if you don't take chances like that one? I don't want
you spending the rest of your life in a fruit canning factory, or
marrying some poor farmer and ending up like..."

A deep laugh rang out behind them, followed by a giggle.
Kwan put her finger to her lips. Mother Pensri stubbed out her
cigarette and peered into the dim light. Two figures turned off
the road, on to the path to the bungalows. A man, pulling a
woman along by the hand. The woman stopped at the edge of
the grass and unfastened her shoes. They crept over the grass to
one of the wooden huts. The man kicked off his shoes, fumbled
in his pocket for a key and unlocked the door. The woman put
her shoes down at the door, then disappeared inside.

"Who was that?" whispered Mother Pensri, fascinated.

"What does it matter, Mama, don't worry about it," breathed
Kwan. "Come on Mama, it's time to go home now."

"Wait a minute Kwan." Mother Pensri tiptoed towards the
bungalow, stopping a few metres from the door. Fashion shoes,
high-heeled, lay outside the door step. One of the shoes had
fallen on its side. Mother Pensri crept a little closer. Red. And
next to them a pair of men's leather shoes. Mother Pensri
opened her mouth wide, arching her neck to better hear the
voices inside.

"What about my sewing machine?" asked the high, flirting
voice.

"You'll get *that* prize in the morning," answered the Chief,
"but first you can give me a kiss..."

Mother Pensri drew back, horrified. She hurried back to Kwan, grabbing her daughter by the hand, pulling her away from the river and the wooden bungalows as a final homemade firework above the village surprised them, rupturing half-heartedly into the air, sputtering faint sparks across the starry sky.

Escape from the Bear, Run into the Tiger

"You should be more careful, leaving your money belt lying around on the stall like that!" scolded Mother Nong. "And you should start locking your door at night too, what with your husband away. A woman on her own."

Aunty Wassana shrugged and tied the belt back around her waist, peering into the deep well of her soup stock. Almost empty, almost time to pack up, wheel her barrow home. And it was only two o'clock. She had plenty of time to get ready.

"There's all sorts going on these days in the village: I hear about everything from Sergeant Yud. It would make your hair stand on end, if you knew what I know. And those *Dai Nok* are at the bottom of most of it." Mother Nong raised her eyebrows, shaking her head. "Yud fired one of them last week, that little one, what's-his-name, the one that danced at the Songkran celebrations last month. Caught him red-handed, about to put a hammer in his pocket."

"A hammer? What would he want with a hammer?"

"A hammer," declared Mother Nong with relish, "is a blunt instrument; he was probably planning to bludgeon someone to death with it and steal all their money. Thought he could worm his way into our community with his dancing, win our trust, then take advantage when we least expected it. Never liked the look of him. Too clever by half." She leant back, folding her thin arms triumphantly across her chest.

"Anyway," said Wassana, cross from lack of sleep, legs aching from standing all day, "I'm not on my own." She tilted her chin to indicate the young girl crouched over two huge basins. Bee was washing up the noodle bowls and chopsticks left behind by the day's customers.

Mother Nong curled her lip at the young girl's back. "Vipers," she hissed, leaning over the soup pot at Aunty Wassana, "'Vipers in the Grass, in the Backyard of our Nation'. That's what the newspapers call them; and if you ask me, they're right!"

"Well, at least they're willing to work!" countered Aunty Wassana, whose experience of hiring the local Thai girls had been unfortunate – they all expected more money than she was prepared to pay, then spent half their time looking for a better job. "Now Mother Nong, I can't stand here gossiping: do you want any noodle soup today or not?" *Two or three more bowls*, she thought, *will just about finish the pot.*

"I'm just trying to be neighbourly!" Mother Nong opened her eyes wide. "Make it two soups then, one with glass noodles and one with wide noodles. Oh, better make that two with wide noodles; one bowl is never enough for Sergeant Yud."

"Taking away?"

"Take away." Mother Nong pursed her lips and waved her hand over the stall at some invisible flies.

Wassana stuffed the noodles into long-handled little baskets and thrust them deep into the boiling stock for a minute to soften. Then she emptied the steaming noodles into plastic bags, filling another bag with the last few ladles of her delicious chicken stock. She twisted elastic bands expertly round the tops and placed them all into Mother Nong's basket, throwing in a few homemade sachets: tiny plastic packets filled with sugar, vinegar and chilli powder, sealed painstakingly by her *Dai Nok* girl, one by one, over a candle flame.

"Thirty baht please."

Mother Nong reached under her blouse and pulled the money out from a little zipped pocket sewn into the bodice of her bra.

"Don't say I didn't warn you," she said over her shoulder, walking across and down the road to the guest house by the river. The teak wood bungalows and the garden restaurant were all finished; the workers had begun landscaping the gardens. They had spent the last few days digging out what would be a large pond. Sergeant Yud was down to four men now instead of five.

Aunty Wassana glanced over at the young girl crouched over the bowls. *There will be no patterns left on the dishes at this rate! And I've still the house to clean, a special dinner to prepare*, she panicked, *and my hair needs washed and set.*

"Hurry up Bee."

"Almost finished," answered Bee, rinsing the last few bowls.

"Stack the bowls away, then come home and start on tomorrow's stock. We need more vinegar and chilli bags making up. I'll go ahead and tidy the house. We haven't got much time. I want everything to be perfect."

Bee nodded, drying her wrinkled hands on the apron Aunty Wassana had given her on the first day. It was huge, making her slight frame seem childish, ridiculous even. She had experimented with tying it differently; crossing the strings at her back and bringing them round to tie again at the front. But then it was too revealing, emphasizing her tiny waist, narrow hips, the round curve of her breasts. She had enough to worry about without men's eyes roving all over her. She rinsed the basins and began to stack the clean bowls inside. She was glad the bowls were plastic. After arriving in Thailand, the first job she and her two friends had found was in a restaurant up near the border: china plates, and drinks served in glasses, not beakers and an alarming array of dishes on the menu, most of which she had never heard of. The owner used to roar orders in a rapid stream of incomprehensible Thai. Bee was afraid to admit she didn't understand so would nod at the orders, invariably bringing customers the wrong food. Then the owner would get angry and Bee would drop plates and glasses, incurring more wrath. Border patrol guards often came to eat at the restaurant, and the owner would threaten to turn Bee and the other girls over to them. It was meant as a joke, one of the girls said, but Bee wasn't sure. The border patrol would strut into the restaurant, clutching by the neck the bottles of foreign whisky with which petty smugglers had bribed them, clicking their fingers, ordering plates of food, ice and soda. The girls had to stand by the table and wait on them, filling up any glass that was almost empty. The guards leered at the girls, comparing in loud, lewd voices the paleness of their skin, glossiness of hair, evenness of teeth, shape of eyes, size of breasts. Tilting their chairs back, they would spread their legs wide under the table, unbuttoning their jackets to reveal soft middle-aged bellies, bleating if the girls poured the whisky-measures too big, too small. One of the guards grabbed Bee's arm one day and tried to pull her down onto his knee. Bee had screamed. The owner ran over and slapped her, apologizing to the man, pushing her into the kitchen. She was fired, the owner shrieked, and could get out, back to the hole she had crawled from. Bee was too scared to ask for her wages. A month's work, fourteen hours every day: all for nothing.

The next morning she had got up early to leave, hugging her two friends, promising to meet them in a year's time. They would all have saved money by then and could return home to their families, back across the border to the Shan State. She decided to head for a village deep in the northern Thai mountains where her cousin Jai Kham had been working for almost a year; he was doing something on a construction site, according to the migrant grapevine, and the conditions weren't bad. And she had heard about a man who, for a price, would deliver her safely through all checkpoints that stood between the border town and the village. She had sold her mother's fine gold necklace to pay for the trip. Two hundred kilometres, five checkpoints. Sitting in the back of his pickup truck, the wind blowing in her face, the landscape of the north didn't seem so different from where she came from. The same mountains, stretching from Thailand across the Shan State and on through India and Nepal, the same trees, flowers, rice fields, wooden houses; some village temples had tiered Shan-style roofs just like the ones at home. The roads were better though, with more trucks and bikes, and people dressed differently, especially in the bigger towns. Many women wore trousers, shirts with no sleeves, short hair. There were no Burmese soldiers, of course, no burnt-out villages, refugees, few beggars. But plenty of checkpoints. The driver would bang on the window when they were approaching one. Bee would lie down, hiding amongst the boxes in the back of the truck. The driver was never asked to stop. He was a policeman, after all, and the guards on duty knew him as one of their own. He had offered to take her all the way to the city, said there was plenty money to be made there. But Bee wanted to find her cousin: *things will be easier, safer*, she thought, *with Jai Kham looking out for me.*

The driver had deposited her in the marketplace. Asking the vendors about her cousin, she was directed to the guest house along the road. The other workers told her what had happened: how Jai Kham had been fooling around with the hammer, making them all laugh as usual, and how the sergeant – who had been in a bad mood – had started shouting at him, accusing him of trying to steal it. Jai Kham had left for the city a few days ago, they said, looking for work. Bee had sat down and cried. How would she find him, with no address and no money to travel any further? Lek, one of the boys, had patted her back and suggested she stay where she was, at least for a while. The village was safe enough and many of the locals spoke Shan. He offered to help her look for a job, knew where to ask. He went round the stalls and shops with her. Before the day was over she had a job with Aunty Wassana. Lek came every day to buy noodles. He would sit and chat to her for a while, watching her serve soup and clear tables, making her giggle with his jokes.

Lek hadn't been to see her that day. Bee looked down the road one last time before setting off for home, leaning forwards as she pushed the heavy barrow laden with all the stall's equipment. It wasn't far to Aunty Wassana's house. Boo, the little lapdog, ran out to meet her, yapping, running around her legs. Boo was doted upon, caressed, cajoled, brushed and stroked more than any other dog Bee had ever seen. Aunty Wassana fed Boo with morsels from her own plate, would turn the fan towards the little dog on a hot day, tied its topknot with ribbons, and even allowed it to lick her face. She would spend hours in the evening combing through its fur for ticks, squeezing them between her fingernails, lamenting the poor dog's suffering as blood spurted out of the swollen bodies. "Poor Boo, poor, poor Boo, Mama's darling Boo, does that feel better now?" Aunty Wassana's special voice for the dog made Bee want to laugh.

Bee parked the barrow outside and went into the house. Aunty Wassana was sitting in front of a small mirror, winding her short hair around foam rollers. A bottle of nail polish lay beside her on the floor and a smart blouse, newly ironed, hung from the door. Her husband, Uncle Ong, was coming home today. Bee went into the kitchen to set about her tasks, nipping her cuticles on the vinegar and chilli she spooned into the tiny sachets, chopping up chicken bones for the next day's stock, peeling garlic, and washing the morning glory. She liked this part of the day, left alone with her own thoughts: this dull routine was somehow comforting.

Someone called her name from outside. She looked up through the back door to see Lek waving from the street. Bee laid down her knife and took off her apron, glancing in the mirror before going out to meet him.

"I brought you some mangoes," said Lek, "they're almost ripe."

"Shouldn't you be at work?"

"Don't worry; Sergeant Yud is at the police station. There's been a robbery or something. How are you?"

"Fine."

"I wondered if you would like to come to the old Hindu shrine tonight. It's a nice walk up there and a great place to watch the sunset. We could take a picnic."

Bee blushed. "I'll have to ask Aunty Wassana. I'm not sure she'll approve."

"What's to disapprove of? Didn't I tell her we were cousins anyway? She thinks we're family, she won't mind." Lek's eyes searched Bee's face so hard she had to turn away.

"I'll ask her later. I'd better get back now before she notices I've gone – and so should you!"

Lek laughed, pushing his long fringe out from his eyes, turning quickly to skip back down the road to the construction site, whistling, hands deep in pockets. Bee went into the kitchen, emptied the bag of mangoes into the sink, turning the heavy fruits over in one hand as she washed them, rubbing the water over the smooth yellow skin with her thumb. She started humming the tune Lek had been whistling, a tune from home.

* * *

The sun was just setting by the time they reached the old monastery. Lek climbed in front, taking the worn stone steps two at a time, a cloth bag slung over his shoulder.

"Just a few more steps, Bee!"

Bee joined him on the top step, breathing heavily. They turned round to look at the view, the valley before them, the village in miniature, the fields stretching out to touch the mountains. Home on the other side.

"Look, there's the temple, and the marketplace... and the police station. Can you see?"

Bee nodded and turned to look behind her. "What is this place anyway?"

116

"It's an old temple or something. There's a shrine over there. Want to see? Come on, I'll show you."

An overgrown path from the top step led to an uneven floor built of huge stone slabs, between which creepers and vines had pushed through, disturbing the stones. Beetles and spiders nested underneath in the damp earth. "Watch out for snakes," warned Lek. A few broken columns remained, an abandoned altar to one side. In the middle of the floor a thick, red-brick pillar rose up to a blunt point at waist height. It was cracked and chipped. Garlands of once white jasmine, now brown and rotting, had been thrown over it. Candle and incense stubs littered the ground around it, alongside remnants of offerings stuck on shreds of banana leaves. Tiny squares of gold leaf had been stuck to the pillar. Bee moved closer.

"What is it?" she asked, her hand resting on the tip.

Lek laughed. "Don't you know?"

She withdrew her hand. "No."

"It's a lingam. Shiva's lingam."

"What's a lingam?"

"Symbol of fertility. I've heard some of the villagers come here when they want to start a family, pray for a baby, that kind of thing."

Bee blushed. "Let's go back and sit down."

She went over to sit on the top step, unpacking the bag. They had bought sticky rice and fried chicken from the market, red hot chilli paste, and prickly red rambutans. Bee unfolded a cloth and laid out the food. Lek pulled a leaf from a nearby tree and placed it on the ground, putting a ball of rice on it. He split the skin of a rambutan to pull out the sticky white fruit, placing it on the leaf, next to the rice.

"What are you doing?"

"It's for the lingam." He smiled at her. "Want to make merit with me? Maybe it will bring us luck."

Bee shook her head. "You go; I'll stay here." He went back over to the pillar, going down on his knees, offering the food with both hands as he muttered a prayer, then bowing, his palms flat on the stone floor.

"Come on, let's eat!"

They didn't speak much, their arms almost touching as they shared the meal, waiting for dusk to deepen over the view. Strains of the national anthem drifted up from the police station. "This is Sergeant Yud, standing to attention," said Lek at last, getting up, puffing out his belly, his hand against his head in mock salute. Bee giggled, covering her mouth.

"Was it easy to get away?" he asked.

"Easy. Aunty Wassana's husband was due home on the last bus so I think she was glad to get me out of the way. She was so excited; I've never seen her like that before. She was all dressed up and everything."

"How long is he home for?"

"Just a week. Must be hard for them, living apart all the time."

"I couldn't do that, not if I was married. I'd want to stay with my wife. Especially if she was pretty." He glanced up at Bee.

"What rubbish you talk!" she said, offering him the last rambutan. "Shouldn't we get back before night falls?" They stood up, brushing off their clothes, and started down the steps. "Watch out! It's more dangerous going down," said Lek. Bee didn't refuse the proffered hand.

* * *

It was different now that Uncle Ong was home: Bee felt glad it was only for a week. Aunty Wassana's excitement at her husband's return had soon given way to rage at the fact he was spending most of his holiday out drinking with his cronies. Uncle Ong had been working for the past three years in Saudi Arabia, for a big construction company. This was only the second time he had been back in all that time. Uncle Ong and Aunty Wassana had spent their life savings on the contract – the agent had taken a huge fee, then there was the passport, visa, work permit, airline ticket. But the wages were high and in five years Uncle Ong hoped to save enough money to buy some land and open a shop. Aunty Wassana talked about it all the time, about what she planned to sell and how her shop would be the best in the village, much more modern than Gimsia's old grocer's shop – it would be a step up from selling noodles, which was ruining her legs. There might even be a job in it for Bee, Aunty Wassana would say.

"I don't care what he says; I'm going out," declared Aunty Wassana to Bee on the last night of Uncle Ong's visit. There was a funeral on in the village: the chance for a few hands of poker. It was not unusual for Aunty Wassana to go out in the evening to play cards. Bee would stay at home to look after Boo. She would lie on the floor, looking through old magazines at pictures of big houses, silk wedding outfits, beautiful models and the famous actors and actresses she knew from the serial dramas on Channel 7. If Aunty Wassana lost she would come home early in the morning in a great huff, waking up Bee to complain about how Uncle Moon or Sergeant Yud had been cheating again, how her luck was never in no matter how hard she tried to be a good person. There was no pleasing her for a day or two. But if she had won it was different, she would hug Bee and dare her to count the pile of coins and notes that filled her pockets. She often bought something for Bee with the money: a blouse, a new pair of sandals, shampoo, her first pair of trousers.

Aunty Wassana had mentioned the funeral earlier and there had been another argument. Uncle Ong was always complaining: he worked harder than Aunty Wassana would ever know in Saudi Arabia, conditions were terrible, it was a huge sacrifice, and all she could do was take the money he sweated and slaved for and throw it away on a card game. Did she think he had a good time there? He even shouted that it was just as well she couldn't have children – she was a cardsharp, a gambler, not fit to be a mother. Aunty Wassana had replied that he didn't understand, he never had, how could he say that, and went running outside to pick up Boo, hugging the little dog to her chest, kissing its head. Bee, who was making the stock, had paused, looking up at Uncle Ong. "Had your fill?" he sneered, catching her eye. He had grabbed his wallet and gone out then, while Aunty Wassana shouted that she didn't need his money, she had money of her own and she was going out too, never mind what he said.

Bee had stayed quiet. She just wanted Uncle Ong's visit to be over. He never spoke to her except to give an order or make a criticism: fetch me a beer, go and buy some papaya salad, there's too much sugar in my coffee, iron this shirt. His eyes followed her all the time as she went about her tasks. Aunty Wassana had changed too. She was short-tempered and edgy, even with little Boo. The dog slept curled up under the balcony now, and wasn't allowed in the house.

That night, after Lek had walked her home and Bee had finished her chores, she unfolded her sleeping mat and went to bed early. She was afraid for Aunty Wassana, afraid of what Uncle Ong might do when he came home and found his wife out at the funeral. *Maybe he will be too drunk to care*, she thought, *or maybe Aunty Wassana will be back first and he'll never know a thing.* Uncle Ong always stayed out very late, coming home smelling of smoke and drink and sweat, stumbling past into Aunty Wassana's bedroom. Bee, on her sleeping mat in the living room, would hear low voices, muffled cries, grunts, moaning from the bedroom. Bee had supposed they were too old for that kind of thing. She would squeeze her eyes shut, trying to block out the image in her head: Aunty Wassana's old green housecoat, hairnet, varicose veins, and Uncle Ong's bald head, the wart on the back of his hand, missing front tooth, rough looking hands. Once or twice Bee had heard Aunty Wassana emerge from the room a bit later, padding out to the balcony to find Boo, cradling the little dog on her lap, sighing and whispering in its ear.

She had almost fallen asleep when she heard Boo yapping outside.

"*Tho-oei!* Fucking runt, I'll wring your fucking stupid little neck!"

Bee sat up, her heart pounding. She heard a scuffle and then Boo set up the slow, steady howl of a wounded animal. *What to do?* She lay down again and pulled the blanket over her, pretending to be asleep.

Uncle Ong pushed open the door and staggered inside, past Bee. He opened the bedroom door and switched on the light. The stench of whisky filled the house.

"Fucking bitch! Useless, ugly, gambling old cow!" He turned round in the doorway, the light on behind him, gazing down at Bee. "Where the fuck is she? Huh?"

Bee sat up, hugging the blanket across her chest.

"I don't know. Gone to a friend's maybe?"

"Only friend she's got at this time of night is a pack of cards! I warned her! I told her not to go." His face was twisted, knuckles clenched. "You can get up. Go and find her. Now. You know where the temple is – go and fetch her, tell her I'm waiting. Tell her that her *husband* is waiting. For his *wife*."

He lurched in the young girl's direction. Bee jumped up, still clutching the blanket, pressing herself against the wall. The dog howled outside. *Surely*, she thought, *someone will hear it and come?* He started to laugh slowly. "What's th'matter? Think I'd touch *you*?" He sneered at her and moved closer, his breath on her face. "Not bad looking are you?" His eyes travelled up and down her body. "Nice and firm, I bet. Not like the old hag. Eh?" He grabbed her face, squeezing her cheeks between his fingers. "Still intact? Eh? Bet you are." He threw his head back and laughed again. "You know, I could sell you. To pay off the old bag's gambling debts. Sell you up at the whorehouse to some old man looking for a virgin to keep him young. Lots of your kind up there." He moved his hand, placing it over Bee's mouth. The dog whined at the door, scratching.

The young girl struggled, her hands pushing against his shoulders, but his bulk was too heavy as he pressed against her, excited by her fear, his anger. He reached with his free hand to push up her nightdress and loosen his belt, forcing her legs apart with his knee. Pinning her to the wall with his hands, he raped her, thrusting hard for only a minute or two, eyes rolling back in his head as he ejaculated, releasing her to collapse on to the floor. Bee sat against the wall, crying softly, hugging her knees. The man turned away from her without a glance. He pulled up his trousers and went into the bedroom, where he lay down on the bed, fully clothed, and fell into a deep sleep.

* * *

Aunty Wassana was behind with the orders. A knot of customers stood next to the stall, all shouting out at once. "Wide noodles, no chilli; two rice noodles; three egg noodles please; come on, I was here first!" Others sat at the tables, arms crossed, watching her hungrily.

Mother Nong, who had been shopping in the market, strolled over to the stall to enjoy the spectacle. She patted the back of her hair, which had been newly washed and set.

"Well Wassana, you're run off your feet today, aren't you?"

Wassana dipped baskets of noodles with one hand while fumbling in her money belt for change with the other. The stall was a mess: the chopping board was covered in bits of food, plastic bands and bags had fallen into the trays of noodles, dirty bowls and chopsticks pushed to one side on tables where new customers were sitting.

"I've run out of egg noodles!" she wailed. "Look, you'll all have to wait!"

"*Aow*, Wassana, haven't you got any help today? Where's your little *Dai Nok* girl got to?"

"She left, Mother Nong. As if you didn't know. Yesterday. I got up in the morning and she'd gone, bags and all, without so much as a word."

"Did she steal anything?" asked Mother Nong, greedy for the details. "Did she take any money or jewellery or anything?"

"No, she didn't." Aunty Wassana said over her shoulder, slopping soup into three bowls and banging them down on one of the tables.

"One of Yud's boys disappeared too. That Lek. Weren't they meant to be cousins or something?"

"Mm."

"They were probably carrying on with one another; being cousins wouldn't stop their kind! Anyway, Wassana," said Mother Nong, unable to contain herself any longer, "they didn't get very far."

"What d'you mean?" Wassana let go of the long-handled noodle basket and turned to Mother Nong.

"Yud heard – they were arrested at the first checkpoint. Guards got on the bus to ask for everyone's ID and they didn't have any, of course. Made them get off the bus. They pretended they'd lost their cards. As if the guards would swallow that."

"So they'll be deported?"

"Taken to the border and sent packing. Good riddance, I say. Want to know how the guards caught them out, proved they were illegals?" Mother Nong smirked.

"How?"

"Asked them to sing the national anthem! Couldn't get further than the first line." Mother Nong laughed out loud. "I warned you, didn't I? We can do without their sort round here."

"*Tho-oei!*" cried Aunty Wassana as she suddenly remembered the long-handled basket, staring at the soggy lump of ruined noodles she had yanked, too late, from the depths of the boiling hot stock.

First Prize in the Strong Man Contest

To contain his nervous excitement, Gimsia is stocktaking. Unable to sleep, he rose earlier than usual, washed and changed into clean pyjamas, executed his daily exercises – thirty arm rotations, thirty knee-bends – and chewed three cloves of raw garlic, washed down with a small pot of jasmine tea. Then he started on the rice sacks, worked his way through the dried noodles and fish sauce bottles, tackled the sardine cans, condensed milk and curry paste, only to reach an impasse with the whisky bottles on the top shelf. *Twelve.* Climbing down the small stepladder he checks the number again in the ledger. *Should be thirteen, not twelve.* He stomps back up the ladder, recounts the bottles out loud, jabbing his forefinger at each one.

"…ten, eleven, twelve… *aiyaa*… have you been selling things and not writing them down in the ledger?"

"What things?" his wife calls from the back shop, where she boils rice for his morning porridge.

"Bottle of whisky missing," grunts Gimsia, blinking at the shelf.

"Only person I've sold whisky to recently is Uncle Moon – his usual bottle, every morning. And I *always* write it down." Mother Pon carries on chopping pickled cabbage.

Gimsia climbs back down, sits at the desk, stares at the ledger. He reaches for his abacus and counts the number of days Uncle

Moon has been in for his daily bottle since the last stocktaking. *Seven. Who else has bought whisky?* Gimsia frowns. *A bottle yesterday for Uncle Daeng.* A wooden ball races across the abacus: clack! *A bottle last Thursday for Sergeant Pan*: clack! Gimsia pauses, staring at the yellow cat perched on top of the rice sacks. The cat yawns.

"You want egg or chopped pork in your porridge?" Mother Pon stands in the doorway.

"*Aiyaa!* Can't you see I'm trying to think?"

She shrugs her shoulders, turning away. "Eggs then."

Ah yes! Two bottles last Monday for Uncle Nun. That's right, old fool had won at the cockfighting. Gimsia had declined his offer of a drink, waving his hand in the air above his head. He didn't drink. Two more wooden balls chased across: clack! clack! But that still left one bottle. He peers at the ledger. *Same last month and the month before. All the way back to February.* A missing bottle of whisky is still not accounted for.

"Here." His wife lays his breakfast on the desk.

Gimsia grunts, picking up a small, ladle-shaped spoon to stir the steaming *khao tom.*

"I wanted chopped pork," he complains.

He raises a spoonful halfway to his mouth and stops. The spoon clatters down on the tray, hot porridge spattering his pyjama jacket. *Of course,* he thinks. *How could I forget?* He had been about to close, it had been a Tuesday or Wednesday, sometime in February – when Sergeant Yud's son, the one who had become a novice, drove up with another boy, asking silly questions, revving up the dust outside the shop with their motorbike. *One of them,* Gimsia decides, *stole the missing bottle. Hmm.* He curls his lip, nodding, and picks up the spoon.

But the boy had become a novice months ago; Mother Pon had gone to the ordination. *Should I tell Sergeant Yud his son is a thief?* Gimsia sucks the hot porridge from the spoon. *No*, he determines, *always stay on the right side of the law.*

"I'm off to market." His wife walks past him, basket across her arm.

"Thousand-year-old eggs!" barks Gimsia at her back.

"I *know*!" she retorts.

Thousand-year-old eggs are his son's favourite. The first time Dee saw the blackened eggs on his plate, the whites turned to a thick jelly, he refused to eat, insisting the eggs were bad. Weren't eggs meant to be white with yellow yolks? Gimsia had gathered his tearful son on to his lap, quickly inventing a story about hungry bandits who had stolen eggs from ducks' nests in the forest. The bandits hadn't realized the ducks were actually giants in disguise. When the ducks returned to the nest and found their eggs missing they grew mad with rage and changed back into giants. The bandits, about to boil the eggs for dinner, heard the giants thundering towards them, shouting through the trees. "We will bite off the heads of the outlaws who stole our eggs!" The bandits were quick-witted though; accustomed to hoarding all kinds of stolen treasure, they managed to bury the eggs deep in the black earth, hiding from the giants in a bush. The giants, more brawn than brain, found neither the bandits nor the eggs. A thousand years passed. One day a beautiful young woman with long black hair was gathering herbs in the forest when she noticed something strange poking out of the earth. She knelt down, dug at the earth with her soft white hands, and uncovered the eggs, which she put in her basket. She took them to the palace to show the emperor. The emperor ordered his cook to prepare the eggs for supper and was so impressed with their delicious salty flavour that he married the young woman.

Gimsia finishes his soup and starts to put the wire racks outside the shop: rubber sandals to the left, soap powder, straw hats and sandpaper to the right. He spots Mother Pensri across the street, in front of the market. He waves, beckoning her to come over.

"What is it, Gimsia?"

"A ticket for this afternoon, please. One hundred baht on the last two numbers, Mother Pensri, two and three."

Mother Pensri reaches into her pocket for notepad and pencil, looking up at him curiously. "Not like you to buy a ticket, Gimsia. Did you have a dream?"

"Dee is coming home today," says the old man, nodding seriously, "and it's his birthday. Twenty-three."

"Twenty-three! I can't believe it! Has he finished college yet?"

"Passed with honours, Mother Pensri, MBA – *Master of Business Administration*."

Mother Pensri hands over the slip of paper. "Congratulations, Gimsia, you must be very proud."

Gimsia folds the paper carefully and puts it in the breast pocket of his pyjama jacket. "Need any bananas today, Mother Pensri? *Gluay hom*: ever so sweet."

"Do you have to pester everyone to buy bananas?" Mother Pon, back from the market, lays her full basket on the desk, smiling at Mother Pensri.

"What are you cooking?" Mother Pensri peers into the basket.

Mother Pon counts the dishes off on her fingers. "Glass noodle soup with tofu and minced pork, steamed chicken with lemon grass, fried morning glory with soy bean sauce and thousand year old eggs with crispy holy basil leaves. Dee's home today."

"Gimsia was just telling me." Mother Pensri looks from Gimsia to Mother Pon. "How quickly they grow up, eh? Seems like only yesterday Dee was running around with the other kids. Always such a polite boy. So tidy and neat, compared to the others." She clears her throat. "How long will he stay?"

"Back for good," says Gimsia, wiping the porridge stain his wife has silently pointed to, "finished his studies, time to help his old father in the shop. Expand the business."

The two women exchange glances. "Well, we'll see," says Mother Pon brightly.

"Nothing to see." Gimsia shakes his head firmly. "Boy's been gallivanting around the city long enough. Should settle down, get a wife. Start a family. Grandchildren." Gimsia wags his forefinger at the shopping basket. "Can't you see I'm stock-taking? How am I supposed to read the ledger when your basket's on top of it?" He turns to the wire racks, fussing with the rubber sandals, muttering under his breath.

* * *

Mother Pon disappears into the rooms above the shop. She sweeps out the bedrooms, wipes the floors and changes the bed sheets. She shakes the mothballs from Dee's mosquito net and takes it downstairs to soak in soapy water. Her son hasn't spent a night at home for two years. Too busy with his studies and a part-time job, he said. Mother Pon has been to visit him though, more than once: a mother cannot wait forever to see her only child. It isn't that far to the city, only four hours by bus. Gimsia always refuses to come with her. He won't close the shop, not even for a day, an afternoon, an hour – not even at Chinese New Year! He won't trust anyone to look after the shop either. Mother Pon rubs the net gently between her hands. In fact, Gimsia never goes anywhere, he pays other people to buy wholesale from the big market in the city. Mother Pon sighs. Her husband has changed so much over the years. She remembers the first time she saw him. Her Aunty Dai took her to the annual flower festival in the northern capital: floats, a big procession, food stalls, beauty contests, a strong man contest. She and her aunt stood at the front of the crowd to watch the men lifting heavier and heavier sacks of rice on to their backs, standing on quivering legs for the allotted two minutes. She wanted the handsome young Chinese man to win because no one seemed to be cheering him on. And he did. When he received his prize – a *pha khao ma* checked man's sarong, ten baht and a small silver trophy– she clapped as loud as she could, willing him to turn round and notice her. When he did she held his gaze boldly for a few moments before her aunt pulled her away. But he followed them around the festival all day like a stray dog. When they went to find the truck to take them home he asked the driver for a lift. "Where to?" the driver asked. "Can go anywhere," said the young man, in a strong accent. He had a large box tied up with string which he lifted on to the back of the truck. "Shirt and a pillow," Auntie Dai said, "that's all the immigrants bring with them – all the way from Guangdong. The Chinese are so poor," she added in a shocked whisper, "they *sell* their own daughters."

Mother Pon rinses the mosquito net and hangs it to dry on the washing line in the yard. Guangdong. She asked him, months later, what it was like in China, in Guangdong, in his village; didn't he miss it? Didn't he have sisters, parents, a sweetheart? By then Gimsia was already in business. The large box he had swung so easily on to the truck contained a sewing machine. He set up a stall by the roadside, next to the market, under the shade of a tamarind tree: just a folding table, a stool, his sewing machine. In the evening he would take soap, shampoo and the *pha kao ma* down to the river to bathe. A hammock, slung under the tree, was his bed. The villagers brought him trousers to hem, sarongs to sew up, frayed shirt collars and cuffs to mend. His prices were so cheap that people grew too lazy to do the work themselves. Before long he had earned enough to rent a room in Auntie Dai's house, giving the young Pon an excuse to talk to her strong man every day. Sisters, parents, yes, he would answer, I have family, but no sweetheart – *you* are my only sweetheart. He bought her sweets, a gold bracelet, a silk sarong, and took her to the travelling cinema when it came to town. After two years in the village he went to speak with her father; by then he had money and gold, enough to open a shop and put a down payment on a truck.

It was a few years later, after Dee was born, that Mother Pon found the picture of his child bride, tucked away at the back of a dog-eared Confucian primer: a black and white photograph of an unsmiling girl with long black braids and accusing eyes, who waited and waited for her handsome husband to return, claim her as his own, rescue her from the smoke-filled factories and the brutality of the Cultural Revolution.

Mother Pon soaks the glass noodles in hot water absent-mindedly. She used to wonder why Gimsia had married her. Had he loved her? Or was it simple pragmatism – to be accepted by the rest of the village, to show he was prepared to assimilate? Was it because her father worked in the district office, could get him a licence to trade? "*Aiyaa*," Gimsia would answer to her questions, "can't you see I don't have time for this? There's a business to run, orders to keep." Sometimes he would mutter under his breath at her in Taochiew. In the end, she decided, it didn't matter. He worked hard, saved money – a considerable fortune, she supposed – and doted on their son. He didn't drink, smoke, gamble or womanize, and he never laid a finger on her, so it could have been much worse. But after finding the photograph she had resolved there would be no more children. Gimsia, exhausted at the end of each day, didn't insist; by then she had already given him a son.

Mother Pon cuts the ends off the morning glory stalks, throwing them outside for the chickens to peck at. *What would have happened though*, she wonders, *had I conceived a daughter?*

She checks the clock on the wall. An hour until the bus arrives. Gimsia always asks, when she comes back from her visits, how the boy is. She usually says, "He's fine, Dee's just fine." She has not dared tell her husband anything else. Not that Mother Pon minds about Dee: she has thought about it carefully and decided it is all the same to her. *But what will Gimsia think?* She pulls the lid off the steamer, jabbing the chicken with a skewer.

* * *

Gimsia stands outside the shop, under the striped awning. He hosed down the street a few minutes ago, cooling the hot tarmac, washing away the dust. The market is finished. Aunty Wassana has packed up and gone home. The lottery won't be announced for another hour, the road is deserted, and villagers are dozing on cool floors. Gimsia peers along the road, hands behind his back. His wife has pulled a stool outside and sits on it with a bowl wedged between her legs, cutting mangoes into slippery orange slices. Both are silent, listening for the bus's roar as it turns the corner up by the police station. Gimsia puts his head on one side, hearing an engine. He narrows his eyes. A figure turns out of the police station on a noisy old bike, growing larger and larger as it comes along the street. Sergeant Yud putters to a graceful stop outside the shop, grinning, his huge bulk balanced delicately on the tiny moped.

"Bottle of the usual for the Chief, Gimsia! He's entertaining again!"

Mother Pon sees Gimsia looking at her. "I can't get it – my hands are all sticky! *You* get it! Anyway, I never know where you hide the good stuff!"

Gimsia glares at her, peering at the end of the road one more time before disappearing inside the shop. He shoos the sleeping cat away from the pile of rice sacks and starts to heave one of the sacks out, struggling, almost falling backwards with the dead weight. He huffs out a breath as he shuffles it across the floor. *Why*, he thinks, *did I have to hide the Chief's foreign whisky behind the rice sacks of all places?* He grabs hold of the next sack down and starts to tug.

"Here he is! Here's the bus!" calls Mother Pon.

Gimsia hears the bus lurching to a stop, brakes squealing, outside the marketplace. He lets go of the sack and turns to look out at the street – the Chief will wait, for once – where Mother Pon is getting up from her stool, wiping her hands down her apron. Sergeant Yud slaps his knee and shakes his head, wolf-whistling loudly. An attractive, oddly familiar young woman is strutting slowly across the road on high heels, dressed tastefully in blue trousers and a white blouse, pink scarf and lipstick. Gimsia stares in amazement as Mother Pon embraces her. He moves forwards to get a closer look at the girl's face, uncomfortably aware of Sergeant Yud's hoots of laughter. The girl pulls free of Mother Pon's arms and walks towards him, putting her palms together in front of her chest to make a deep *wai*. Gimsia groans. "Papa," says the apparition in a low husky voice, "aren't you going to wish me a happy birthday?"

Mali Foi Thong

Quick, run to the sala. Safer there, safe from the dogs barking at your heels, the people calling out names, the voices shouting and laughing. If you're careful, careful, careful, they will be appeased, pleased, applaud the piles of stuff you have collected for them; the bamboo and wood, the plastic bags, the scraps of food, the odds and ends, the this and that, the ifs and buts, the butts, the endless butts, smoked down to the stumps, the roots, sooty old roots, and the root-toot-toot of the dustcart and Uncle Moon jumps down and smiles and laughs and for a moment you feel good, he is kind, you are good, he says so, not a poor boy, a lonely boy, a boy who was born out of an egg, a bad egg, a big bad egg. Where's your mother Gop-Guu? Did you kill her? Split her open with your egg? Must have been you, you odds-and-ends boy. Who else, there is nobody else, nobody loves you, not him in his shed with his knife and the blood, the blood, the red, red blood that spills over into the yard and creeps like a red stain over your bare little toes.

* * *

Her name was Mali, which means jasmine, and she wore her hair in a side parting to hide a strawberry birthmark, about the size of a five baht coin, on her left cheek. The birthmark, her father claimed, was the result of a sinful episode in Mali's previous life.

Nothing as bad as murder, he would muse, brushing back Mali's hair each night in front of the dressing table mirror, maybe just some lying, a little light thieving. Laying down the brush, he often stroked his hand meditatively over Mali's blemished cheek. "It will keep you safe," he liked to say with a little sigh. "Not like your poor mother." Mali, left sitting with her reflection, would put hand to face, tracing out the small red stain, still warm from her father's touch. *What terrible lies*, she worried, *did I tell? Whose belongings did I steal?* Whispering a prayer for forgiveness, she would lie down on her bed, pulling out a magazine from the secret place under the mattress, while the jungle creaked and groaned outside and cicadas whirred through the trees. Then she would stuff cotton wool in her ears to block out the sounds of her father working through the night in the shed.

Mali and her father lived a mile apart from the rest of the village, at the end of a rough path that led from behind the morning market, out of the village, and just beyond the jungle's perimeter. The path ended at their house, which was built on stilts to keep wild animals, snakes and poisonous insects at bay. Covered with a roof of woven nipa leaves, it perched on a small patch of cleared land surrounded by coconut and banana trees. Don't ever go far into the jungle alone, her father would warn her, it's dangerous, stick to the path – you never know what might be lying in wait.

Mali's father was a butcher. The local farmers paid him to slaughter their animals: cows, pigs, the occasional buffalo, which he killed at night when the air was cool, the villagers asleep. He would spare the beasts all but their sense of foreboding, coming upon them from behind, clasping their heads tightly, drawing his huge knife quickly and expertly under warm throats. Their legs would tremble at the cut, some animals would sigh and others scream, eyes rolling back as they folded in on themselves, crumpling, thudding to the ground in their hot blood. The villagers, distant and slumbering, twitched in their sleep. The meat was hung, skinned, filleted and dissected in the shed. No matter how clean her father kept his work place, ordering Mali to pull bucket after bucket of water from the well to wash the blood-soaked earth, the small compound stank of raw meat, of warm offal, of death. Stray dogs slunk around in hungry packs, snouts poking through the undergrowth; oversized flies buzzed over the shed in a black cloud.

Every morning Mali's father would use a hand cart to wheel the cuts of meat, offal, bones, and neatly measured bags of blood along the path, dogs creeping behind him, to make his deliveries to the villagers. He would come home a few hours later to fall into a fitful sleep, tossing and turning on his mattress, the animals' eyes haunting him through clammy dreams. A man with lonely habits, he had never recovered from the death of Mali's mother. The villagers might be grateful to him for butchering their animals, but they did not seek out his friendship or shake his bloodied hand. In those days most butchers were Muslim: few Buddhists risked their fragile karma on such acts of violence. But it was more than that. The butcher's wife had died at home in childbirth: some villagers even swore they still heard her screams at night. No good could come of being friends with Mali's father. "It's as well that house is set apart," they would whisper to one another. Who was there amongst them that didn't fear the desperate ghost of a woman who has died in the act of giving birth?

Every day, as Mali walked to and from school along the path, she carefully avoided the footprints of the animals that had walked to their death the night before. It was a sin to kill. Mali knew all about sin. She learnt about it at school from her teacher, at the temple from the monks, at home from her father, and she wore its mark on her left cheek. Mali tried to be meticulous in her pursuit of merit, determined to diminish the large fund of transgression she had inherited from her previous life. She studied hard at school, respected her teacher, and helped her fellow pupils. She relinquished many hours of play to help her father with the household chores. She even suppressed her natural aversion for her father's trade to assist him in the shed. Her friends often found her at the temple, in a corner of the main hall, her legs tucked neatly behind her, praying. Even the Abbot remarked on her piety: unusual in a girl. Whilst her schoolmates sat dangling their legs from the wooden bridge crossing the river at the valley's edge, Mali studied meditation and learnt difficult prayers by heart. She had resolved to become enlightened. Her only weakness was her subscription to the monthly movie magazine *Dara Nang Ngern* – "Stars of the Silver Screen". The magazine, published in Bangkok, featured pictures and stories about the latest films, both Thai and foreign, and the most popular actors and actresses. Mali knew the names of all the big American and British stars. She would roll the foreign sounds around on her tongue like exotic fruits: *ah-jay-mes stew-art, ah-weewian lee, ah-cayree gran, ah-mareelin monro…*

Her passion for films had begun when she was twelve and her father took her on her first (and last) trip to the city. Word had come that an old spinster aunt, her mother's sister, was lying sick, delirious in the city hospital. At that time, the road to the city was little more than a dirt track. There were no buses, and few people in the village owned a truck or a car: so journeys to and from the city took days of walking and nights of camping, lighting fires to keep away wild animals. The villagers rarely encountered strangers, apart from the occasional forlorn missionary with his bag of bibles, a bandit or two, and itinerant salesmen with their magical cure-alls. But Mali and her father were lucky enough to get a lift to the city with Gimsia, the handsome young Chinese entrepreneur, who was setting up the village's first grocer's shop – although by the time Mali and her father arrived in the city, the aunt was already dead. They stayed for the funeral, helping to sort through the woman's effects, discovering amongst the old clothes and keepsakes a hoard of *Dara Nang Ngern* back issues. Whilst her father and the other relatives chatted and played cards, Mali pored over the magazines, lost in a new world of glamorous men and women, huge automobiles and red carpet events. And on their last day in the city Mali went to the cinema with some older cousins while her father went looking for a gleaming new cleaver in the huge market by the river. The cinema, run by a businessman who had made his fortune during the war procuring prostitutes for Japanese soldiers, showed the same old films over and over. That week it was *Nang Sao Suwan*, the love story of a young couple fighting against insuperable odds, the exciting culmination of which was the heroine's train ride from the south to the north of the country just in time to stop the executioner from chopping off the hero's head. From that moment on, Mali was hooked on movies. Not that she was under any illusion of ever becoming an actress: she was the daughter of a village butcher, and she had a strawberry birthmark on her left cheek.

At the age of fourteen, Mali left school. Her father had arranged for her to go and work for Grandmother Rung in the village. Grandmother Rung was a spinster: deaf, lame, outspoken, and excessively fond of cats. "Give me a cat over a man any day of the week!" she would often shout at Mali, waving her wooden stick in the air. Widowed and childless, Grandmother Rung had surrendered her energies to mastering the delicate art of confectionery. The village children made up cruel stories about her: she had hair growing between her toes, she put poison in her sweets, she cooked the cats and made desserts from them. Under the tutelage of Grandmother Rung, Mali learnt dozens of secret recipes. Within a year she had learnt how to beat egg whites to exactly the right level of stiffness, boil mung beans to within a second of over-cooking, steam sticky rice to perfection, prepare lotus seeds and cassava, barbecue bananas in their skins and scrape the flesh from coconuts to wash through muslin, using precisely the right amount of hot water to extract the thick, sweet cream. She learnt how to soak jasmine and other sweet-smelling flowers in water and use the scented water to make syrup. She learnt the art of infusing cakes with fragrance by burning aromatic candles next to them, or by storing them with flowers overnight. She learnt how to carve the skins of fruit and vegetables into the shapes of tiny flowers, how to cut intricate slivers of gold leaf to garnish sweets for weddings and other grand occasions. But Mali's speciality was *foi thong*: golden threads of egg yolk cooked hard in sugar syrup, flavoured with jasmine essence. Mali's *foi thong*, even Grandmother Rung was forced to admit, was better than her own. The old woman was delighted with the young girl's aptitude for the ancient trade. When her arthritis grew so bad that she could no longer walk from her house to the marketplace, she entrusted her stall and all its equipment to Mali. Mali became one of the market women, rising early in the morning to prepare her wares, setting up her stall before dawn, selling sweets and desserts right through to late morning when she would pack up and go home to soak more beans, mash more coconut, boil more eggs. She gave most of her earnings to her father, keeping just enough for her modest needs: some toiletries, the odd new blouse or sarong, her monthly magazines and donations to the temple. The market women liked her quiet nature, her willingness to lend a hand. They christened her Mali Foi Thong. Amazing, customers would say, nodding as they bit into the sticky sweetness of her speciality, that one so young should be so gifted with her hands! More like a blessing, her father would say as he slung the carcasses around in the shed; with Mali's face it was unlikely she would find a husband to provide for her. Not that it mattered, he said, turning to her with a smile.

* * *

"Hey, Mali Foi Thong," shouted Aunty Gaysuda from behind her vegetable stall, "have you heard the news? The *Nang Khai Ya* has come to town!"

"I can't wait," cried Aunty Dai, weighing out oranges, "I'm going to find a cure for my varicose veins!"

"Oh never mind that – I just want to see the film!" said Aunty Gaysuda.

There was talk of nothing else in the village that day. The herbal medicine salesman had arrived the night before in a pick-up truck gaily decorated with mud-splashed billboards. One side showed advertisements for an array of magical remedies: opiates, snake oil, ginseng roots, bird's-nest soup and powdered deer antlers. The other showed a badly painted picture of a dashing farang man with a fine moustache carrying a beautiful woman in his muscled arms, a torched city blazing in the background. The herbal medicine salesmen always brought a film to show before starting their sales pitch, to attract as many potential customers as possible.

An epic! – boomed the loudspeaker attached to the top of the truck – an epic story of unrequited love set against the backdrop of civil war! Not to be missed! Romance! Tragedy! War! Action! Guaranteed to set hearts on fire! Aunty Gaysuda and Aunty Dai were in a state of excitement, having spent the morning enacting possible scenes from the movie, dancing between the marrows, declaring undying love to the jackfruits, sword-fighting with a banana and a cucumber, laughing and shrieking. Mali watched them from behind her sweets, giggling at their capers. She knew all about the film, had read about it in the magazines. It had become a classic, winning eight Academy Awards when it was first released. *Ah-calark gabeel*, thought Mali automatically, and *ah-weewian lee*.

"So, Mali Foi Thong, are you coming with us to see the picture show tonight?" They turned to her, fanning their faces, resting against stalls, weak with laughter.

"I don't know," said Mali, "there's always so much to do… and… my father might not like it."

"Oh, come on Mali; there's more to life than work!" cried Aunty Dai, linking her arm through Mali's, "and the travelling cinema comes so rarely. We are taking you with us whether you like it or not!"

It was hard to refuse such an invitation, and Mali didn't want to hurt their feelings. But much as she yearned to, she had never dared to watch a film in the village before. It was because of her father. Films? *You* go, he might say, turning back to his work, *I've* too much to do here. There was something in his voice, Mali didn't know what, that made her feel it was wrong to go. For other young men and women the films were an excuse for courtship. Boys would invite girls to sit next to them, wooing them with sweets and cakes; confident boys fumbled for their sweetheart's hand halfway through the picture. The girls would scream at the frightening parts – an excuse to clutch the boys' hands more tightly – and sigh at the romantic parts, when they would rest their heads gently on heroic shoulders. There was usually a flurry of engagements, sometimes a hasty wedding, after the cinema had been in town. But no boy had ever invited Mali to see a film. She would sit outside the house at the edge of the jungle instead, listening through the night air to the vague boom of the soundtrack, the actors' ghostly voices drifting over the treetops, the music's rhythms and crescendos throbbing through the undergrowth. She would lie back, close her eyes, imagining the rest. It wasn't difficult: she knew most of the plots by heart.

That afternoon, when she returned home, she found her father working in the shed, cutting up joints of beef. He turned his tired face to Mali, hands bloodied, wiping a bead of sweat from his forehead with his wrist.

"Good day?"

Mali nodded. "Only a few cakes and some *foi thong* left." She started to break up coconuts for the next day, saving the milk in a pitcher, grinding the hard flesh through a small metal mill, her mind busy. As father and daughter worked they could hear, in the pauses between the coconut grinder, the muffled boom of the loudspeaker as the truck drove around the village. Epic! Romance!... Mali glanced up at her father.

"The women in the market," she began, "have invited me to go with them to see the film tonight."

Her father clicked his tongue.

Mali bit her lip. "Please?"

He thought for a moment, knife suspended over a red slab of flesh. "Oh, all right then. You are going with the women, after all. But don't be late."

Mali nodded, barely listening. "Of course, Papa."

* * *

She ran down the path at dusk to find her fellow vendors sitting on a rattan mat spread out on the grassy clearing in front of the district office. The women had brought leftovers from their stalls: bunches of longans, banana fritters, green papaya salad, sticky rice, water flavoured with pandanus leaf. Mali had brought a few coconut cakes and the leftover *foi thong*. The whole village had turned out to see the film and listen to the salesman peddle his unguents and medications, mothers with babies asleep in their laps, groups of men sharing moonshine as they exchanged witty quips, young couples leaning their heads together in dark corners, small children chattering at the front. An older man in a distinctive bowler hat was hanging up a huge sheet that functioned as a screen, securing the tops of it to the balcony of the district office, whilst a younger man set up the projector at the rear. Aunty Dai nudged Mali and turned round to the young man.

"When's this film going to start? We've been waiting ages! Can't you work any faster – don't you know it's past my bedtime?"

"Sorry ladies!" he shouted back. "I'm going as quick as I can! Spare a thought for a poor fellow far from home who works so hard he hasn't even had time for dinner!"

"No dinner?" cried Aunty Gaysuda. "Why didn't you say? You can come over here and share some dinner with us!" Aunty Gaysuda simpered, batting her eyelashes, as the rest of the women hooted with laughter.

"I might just do that, ladies," answered the young man quickly, his white teeth shining in the dark, "just wait until I get the first reel rolling!"

Seconds later the film crackled into life; all heads turned towards the huge screen. From the opening credits, Mali was transfixed. The story of Rhett and Scarlett was much more beautiful, infinitely more exotic, than *Nang Sao Suwan*. She hardly noticed the young man who came to sit next to her on the mat, nor the way he winked cheekily at the other women and helped himself to their food. It was only after an hour and a half had passed, the film juddering to an uncertain stop, that Mali realized she had been sitting next to a young man at all. He jumped up, mouth full of *foi thong*, to change the reel, the audience hissing and booing at the delay. "Are you enjoying it?" he whispered to her as he sat back down. He had never seen anyone quite so enthralled. She nodded, her hand instinctively over her cheek, even in the dark. "Good," he said, "the second part is even better." Mali nodded, turning back to the screen. She already knew what would happen next.

At the end of the film the young man packed away the reels, grinning at Mali, hoisting the heavy equipment easily on to the back of the truck, while his uncle started to unpack the potions and cure-alls he had brought to sell. Oil lamps were lit around the truck, illuminating the man's face, his moustache and bowler hat. He cleared his throat.

"Good ladies, kind gentlemen, I hope you have enjoyed the film. Before you leave, however, I would like to take this rare opportunity to introduce to you, tonight, and only tonight, a new tonic." The man paused, holding aloft a sample bottle, casting his eyes around the crowd. "Not just any tonic, but a tonic that delivers a cure for every ache and pain known to man and woman, a treatment for every disorder. There is no disease, physical or hysterical, that this medicine cannot treat. And all for fifty *satangs* a bottle!"

"Will it help my husband?" shouted Aunty Dai. "He's losing his hair!"

The peddler smiled indulgently at Aunty Dai, then removed his hat, revealing a full head of thick black hair. "Lady," he said, placing his hat over his heart, "I too was once bald. Bald as an egg. Before I discovered the tonic. And now look at me!" A low murmur went through the crowd, and men turned to one another to nod. "Baldness, back pain, stomach pain, headaches, fevers, toothache, cuts and grazes, bites and stings, boils, pimples, rashes, incontinence, freckles…"

Mali listened to the man, staring at the bottle. *No disease? Physical or hysterical? All disorders? What*, she thought, *if I rub it on to the birthmark? Might it, could it… disappear?* The

146

villagers were already starting to sidle up to the truck, picking up the bottles, straining to read the labels in the lamplight. *What*, she panicked, *if the bottles sell out?* She fumbled in her pocket, digging out her purse. A soft voice whispered close to her ear.

"Do you want to buy a bottle? Shall I get it for you?" It was the young projectionist.

Mali nodded, handing over the coin.

The young man went over to his uncle, pushing through the eager villagers, coming back with a bottle for Mali. She looked at the picture on the label: a foreign looking apothecary in a white coat, whiskers like the peddler's, arms folded seriously, was standing authoritatively in front of a shelf full of bottles. Snakes, mysteriously entwined, twisted around the label borders. A row of scorpions was at the top. The writing on the back was Chinese.

"Thank you."

"What's your name?" he asked.

"Mali."

"Mali Foi Thong's her proper name." Aunty Dai shook her finger at the young man.

"Did you make those delicious *foi thong* then?"

Mali shook her head shyly.

"'Course she did, there's nobody else for miles around that makes *foi thong*!" said Aunty Gaysuda, pulling the girl's arm. "Come on Mali, time to get you home else your father will be wondering what's happened to you!"

"Good night then!" said the young man softly. "I'll see you in the market tomorrow to buy some more of your *foi thong*! Sweet dreams, Mali!"

Mali walked back through the village with the women, smiling in the dark, her fingers tucked around the bottle in her pocket, listening to the chatter about the film.

"Wouldn't mind if *my* husband was that rich!"

"Imagine having to wear a corset though!"

"But wasn't she the prettiest thing? Such a tiny waist!"

"I hope this potion can help me get my figure back! My husband says I have a back-end like a buffalo!"

"I wonder if there's a potion that can cure my husband's bad temper?"

When they reached the marketplace Mali bid them goodnight, weaving her way quickly through deserted stalls, along the familiar path, the moon shining like an old friend through the treetops. The film soundtrack and the young man's voice reverberated in her head, all muddled up. Without realizing, she broke into a skipping run.

* * *

The next day, after a night of restless dreams, Mali rose late, an hour before dawn, just as her father was wheeling the meat away from the shed, down the path. She flew about her tasks, preparing a fresh batch of *foi thong*, washing her hair, raking impatiently through her few possessions for her prettiest clothes. She pulled the bottle out from under her pillow and sat at her mirror, staring at the label, unable to decide whether she should swallow a spoonful of the potion or rub a small amount on her birthmark. In the end she decided to do both. There was no immediate improvement, but she comforted herself with the thought that such cures took time and perseverance. Distracted, she completely forgot about the monks' early morning alms round. The monks made a special detour every morning to pass Mali's house, sure of a regular donation of food from the butcher's daughter. Mali usually waited for them, standing in front of the house with a bowl of curry and rice. That morning, however, she had been so busy; it wasn't until she heard the monks chanting outside the window that she came to her senses, scrabbling around for something, anything, to offer them. She looked over at the fresh batch of *foi thong*; it would do, she supposed, but then she wouldn't have enough left for the stall. *Does it matter?* she asked herself. *It shouldn't... but today it does.* Overriding her conscience, she grabbed a bunch of bananas and some green mangoes instead. *Never mind,* she reasoned, stepping out of her sandals to kneel before the monks, *I'll make an extra big portion of curry to give them tomorrow.* Her toes twitched impatiently as she listened to the blessing. The monks gone, she dressed in her best sarong and the new white blouse intended for the end of Lent celebrations. Loading her barrow quickly, she set off down the path. *What if I miss him? What if he's gone back to the city already? What will he think, in the hard light of day, of my birthmark?*

Mali stopped at the back of the market and rested her barrow. She looked around at the bushes, hands fluttering, then picked off some bright orange marigolds and a few sprigs of jasmine. When she got to her stall she laid it out with unusual precision, the flowers woven neatly around and between the rows of sweets. In the centre she set up her small mountain of golden *foi thong*.

Aunty Dai leant over and whispered in her ear. "*Oh-ho*, Mali! Don't you look pretty today? And so does your stall! What's the occasion then?"

"Nothing! I just... It's that... you know, I wanted to... make an effort," Mali concluded, blushing, busy rearranging.

"Expecting a special guest are you?" Aunty Dai smiled, as if recalling an old joke. "And why not? Pretty young girl like you!"

"Don't say anything to my father!"

"Don't worry, little Foi Thong, your secret's safe with me!" Aunty Dai nudged Mali, nodding in the direction of the street. "That wouldn't be your special guest now, would it?"

Mali glanced up quickly, heart pounding. The young man was standing next to the pick-up truck, one hand shading his eyes, as if searching for something, someone. He waved at Mali and strolled across, stopping to chat to the other vendors. "Lovely vegetables aunty! Did you grow them yourself? How much do you charge for those oranges? *How* much? Can I taste one first?" The women simpered and shook their heads, giggling as he threaded his way through the stalls. Mali kept her eyes down, painfully aware of his approach.

"Hello again, Mali Foi Thong, how are you today? Did you sleep well last night? *Aow*, what a lovely stall you have! And what a selection of sweets! Did you make them all yourself?"

Mali nodded, fumbling at the coconut cakes.

"Will you sell me some of your delicious sweets?"

"Of course," she whispered, "what would you like?"

"Oh, make it two of everything! And a dozen of your wonderful *foi thong* please. I can eat them on the journey back to the city, they will remind me of this pretty village..." the young man's voice dropped low, "and of the pretty girls who live here."

"You're going back today?"

"Midnight. My uncle prefers to drive at night. It's cooler."

Mali's hands trembled as she packed the sweets into banana leaves. "And will you be back soon? With another film?"

"Would you like that, Mali?"

"Of course, I mean... I... like films."

"What films d'you like then?"

"All kinds. I mean, I haven't *seen* many films but I *read* all about them. I get this magazine, you see, from Bangkok." Mali pulled the latest edition from the bottom of her basket to show him.

He flicked through the pages. "Reading about films isn't the same as watching them, is it? Not nearly as exciting."

Mali shook her head. "So, will you be back with another film soon?"

"Of course! I have to come back, don't I, to get more *foi thong*." The young projectionist stood so close that Mali could smell the soap from his skin. "How about I show you the brochure for all the other films we can get? Would you like to see that? You can help me choose which films to bring. My uncle lets me pick all the new films."

"Well, I don't know..." Mali blushed, handing over the package of sweets, her mind racing. *Hasn't he noticed my birthmark? Doesn't he mind?*

"I don't even know your name!" she said at last.

"Moon," he replied, stretching out a hand, farang style. "Pleased to meet you, Mali!"

Mali giggled, shaking hands. Moon's hand was warm. She could feel his thumb gently tickling her palm and knew she should pull away.

"What do you say Mali? Where's the harm in looking at pictures?"

151

Withdrawing his hand at last, he fumbled in his pocket, pulling out a five baht coin. He walked round the stall to stand behind Mali. With one hand on her waist, he leant over her shoulder to drop the coin into her apron pocket.

"I'll meet you later," he breathed into her ear, "about seven o'clock – behind the market, at the edge of the jungle." Picking up the package of sweets, he strolled out the market, whistling the theme tune from the movie the night before.

Mali stared at the five baht coin in the palm of her hand, still hot from his touch. Her knees were trembling. *Five baht*, she panicked, *is far too much! Now I will have to meet him just... just to give him his change.*

* * *

Uncle Moon stops the dustcart at the *sala* to wait for Gop. It's not like Gop to be late. Uncle Moon hopes nothing has happened to him. He reaches into his back pocket for whisky, licking his lips. *A half bottle a day isn't bad*, he reasons to himself, *it could be much worse*. He has no wife to worry about, and plenty time to sleep it off in the afternoon after he's been to the tip. A man needs a drink inside him, he often remarks to his cronies, just to stomach the stink up there. Uncle Moon plays absent-mindedly with the penis amulet around his neck, looking up to see Gop approaching, laden with rubbish as usual. Uncle Moon peers at Gop's shaggy head, noticing grey hair for the first time. *How old is he anyway? Tho-oei, must be... let's see... about thirty-five now*. Pushing back his cap to scratch his head, he counts the years off on his fingers. It's fifteen years now that he's been driving round the village collecting garbage, waiting for Gop at the end of the round. Uncle Moon shakes his head, takes a long swig from the bottle and jumps down from the cart. *How time passes.* He swaggers towards Gop like a cowboy, pulling imaginary pistols from his waist.

"*Aow*, stranger! You the new sheriff? What's that? You've come to save the village?" Moon bows elaborately.

Root toot toot: here he is, the other one, the kind one, no blood, no knife, just smiling and laughing and admiring the things you have brought, back to the safe, the cave, you are brave, he knows you are brave.

"You've got a lot of stuff today, haven't you? Can I take a look? *Oh-ho*, isn't this ancient treasure though? Washed up from a shipwreck? Are you a pirate then?" Moon hops around on one leg.

Look, look, bamboo, wood, bags and food, odds and ends.

Uncle Moon collapses on the steps of the *sala*, suddenly tired. The sun is high and the rubbish in the cart will start to stink if he doesn't shift it soon. He considers the whisky bottle carefully before swallowing the last few drops. Raising a finger, heavy with secrets, he turns to Gop.

"I remember her, you know, even though we only met twice. Like it was yesterday. I've never wanted any other woman but Mali. Mali Foi Thong. She made the best *foi thong* I ever tasted. And she was a pretty girl, don't let anyone tell you different. Even that birthmark she tried so hard to hide was pretty too, in a funny sort of way..." Uncle Moon pauses, taking a gulp of air, "...believe me boy, I didn't mean to go that far but we were talking and laughing and the moon was full and it was just meant to be a kiss and then..."

Where's your mother Gop? Did you kill her, did you? Split her open with your rotten bastard egg?

Uncle Moon frowns at Gop, who is pulling the rubbish out from under his shirt, arranging it in neat piles, muttering all the while. "Must have been hard for you, never knowing a mother. Living in that old house in the jungle. Nobody liked going there. Only that strange old man to look after you. They say he never got over his wife's death, and went mad when Mali died too." Moon shakes his head and shivers. "I remember the day *he* died. Terrible disease. Screamed like a pig. Some people said it was retribution. For killing all those poor beasts or something."

Uncle Moon squints up at the mountains, and rubs the back of his hand across his eyes. "I know. I should have come back before, I did mean to. Come back and see her, bring another film. I loved her, I really did. I would have looked after her, if I'd known. But the rains started and part of the road was washed away. I couldn't have got the truck up here if I'd tried. And when my uncle got the chance to open his own cinema in the south, I had to go with him." Moon turns back to Gop, hands outstretched. "What else could I do?" Gop, too busy with his own stuff, offers no answers.

There is nobody else, nobody loves you, not him in his shed with his knife and the blood, the blood, the red, red blood that spills over into the yard and creeps like a red stain, a red-hot stain over your bare little bastard toes.

History Lessons

Sia Heng appointed Mother Pensri as the supervisor of his production line: a clever choice, pleasing the female workers and throwing the male workers off balance. There was less chance of any slacking or cheating with a woman in charge. He sat back in his little office at one end of the workshop, a pile of new orders on his desk, looking out over his small but lucrative venture. *With time and patience*, he told himself, *the mulberry leaf becomes a silk gown.* The Relic Committee had been awarded a business grant by the province, and with the exception of two or three dissenters had been easily persuaded to fund half the enterprise. Sia Heng had put up the rest and the profits were split down the middle. The Committee's share would go into a community fund for local projects: festivals, student bursaries, road and drain improvement, and a new dustcart.

The workshop produced imitation relics, made from simple clay castings filled with molten metal. Uncle Daeng, out of work since selling his rice field to a rich neighbour, operated the small forge. A few *Dai Noks* worked on polishing and buffing the coins, packing the different sizes into tissue paper-lined boxes. The boxes were red, emblazoned with a golden dragon: Sia Heng's logo of choice (he had been born in the Year of the Dragon). Average output was fifty relics a day but Sia Heng was ready to expand. Mother Pensri kept everyone up to speed, organized lunch breaks, checked numbers (for which she had a natural flair) against orders, calculated the wages, planned the staff rota and reported any enquiries to Sia Heng. She had wangled a part-time job for her husband too, sweeping and cleaning the workshop, which curbed the hours Uncle Nun could spend at the whisky stall. She made sure all his wages went straight to her. Demand for the imitation relics had grown; devotees from across the country, having read of the miraculous discovery in the newspapers, were flocking to the village to visit the sacred spot where the original had been found, and most of them wanted to buy a copy. There was talk of setting up a souvenir shop at the shrine. *T-shirts*, thought Sia Heng, *commemorative plates, Kodak and Fuji film, cold drinks, snacks, maps and postcards. Foreign tourists will lap it up – it'll put the village squarely on the map!* He was planning a colourful poster of this year's Songkran beauty queen cradling a relic in her lovely lap. But he would have to ask the Police Chief first. Sia Heng had even come up with the brilliant idea of levelling out the old steps and having a new walkway built to make the ascent easier for older devotees and tourists. It would mean destroying the original steps and cutting down some ancient trees, but business was business and change was inevitable.

Worship of the lingam in the old ruined shrine had flourished; several women had given up their market stalls to weave jasmine garlands for the worshippers. By the end of the day the lingam was often buried under wreaths of snowy-white blossoms. Aunty Wassana had considered moving her noodle stall up to the ruins – there was a fortune to be made – but she couldn't navigate the steps. No one had listened to the Abbot when he pointed out that while the relic was a sacred Buddhist artefact, a symbol of Enlightenment – the lingam was something else altogether. So what? people exclaimed; where was the harm in worshipping both? The Abbot had tried to scupper the project right from the start. So had the Schoolteacher – so enthusiastic at the beginning, poring over his books to discover how old the relic was and where it originated from; but since the factory had opened the Schoolteacher had resigned from the committee. *Had got to his feet during one meeting*, Sia Heng remembered, *and shaken his fist at me and the other members, calling us all capitalists, shouting that the fund should all be given to the school! Something about a school library? Who did he think he was? Anyway, what was wrong with the way things were turning out? Didn't everyone benefit?* Sia Heng shook his head with a wry smile, turning to look out the window. The weather had been close and humid for days now. It was agonizingly still in the valley, but dark purple clouds were coming in from the east, gathering over the mountains. He picked up a small white flannel from a pile on his desk and wiped his brow and neck, tossing the used flannel into the bin – a small enough luxury, but one that Sia Heng knew many women found irresistible.

"Sia," said Mother Pensri, entering the office with a barely perceptible curtsey, "the Headman left a message for you."

"What message, Mother Pensri?"

"The Relic Committee has called an emergency meeting. In twenty minutes. At the school."

"The school? Why the school?

"No idea," answered Mother Pensri, mopping her brow, "but the Headman looked quite worried."

Sia Heng fiddled with one of the lucky ceramic Chinese cats on his desk. It sat up on its hind legs, a front paw raised, beckoning prosperity. *Aiyaa*, he thought, *what are they fretting about now? Isn't everything going along smoothly?*

"Ah well, I expect it's a storm in a teacup. Thanks Mother Pensri. And while you're here – go and get me some noodle soup. This meeting might drag on for hours – they usually do. You know how I like my soup. Plenty of chilli. *Aow*, and some of those nice red bean dumplings as well." He pulled out a large banknote and fluttered it at Mother Pensri. "And get some for the workers while you're at it."

Mother Pensri folded the note carefully, sticking it under her bra strap as she walked out the factory. *Aunty Wassana will be furious*, she thought with a smirk, *at having to change such a big note.* She opened her umbrella for shade from the hot sun as she walked across the street. Sergeant Pan and Sergeant Yud were perched on bar stools at the moonshine stall, drinking, crunching on ice cubes to keep cool.

"Mother Pensri! Got any tips for next week's lottery?" shouted Yud.

"I've no time for the *lottery* these days," she replied in a voice loud enough to reach Wassana's ears, tossing her head and sniffing.

Sergeant Yud laughed, nudging Sergeant Pan. "It's all change round here since that relic was discovered! I reckon the Police Chief is expanding his guest house too; heard he got another big delivery of wood last night," said Yud, winking, "*during the night*, that is! How many bungalows is he planning to build?"

"Not for us to know, Yud. Just do your job and keep your mouth shut, you should know that by now," said Sergeant Pan philosophically, raising a glass to his friend and downing the liquor in one swallow. "He probably expects a tourist invasion now the village is officially *historical*. Two more Widow Ghosts please, Lai."

"Hey," called Sergeant Yud, spotting the Schoolmaster riding past on his bicycle, "fancy a glass, Schoolmaster? A quick Widow Ghost before dinner?"

Sergeant Pan sniggered at the innuendo. The Schoolmaster carried on cycling; a folded-up magazine was tucked into the back of his trousers. A voracious reader, he subscribed to a wide range of publications: history, arts, politics, literature. The journal he had collected that day was about archaeology; he had become absorbed in the subject since the discovery of the relic. Flicking through the pages at the shop, he had found an article that he was most anxious to show the Relic Committee. *They'll be sorry now*, he fumed, pedalling harder.

"No thanks, in a hurry!" cried the Schoolmaster, almost knocking Gop to the ground as he took the corner by the market too quickly.

"Where you off to, Schoolmaster?" shouted Pan.

"Relic Committee – special meeting!"

Gop, startled by the near accident, had dropped his day's bundle. He bent down to pick it up, stuffing the bags and papers under his shirt.

"*Ai* Gop, fancy another day in the cells?" said Sergeant Yud, chortling. He clambered off his stool and started to give chase, lumbering towards Gop, arms outstretched. Gop turned tail and scuttled off, booty scattering on the road, scared they would lock him up again. Not that the occasion hadn't provided him with rich pickings. While the village slept in after the handing-over ceremony, Gop had pulled down the red, white and blue bunting from where it sagged between the trees, laughing, dancing, dragging it along the road to decorate his *sala*. The district office grounds had been covered in scraps of food, cigarette butts, paper cups, discarded flags, all crumpled and trodden underfoot. After the governor had gone everyone relaxed: Lai opened up his stall and all the men got dead-drunk, including Uncle Moon, who was in such a bad state that he had driven the old dustcart into the river. The villagers had been without a dustcart for weeks now; many had started to grumble. Wasn't the Relic Committee supposed to be using its funds to buy a new one? Why was it taking so long? In the meantime, Gop's *sala* was stuffed full.

"There he goes," wheezed Sergeant Yud, his hands on his knees, sweat pouring down his face, "Gop-Guu – the best public servant this village has ever had!"

Sergeant Pan laughed so hard he almost fell off his stool.

* * *

The Schoolmaster paced up and down the empty classroom, the magazine rolled up in one of his hands. The article he had come across was about a shipment of antiques bound for Hong Kong that had been intercepted by customs officials in the Klong Toey port in Bangkok. Photographs showed uniformed men standing with straight backs and folded arms beside Buddha statues, ceremonial swords and daggers, stone images of the Hindu gods, antique jewellery. Individual photographic enlargements had been taken of the smaller pieces of plunder, and amongst them the Schoolmaster had spotted the familiar dull metal object. "Unbelievably Rare, Original, Ancient Metal Buddhist Talisman" ran the quote from a government expert.

What are the chances, the Schoolmaster asked himself, *of seeing two such relics in such a short space of time?* He threw the magazine down on one of the desks and ran his hands through his hair. *Could they both be genuine? Impossible.* He had found nothing in his reference books to indicate the relic was anything more than a previously undiscovered original, probably left behind by a pilgrim monk visiting the remote mountain area. *So which one was the fake? Not the one in the magazine – the experts would have spotted it straight away! In which case, who swapped it for a copy?* He blew out a breath and gazed at the blackboard, which was still covered in the day's lessons. Modern Thai history: democratic reform. Above the blackboard was a portrait of the King, flanked on either side by two flags; the red, white and blue national flag, and the yellow flag of Buddhism. Everything as it should be. He turned round. On the back wall there was a picture of Jit Phumisak – his treasured old photograph of the dead revolutionary. The Schoolmaster had pinned it up a few weeks ago out of scorn for the committee, for the factory and the whole sordid commerce of what was taking place. He knew his picture could be misconstrued. There was no mention of Jit Phumisak in the national textbooks, though every man, woman and child in Thailand knew by heart the lyrics of his revolutionary songs. The Schoolmaster decided to leave the picture where it was. He'd compromised enough. *Let them see it*, he seethed. He strode over to the window and watched them arrive: Sia Heng first, in his new Japanese car, with the District Officer in the passenger seat; the Headman on his noisy moped; the old Abbot on foot. There was no sign of the Police Chief. *He's probably too busy catching criminals*, thought the Schoolmaster, snorting out loud.

He hadn't given a thought to the seating arrangements, so the first few minutes of the meeting were spent in deciding who should sit where, which seat was higher (for the Abbot), whether the window should be left open and the fan switched on. The sky was now completely overcast; a strong wind had started to bend the trees lining the playing field, and the branches were being whipped back and forth. The first storm of the year was approaching, bringing with it heavy rain.

"So what's all this about then," said Sia Heng crossly, after matters of protocol had been attended to, looking at his watch.

"I think we should wait for the Police Chief, don't you?" The Schoolmaster clasped and unclasped his hands, folded them under his armpits, sighed loudly.

"*Aow*, can't we just get on with it?" moaned the District Officer. The meeting had interrupted his afternoon nap: his uniform was sticky, and his patience was wearing thin.

"OK, OK, OK." The Schoolmaster got to his feet and unfurled the rolled-up magazine, opening it at the article. "How would you like a short history lesson, gentlemen?" he said, folding back the pages, "about something that happened not that long ago? Something concerning a certain *relic* of ours?" He held the magazine up, pointing at the photograph on the page. "A relic so *ancient*, so imbued with magic that it can turn up in two places at the same time?" He paused, eyebrows raised, before slapping the magazine down on the desk in front of the District Officer. "Just take a look at that, will you!"

The District Officer sighed, shrugging his shoulders at the other men. Holding the magazine at arms length, he narrowed his eyes to lazily glance at the page. After a few seconds, his expression changed. He leant over the page, eyes quickly reading through the article. He looked round at the other men, mouth hanging open. Silent, he passed the magazine over to the Headman. One by one the committee members took it in. The Headman cleared his throat. The Abbot shook his head sadly. Sia Heng looked like he'd swallowed a large chilli pepper. Forked lightning ignited the sky.

"Don't you see?" said the Schoolmaster. "It's all a sham. The relic in the provincial museum is not real!"

A loud peal of thunder made the men jump.

"But... how?" asked the Headman, throwing up his hands, turning to the others, "and when?"

"Don't you mean *who*?" came the Schoolmaster's sardonic reply.

"Aren't we jumping to conclusions?" tried the District Officer. "Just because the relic was kept in the police station... doesn't mean..." His voice tailed off.

"That," said the Schoolmaster, "is precisely what it does mean. The Chief was the only one with access to the relic! He must have made a copy of it before the presentation ceremony! I bet he sold the original to one of his shady colleagues or something. What fools we were to trust him. And what fools we are going to look when this all comes out, when the provincial office discovers the precious relic is nothing more than a cheap imitation!"

"But," pleaded Sia Heng, "no one has to know! It might never come out – I mean, how many people actually read these magazines?"

"*Tho-oei*! There's no way this can be hushed up – not now – not with your factory and all the visitors and tourists and nonsense up at the old shrine! We will have to inform the provincial office straight away – before someone else does!"

"I wouldn't be surprised," said the Abbot enigmatically, casting his mind back to the presentation ceremony, "if the Governor didn't know already."

"You're right, Abbot. News like this always travels fast. And the papers won't miss the chance for a scandal."

A loud knock rattled the classroom door. The District Officer leapt out of his chair with fright. *Was it the Chief? Had he overheard?* The Schoolmaster strode over and opened the door. Mother Pensri stood on the other side, hot, out of breath, and cross.

"Sia, Sia, how long are you going to be? An official from the Forestry Department is waiting to see you. Something about clearing trees for a new path up to the shrine?"

Sia Heng groaned, covering his face with his hands. Outside, the storm clouds burst.

* * *

It had been raining for three nights and days. The drains along the main road were overflowing. Children, warned to stay away from the fast-flowing river, crouched by the roadside waiting to catch the startled fish catapulted from the river by the dangerous current. Gop's *sala* had flooded, and because there was no dustcart, the main street was swimming in debris. The garland sellers had deserted the old ruin, Aunty Wassana had been forced to close her stall, and Gop was nowhere to be seen. Lai was running odds on how long the rain would last. The storm had blown trees down along the mountain road, damaging power cables and phone lines: the electricity was off and telephones silent. Gimsia was selling candles at a tremendous rate. Everyone was starting to sneeze and shiver. The factory had been closed without explanation. The *Dai Nok* workers had nowhere else to go and were sleeping rough at the back of the market; Mother Pensri took them some food each morning.

The Schoolmaster, Sia Heng, the District Officer and the Headman were sitting in the Police Chief's office. (The Abbot had wanted nothing more to do with it.) They had been waiting for ten minutes already, the air conditioning blasting out freezing cold air. They shivered, watching the Chief through the glass door; he was speaking to a sheepish-looking Sergeant Yud. At last the Chief came in.

"Well gentlemen, what can I do for you today?"

"You missed the committee meeting at the school," blurted the Schoolmaster, unable to stop himself. "The relic in the museum is a fake – someone copied the original and now the original has turned up in Bangkok!" He threw the magazine on to the Chief's desk.

"I'm sure there's a very good explanation for… *all this*," said Sia Heng, waving his hands around vaguely, horrified at the Schoolmaster's tone of voice. The Chief sat back in his seat, folding his arms across his chest, ignoring the magazine.

"Em, um, perhaps someone… from the provincial office… you know, switched the relic… em, no, now that I think about it, that's probably not the case," mumbled the Headman.

"I hope you are not suggesting that the Provincial Governor was in any way involved!" said the District Officer, outraged, "I've known him for years and his record is impeccable!"

"Oh yes," said the Chief dryly. He knew all about the Provincial Governor's record. "I wonder who that leaves then?"

The Schoolmaster was on his feet before anyone could stop him. "That leaves you! *You* were the only one with access to the relic – it was passed into *your* safekeeping!"

The faces of the other men had turned pale. How could the Schoolmaster say such a thing? To the Chief? This was not the way to go about things, not the way at all. But he'd said it now! What were they going to do? He had implicated them all!

"Now, now, now," implored Sia Heng, remembering the visa stamps in his Chinese passport were well out of date, "the Schoolmaster is not himself today, I'm sure he doesn't mean anything, Chief."

"That's for certain!" said the Headman, nodding, "we all know what excellent work you have done since you came to the village. There is no suggestion that—"

"You hypocrites!" shouted the Schoolmaster, turning to the other men. "Why won't any of you back me up? You know I'm right!" He pointed his finger rudely at the Chief. "I mean to take this further – I'll be on the phone to your superior officer – you mark my words!"

The Chief cleared his throat. "Go ahead," he said lazily, waving his hand at the Schoolmaster, "and phone who you like."

The Schoolmaster jumped to his feet, upturning his chair. "You haven't heard the last of this!" he threatened, barging out of the office, banging the door behind him.

The Chief sighed and smiled, leaning forwards, arms on the

desk. "He's going to have trouble making phone calls with the lines down, isn't he?"

The others laughed nervously, a little too loud.

"How about some whisky, gentlemen? What with this bad weather and all, I'm sure we could use one."

They nodded, relieved, as the Chief produced a bottle of foreign whisky and some glasses from a drawer. He went over to open the door, calling for Sergeant Yud. "Ice and soda, Yud! And while you're at it, bring in the photograph!"

* * *

Everyone at the morning market watched him leave out of the corner of their eyes, struggling with all his bags and boxes of books onto the first bus. No one went forwards to help him. No one said goodbye. Mother Pensri stood next to Aunty Wassana, who was stirring her soup stock.

"Imagine," said Wassana, as the bus pulled away, "putting up that picture in the classroom – filling the heads of our schoolchildren with dangerous revolutionary ideas!"

"I suppose."

"Just as well he was found out in time! Turns out the Chief ran a check on him and he was involved in all that democracy stuff in Bangkok – you know, the student thing a few years ago."

"Against the government?"

"Something like that. Anyway, he even spent time hiding in the jungle! I guess that's why he moved up here – get away from all that trouble, thought he could hide away in the mountains. But your past always catches you up, eh?"

Mother Pensri wrinkled her nose, unconvinced.

"You know what my Ong always says? Bring back the military. At least you knew where you were with them."

Mother Pensri sighed. She dug into her pocket for her notebook and thumbed through the pages wearily. "Any numbers for next week Wassana?"

The rainstorm had stopped the day before and the village was returning to normal: the hot sun was drying out the flooded main street in no time at all. Sergeant Yud and Sergeant Pan, on orders from the Chief, were supervising the clearing up of all the rubbish clogging the drains. The old dustcart, which only just escaped being swept away in the flood, had been pulled out of the river and was being patched up. It didn't look likely that the village would get a new one now.

Sia Heng had gone to stay with his cousin, at least until the scandal died down. He planned to sell the stock of relics at the Chatuchak weekend market in Bangkok at discount prices. The Headman and the District Officer had taken to their beds, having fallen ill with frightful colds. The Chief had informed the Provincial Governor that the Schoolmaster must have swapped the relic for the fake one during the time he had spent examining the original, supposedly to find out its origin. It was thought the Schoolmaster had sold the original to a dealer, contributing the proceeds to Communist Party funds! The Provincial Governor had contacted the Department of Education; the Schoolmaster was immediately stripped of his position. Lack of concrete evidence meant he had escaped prosecution, but he would never teach again. A new teacher had been appointed – a woman this time. The original relic, the authorities had decided, would be retained in the National

Museum in Bangkok. Since the story had hit all the newspapers, visitors to the village had petered out. The Abbot had organized a special sermon on the evils of theft to coincide with the Lent Season, but few people attended. Morale was low now that the village was no longer a famous historical site.

Gop had been found inside the locked up factory, surrounded by neatly stacked piles of imitation relics, all pulled out from their boxes. He had survived on a bag of red bean dumplings. He had taken over the old shrine again, now that it was quiet. It had taken him several days to clear away all the mess left behind by devotees. He leant back against the cool lingam, naked now of all its frothy white blossom, watching the spiders and beetles creep in and out from under the huge stones. Fresh storm clouds were starting to gather, darkening the sky. An overripe jackfruit hung heavily from the big old tree, rancid, rotting slowly in the heat. Gop's eyelids started to droop, and his head fell to the side. The dreams began: the voices loudly accusing.

The Hot-Air Balloon

Mother Nong was crouched at the door of her kitchen, pounding garlic, ginger, chillies and shallots in a huge stone mortar to put in a curry for the evening meal, when she noticed a small hot-air balloon floating above the village, drifting slowly across the tops of the great banyan tree in the temple grounds. The festival of Loy Krathong was to start the next day, and more than a dozen hot-air balloons, which the villagers had made themselves, were strewn across the temple grounds, ready for the celebrations. A prize would be awarded by the District Officer for the most gaily decorated one. They were to be fired up and set adrift the following night, symbolically carrying the villagers' sins as far away from earth as mere human endeavour would allow. But it was most inauspicious to set the balloons adrift early and Mother Nong couldn't think who would have done it. The balloon appeared to have some small object dangling from its string, but it was too far away to see what the object might be. *It's probably something to do with Mother Suree's boys*, she thought, *they are always up to some prank or other*. Mother Nong felt sorry for Mother Suree but lately she had begun to run out of patience; she had even started to turn the other way when Mother Suree passed her in the market.

She glanced at the clock and started to pestle a little harder. Sergeant Yud would soon be home from the police station and he was always hungry. Few things pleased Mother Nong more than watching her husband tuck into his food, and the size of his belly, she felt, was evidence of her success as a wife. Only last week he had asked her to sew new panels into the trousers of his uniform. She stood up and lit the gas stove, pouring oil from a large tin can into a wok. She transferred the mortar's contents into the wok and added diced pork and chopped spinach, stirring and tossing the mixture with the spatula in her right hand as her left splashed in a liberal helping of oyster sauce. The lid of the pot in the electric rice-cooker was trembling and steaming. *Almost done,* she thought with satisfaction, *and time for a wash before he gets in.* She turned off the gas and went into the bathroom. She had been to the hairdresser's that day, so she covered her head in a plastic cap. She slipped out of her blouse and sarong and scooped cold water from a huge earthenware dragon pot, throwing the water over herself, soaping and scrubbing vigorously. Rather than use a towel, she wrapped the sarong back around her wet body to prolong the sensation of cool for as long as possible, and went upstairs to sit in front of her mirror. Taking off the shower cap, she combed her hair. *Nothing to be ashamed of,* she mused, gazing at her reflection. *I haven't let myself go – not like Mother Suree.*

In the beginning, when her friend had confided to her one day over a bowl of noodles, Mother Nong had pointed out that a husband will stray only when his wife stops making an effort to look nice for him. She had taken Mother Suree to the hairdresser's and they had even gone on a shopping trip to buy some new clothes, but her efforts had been in vain. Within a few days Mother Suree was back in her usual drab outfits, with her hair swept carelessly up into a straggly bun at the back of her head. *Really, the woman has no idea,* thought Mother

Nong, smoothing cream on her face and neck. Mother Suree had defended herself by saying she had no time to spend on her appearance, what with working all day in her green papaya salad stall. What was the point, Mother Suree had said, in dressing up in nice clothes when she had to cover them up with a big apron to stop the lime juice and fish sauce splashing all over them as she mixed the salads for her customers?

Mother Nong dressed and went back downstairs. It was six o'clock. She could hear the national anthem playing from the loudspeaker in the police station. Sergeant Yud would be lined up with the other officers on the clipped lawn in front of the station, saluting to the flag. *He is a good man*, she reflected. They had been married for twenty-five years already and had two children. Her daughter Maew was engaged to be married now and her son had entered the monkhood at the beginning of Lent. She glanced at his picture on the wall, dressed in his saffron robes. The day of his ordination had been one of the proudest moments in her life. Mother Nong lit a candle and three sticks of incense and knelt down in front of the household shrine, repeating the words of an obscure Sanskrit prayer. The fact she had no idea what it meant did not worry her in the slightest; she knew that by repeating it once every morning and once every night she would guarantee her family's continuing prosperity. She had bought the prayer for a small fee from the Fortune Teller who lived in a cave in the nearby forest and was famous for the accuracy of his predictions and the efficacy of his cures. He had arrived in the village too many years ago to count, having walked barefoot across the border from the Shan State in Burma, smoking a foreign-looking pipe, with nothing more than a cotton bag over his shoulder. It was rumoured he had been an important general in the Shan State Army, had fought alongside Aung San's Burmese soldiers in the war for independence against the British. He shared his cave with ridiculously large spiders, kept at bay by a posse of stray cats that the less tolerant villagers had chased away. He had prayers to answer every condition. He wrote them down from his prodigious memory on pieces of lined school paper and sealed them up in plain white envelopes. Mother Nong had taken Mother Suree to see the Fortune Teller when she realized something more than a visit to the hairdresser was called for. The Fortune Teller had asked Mother Suree the day and time of her birth and had set out the numbers in a triangle, which he surrounded with other numbers corresponding to the positions of the planets at her birth, counting furiously around the numbers with the tip of his astrologer's pencil.

"Five, six, seven, eight, nine... ah yes. Well, this is not an auspicious year for you in matters of the heart. You should be very careful, you know, until the middle of next year when the position of Jupiter will change."

"Is there nothing I can do?" Mother Suree had asked.

"The reason your husband is seeing another woman," he had said, smoothing back his white hair and sifting through his pile of envelopes, "is because you stole someone else's husband in your previous life. It's very simple really. I can give you a prayer to repeat every night and every morning and that will probably help, but it's also a good idea for you to make some merit. According to your horoscope, your fund of merit at the moment is dangerously low. You really should have done something about this sooner. You should make a special offering as quickly as possible to the monks at the temple and buy seven catfish to set free in the temple pond."

So the two women had gone to the market to buy the seven catfish thrashing hopelessly around in a tub of water, and gifts for the monks. Mother Suree had taken all the money she had saved that month from her green papaya salad stall and had spent it on new robes and towels, instant noodles, tobacco and toothpaste, incense, candles, tins of condensed milk and sardines in tomato sauce, which she packed into baskets. On the morning of the next day Mother Nong had gone to collect her neighbour and had been pleased to see that Mother Suree had at least made an effort with her clothes and hair. As for herself, Mother Nong had put on her third best sarong for the occasion, made of a dark blue silk with delicate gold threads running through it – but Mother Suree hadn't even complimented her on her choice of sarong.

"He didn't come home again last night, Nong! I couldn't sleep a wink, waiting for the sound of his bike, his footsteps outside the door."

"That's not so bad, is it? Even Sergeant Yud doesn't come home *every* night. But men are like that. It doesn't mean anything, Suree."

"But do you know where Sergeant Yud is when he stays out all night? Does he tell you where he's been?"

"Oh, I don't care to ask." Mother Nong smoothed out an imaginary crease from her sarong. "Men don't like a woman who pries and nags, and asks too many questions. Besides, he's a policeman and sometimes he has to, well, take care of things. Things I might not understand."

"But don't you worry he might be with another woman? In the brothel or the karaoke bar?"

"Of course he doesn't go to the brothel! I know he goes to the karaoke bar sometimes but only because the Chief invites him – he can't turn down his boss now, can he?"

"But what's the difference? The karaoke bar is full of girls! Those young girls dressed up in mini skirts and high-heeled boots! Singing and dancing and who knows what else! And you know what men are like when they have had a drink!"

"Exactly, Suree. If anything was to happen – and I'm not suggesting that it does – then it would be because of the alcohol and nothing more. Or because those girls are asking for it. Anyway, at our age we should be glad to be relieved of… well… our responsibilities, if you know what I mean. It's been a long time now since I've been interested in such *capers*. I can't help thinking that if Sergeant Yud spends a few nights somewhere else every so often then it's in my best interests!"

Mother Suree had fallen quiet then as the two women had walked through the village. Mother Nong was glad of an excuse to visit the temple, hoping to catch sight of her son. She spotted him sitting cross-legged in the great hall, his shaven head bowed, his thin shoulder-blades protruding from his robes, chanting sacred verses along with the other novices. It was such a relief to Mother Nong to know her son was safe. In the months running up to his ordination he had fallen in with a group of wild boys who drove their noisy mopeds too fast around the village, smoking and drinking and playing loud music. He had constantly asked her for money – too scared to ask his father – and it had been hard to refuse him because she loved him so much. She preferred not to think about what he was spending the money on. Anyway, all that was over now. Nothing bad could happen to him whilst he was in the temple and it had made her so proud to see him in his robes. Being ordained was the greatest compliment a son could pay his mother, and he had brought merit to the whole family.

"Do you feel better now?" Mother Nong had asked as the two women walked back from the temple with empty baskets, the seven lucky catfish swimming happily around the temple pond.

"I suppose so."

"And what about your prayer, Suree? Are you repeating it twice a day?"

"Yes, I'm doing all that."

"Well, if all this doesn't work then nothing will!" Mother Nong had linked arms with her neighbour then, feeling she really had done her best to lend a helping hand. And there was merit in that too, after all.

Well, she reflected, *that was all in the past*. Mother Nong spread a mat down on the floor and arranged the plates and cutlery on top; she would have enjoyed some green papaya salad as a garnish to the main dish, but these days it was best to give Mother Suree a wide berth – the woman was cracking up under the strain of her marriage. It was rumoured that Suree's husband was spending all his money on his minor wife now, forcing Mother Suree into selling her gold necklace to help make ends meet. Apparently, she had even been seen shouting at the minor wife in the middle of the street. *Such a loss of face*, thought Mother Nong, *Suree will never live that down!* A joke was going round the village that her papaya salad was the sourest in all Thailand, no matter how much cane sugar she put in. Mother Nong couldn't help smiling at that.

She went into the kitchen and looked outside to see if her husband was on his way. *Maybe he had to work late*, she reasoned. There was no sign of him, yet there was something unusual going on in the village. She went out into the road and peered along it. Men and women were leaning eagerly over their garden fences, while at the end of the road, outside Mother Suree's house, a knot of people chattered and gesticulated. *Those boys again*, she thought, *I bet it's to do with that hot-air balloon!* Mother Nong shaded her eyes against the yellow sunset and took a few steps in the direction of the hullabaloo. She drew in her breath. *Why, isn't that Mother Suree being pulled out of her house by a policeman? What on earth has she done?* Mother Nong gathered up the ends of her sarong and ran along the road to join the crowd. Sure enough, there was Mother Suree, laughing like a mad woman, her hair undone, the white apron she wore all day at her stall hanging from her neck, covered in stains. Mother Nong spotted Sergeant Yud in the middle of the throng and pushed her way through to pull at his arm.

"What's going on?"

"You'll never guess what's happened! I can't believe a woman could be so... heartless!"

"What is it? Has she killed him?"

"Killed him? As good as! That Suree woman – that so-called *friend* of yours..." Sergeant Yud shivered. "It's too horrible! How could anyone do such a thing?" He flung his arms before him. "The doctors can't help him now!" he warned.

Mother Nong tugged at her husband's arm. "What do you mean? What has she done?"

"She drugged her husband, then cut off his penis while he was sleeping! Cut it right off with the same knife she uses on her limes!"

"*Tho-oei!*" shrieked Mother Nong.

Yud seemed to be trying to absorb the horror. He struck his fist into the palm of his hand. "I swear I'll never, ever... eat green papaya salad again!"

Mother Nong clutched her throat. "But surely he can be taken to hospital and... and... have... it... sewn back on?"

"Oh no, she's too vicious for that! It's up there!" He was pointing madly into the sky. "After she cut it off she tied it to a hot-air balloon and now it's floating away somewhere over the valley!" He pushed his wife to one side. "There's no way I can face my dinner now! I have to go back and follow the penis!"

Sergeant Yud started up his moped and drove off, leaving Mother Nong open-mouthed in the middle of the road, watching the trail of trucks and bikes and dogs and children chasing a tiny gaily coloured dot that had drifted across the village on the back of the gentle evening breeze, and was slowly heading into a golden sunset above the rice fields.

Hair

Once again it was no longer safe for Gop to climb the old steps
to sit by the lingam, not even at night. All those people, all that
noise, equipment, fuss. The farangs tried to lure him up with
fried chicken – they wanted pictures – but Gop refused to leave
the *sala*, pulled his knees up to his chin, folded his head in his
arms. They gave up in the end: someone else took their fancy.
They shot Aunty Wassana, who grinned and simpered, dishing
out noodle soup. They spent a long time filming Grandmother
Gaysuda as she made coconut cakes on a griddle, clapping
their hands with delight whenever she puffed on her cheroot or
smiled toothlessly at the camera. Then they turned to the men
drinking at the moonshine stall, caught them raising glasses,
smiling, slapping backs. Getting up very early, they shadowed
the monks on their alms round, creeping along behind long-
legged cameras. They loaded equipment onto trucks and
drove out of the village to capture the red glow of sunset over
rice fields. Hunting out the cave in which the old Fortune
Teller lived, they gestured for him to lift his shirt and roll up
his trousers – someone had gossiped about his tattoos. They
sought the ricketiest houses and the cutest children, chased
after the saddest buffalo and the thinnest dog, tireless in their
pursuit of the authentic.

* * *

"I can't fit you in, Mother Nong! I'm too busy attending to the stars!" Dee stood with one hand on his hip, the other waving a comb in the air.

Mother Nong nodded, hardly listening, peering inside the new beauty salon at the foreign actor sitting in the plastic chair.

The salon was prospering. The film crew's hairstylist had fallen sick on the first day of filming – food poisoning or malaria, no one was completely sure. Dee had stepped in with his new business. He had renovated his father's old store, installing a new shelving system for all the whisky bottles, rice sacks and fish sauce, freeing up enough space to turn half the shop into the village's first proper beauty salon. There was a row of mirrors along the back wall, a sink for hair washing and a bed for facials. Low investment, he had convinced his father, steady trade, regular customers – everyone needs a haircut eventually! Gimsia had given in easily enough: maybe the boy had learnt something about business after all, and he was an extra pair of hands to help in the shop. Since the boy had come home, business had picked up. Gimsia had retreated to his battered deckchair in the back, sleeping through the hot afternoons, buried under a pile of Chinese newspapers. Dee was much better with the customers, was always ready to chat and could gossip for hours. As for the new salon, it was proving such a hit that the old hairdresser at the other end of the village had hung up her comb and scissors, and had taken over Mother Suree's green papaya salad stall instead.

"Is that the famous one?" asked Mother Nong, indicating the actor with a tilt of her chin.

"Yes! Isn't he wonderful?" Dee sighed, gazing at his client's reflection in the mirror as he worked some mousse into the man's short blonde hair. "That colour's *natural*, you know."

"What's this movie about then?" continued Mother Nong, inching her way inside.

"Oh, it's so exciting!" Dee laid down the comb. "He," he began, nodding at the actor, "is an American soldier who has lived a long time in Vietnam. He's on a special mission to rescue an important colonel, an engineer, who never came back from the Vietnam war. *Apparently*, this colonel was captured by *communists*, and forced to build bridges and dams for them! The hero searches for him across the country," said Dee with a dramatic sweep of his arm, "surviving great danger. All the clues he finds," said Dee, pausing for breath, "point to a secret place near an ancient Hindu shrine."

"So where does the heroine come into it all?" asked Mother Nong.

"Oh, there's no *heroine*. This film is full of *men*," said Dee, with evident satisfaction, "but the reason the hero takes on such a dangerous mission is *because* a woman broke his heart! He came back from the horrors of the Vietnam War to find his girlfriend in the arms of another man! Just imagine," Dee continued, looking sympathetically at the man in the chair, "how he must feel! So he comes straight back to Asia to forget all his troubles, learn about meditation, martial arts, the *ancient ways*. He ends up living with a local hermit, who teaches him *everything*. Do you know, Mother Nong, they asked the Fortune Teller to play the part of the old hermit and he *refused*?"

"No!"

"*Yes!*" Dee opened his eyes wide. "I would *die* for the chance to be in a film! Wouldn't you, Mother Nong?"

"Oh, I'm going to be in the film! Haven't you heard – there's going to be an audition. There was a meeting up at the district office this morning!"

"When's the audition?"

"This afternoon – up at the old shrine. Apparently, they're shooting some big scene up there later and they need people to be the crowd. That's why I'm here – I want to look my best! Are you sure you can't fit me in for a wash and set?"

"Mother Nong, give me twenty minutes – and I'll be right with you!" Dee smiled at the actor in the mirror and quickly began blow-drying his blonde hair. He chattered away in English, while Mother Nong sidled into one of the other chairs, watching, listening, fascinated by the foreign words. The actor was animated, talking with his hands.

"What's he saying?" interrupted Mother Nong.

"He says he *loves* it here – the village and the mountains, the simple lifestyle – it's very beautiful, and everyone is always smiling and laughing."

Mother Nong nodded in approval. "Ask him if he's been to the waterfall."

Dee consulted the actor for half a minute, turning back to Mother Nong. "Not yet! But don't you worry, Mother Nong, I've offered to take him there later on this evening! We might be there in time for the sunset. Don't you think, Mother Nong," said Dee, clasping his hands together under his chin, "that the waterfall would be the perfect backdrop for a love scene?"

"Ah, if only there was a heroine!" said Mother Nong coyly. "You need a heroine for a love scene, it would really be perfect – just imagine, our waterfall in a Hollywood film! Gimsia,

Gimsia!" called Mother Nong, catching sight of the old man in the back shop. "What do you think of that? Our waterfall in a Hollywood film!"

Gimsia shuffled through, hands behind his back.

"Good for business," he pronounced, "good for my shop, good for Dee, good for the Chief." He stood in the doorway, looking across the road to the market. "Good for Aunty Wassana too." The noodle stall was very busy: the film crew couldn't get enough of the delicious soup. "Won't last forever," Gimsia concluded, bending down to stroke the yellow cat rubbing against his legs.

Dee tossed his head, fluffing up the actor's hair and spraying it liberally to keep the style in place. Mother Nong folded her arms, waiting for her turn. The yellow cat jumped away as the dustcart turned the corner by the bus station, Uncle Moon at the helm. He swung down from the cart, hitching up his trousers as he crossed the road, grinning. Gimsia went to fetch his bottle of whisky from the top shelf.

"Morning Mother Nong, morning Missy Dee, morning Gimsia!" He pulled off his gloves, pushing his cap back on his head. "Hollywood, eh? Who'd have thought that our village would be in a film? Of course," he said knowingly, "no one will have a clue that it's our village. Could be anywhere."

"What do you mean?" asked Mother Nong.

"Supposed to be Vietnam, isn't it? But they can't get permission to film there now, can they?" He stared at the blonde actor and puffed out his own thin chest. "*Oh-ho*. He looks strong. But not a patch on the old stars, not nearly as handsome as *ah-maalon ba-rando*. Not famous either – I've never even heard of him."

"How would *you* know?" Dee turned to him, exasperated.

"*Aiya*, Uncle Moon is movie expert, Dee! From long, long time ago!" Gimsia handed over the whisky, shaking his head.

The actor pushed back the plastic chair, standing up. He peered in the mirror, checking his reflection this way and that.

"*Real* stars would have their own entourage," explained Uncle Moon, "this must be a *very* low budget production." He unscrewed the cap of the bottle and took a long swig. "A 'B' movie," he said mysteriously, turning to go. "I'll settle up at the end of the week, Gimsia!"

"What's a 'B' movie?" asked Mother Nong, watching Uncle Moon throw the contents of the dustbins outside the market on to the back of the cart.

* * *

Almost everyone was up at the shrine, even the monks and novices. The film director had bought them all new, bright orange robes. Their old robes, it transpired, were too dull for Hollywood: the director wanted a splash of local colour in one of the village scenes to be filmed the next day. The smallest village children were clustered round the legs of adults, while some of the older ones had climbed up the old jackfruit tree to get a better view. The director swaggered about, a baseball cap set backwards on his head, barking instructions and waving the villagers back every so often from the impromptu set which covered most of the huge stone slabs on the uneven floor. Lights had been set up in each corner: it had been quite a struggle getting all the equipment up the steps. Two cameramen stood at either side of the lingam, the soundman with his earphones and boom in the middle. A small group of Chinese actors was standing to one side, practising an elaborate-looking martial arts routine: they had been brought in from Hong Kong to play the Vietcong.

Mother Pensri and Aunty Wassana stood as close to the actor as they dared, giggling over his huge muscles, marvelling at the line of his nose, his wavy-blonde locks. He had been tied to the old lingam with a thick rope by the Vietcong. Dee was putting the finishing touches to the actor's hair. The idea was that the hero would burst out of the ropes and defeat his captors with a display of spell-binding fighting skill. There had been a fuss earlier when Dee noticed a large spider crawling out from between the stone slabs. Screaming, he had called out to the hero, who kicked his legs up and down – someone had tied the ropes a little too tightly. It was Sergeant Yud who dealt with the crisis, crushing the spider under his boot, holding the mangled body up for the crowd to see. It had taken some time for the director to persuade Dee to go back over to the lingam.

A few of the villagers had expressed concern when they heard about the proposed scene at the shrine. They had presented their case to the village Headman earlier on in the afternoon: was it not disrespectful for a farang to be touching, let alone *strapped* to, their ancient symbol of male potency? The Headman had listened carefully to the arguments but assured them the village was being well paid for the inconvenience; some of the money was being put aside for special ceremonies to appease the spirits once the film crew had gone. The spirits would understand, the Headman had said vaguely; it was in the villagers' best interests. Anyway, he had added, it might have been much worse – what if they had wanted to strap a female farang to the lingam?

Dee stepped back from the actor, dropping his comb into the

yellow vanity case at his feet. The director beckoned him over; the villagers watched them talking together.

"What's all that about?" said Mother Pensri, pointing at the two men and nudging Aunty Wassana.

Aunty Wassana shook her head. Now the old Schoolteacher had gone, the director was lucky Dee was around to translate. None of the film crew, not even the director, could say more than "Please", "Thank you" and "Cheers" in Thai.

Dee raised his hand, clearing his throat.

"Would the villagers taking part in this scene please come forwards?" he said, trying to ignore the burly cameramen simpering behind him in imitation, hands on their hips, calling out names. They had been teasing him all day.

"What are they saying?" asked Aunty Wassana.

"*Ladyboy*," said Mother Pensri, "I think they're calling him a *ladyboy*."

"Sssh," hissed Mother Nong, "I can't hear the instructions!"

Dee was holding up a large sack. "Please come forwards and pick up your hats!"

"Hats?" said Mother Nong, pushing to the front. "Why do we have to wear hats?"

Mother Pensri put her hand over her mouth to laugh. "Look at that," she whispered to Aunty Wassana, "Mother Nong had her hair done and now she has to wear a hat!"

"What kind of hat is this?" asked Uncle Nun, who had also passed the audition. He tried on the deep, conical hat, tying the ribbon under his chin.

"Vietnamese!" shouted Uncle Moon drunkenly from the back. "It's a Vietnamese film and you're all going to be Vietnamese farmers!"

"But I can't speak Vietnamese!" whined Uncle Nun from under the brim.

"I refuse to wear a hat!" cried Mother Nong, putting a hand up to her hair.

The actor roared in fright as a rhinoceros beetle scuttled across the stone slabs towards him. The director groaned, head in hands, as Sergeant Yud pushed through the crowd to chase the offending creature. The Chinese actors mistook the actor's roar for their cue and leapt forwards, whooping, kicking their feet high in the air around the lingam.

"The director says you will all have to go and change," Dee was now shouting, putting up his hands to appeal for calm. "You're too smart to be peasants, you'll have to go home and put some old clothes on. You're meant to be *poor*," he explained in exasperation, hands on his hips.

* * *

The director rolled over in bed, dropping an arm over his eyes to shut out the sunlight filtering through the bamboo blinds. *What time did we get back to the guest house?* He had no idea. The night out had been arranged, he guessed, to compensate for all the inconvenience up at the shrine. He groaned, remembering how they had to shoot the damned fight scene over and over again: no one seemed to understand what they were supposed to be doing, the extras kept shouting out and laughing, the Vietcong missed their cue, the actor freaked out over every insect... The director had lost his temper, shouted a little, waved his arms to show he meant business: but the Vietcong shrugged and the villagers all looked the other way.

He had read somewhere that the Thais didn't do anger, but he did. He had screamed at the ladyboy to send for the Chief. He had been promised total cooperation right at the start – whatever he wanted, he just had to say the word? Shit, he had yelled, I'm paying enough for it! The Chief had turned up with a group of young men, construction workers by the look of them: replacement peasants – *they sure as hell didn't make any fuss about wearing the goddamn hats.*

That darned whorehouse, he remembered, *was some place though: wouldn't mind getting a camera in there!* He and the guys had piled out of the police truck, already high on the Chief's free beer and whisky, hooting and hollering, pushing one another through the door, whistling at the row of girls inside. *How old were they? Gee, it was hard to tell, 'specially with Asians: hopefully older than they looked.* Some of the girls had stood up, smoothing down their little skirts, smiling, moving forwards to take him and the guys by the arm. The younger-looking ones hadn't shifted off their seats, hadn't looked up, just sat there hugging their chests.

The director grinned, recalling how well the fat sergeant knew his way around, going over to speak to an older broad sat smoking in the corner at a table, dyed black hair piled high on her head, greasy make-up, red lipstick. *Must have been the Mama-san: she looked like she'd seen a thing or two.* She had got up, pulling the two best-looking young girls off their butts, pushing them over towards him. He had no idea what the sergeant said to the Mama-san, but he and the guys didn't pay a dime.

The director belched and rubbed the sides of his head. He could still taste the cheap brandy. *I should get up*, he told himself, *get a drink of water, a coffee.* It was already hot in the bungalow, must be even later than he thought. *Where'd I put my watch?* After the brothel, the two girls, that small room with the mattress, the teddy bear on the bed, red-and-gold shrine high on the wall in one corner, it all became a little hazy. He threw back the thin cover and stumbled over to the bathroom, catching sight of his face in the mirror. *Shit.* He stuck out his tongue and shuddered, remembered his wife, his two teenage daughters back home. Gathering up some phlegm, he spat into the toilet bowl, head thumping now. He could always be more-or-less honest – *women go for that,* he reasoned, *don't they? It's not as though I've ever done anything like this before. I could explain to her I was drunk, and it would have been kinda rude to turn down the Chief's offer.* He examined his reflection, the row of small teeth marks on his neck, and shook his head. *Nah, it was a one-off, why mention it? Why upset her with something that didn't matter?*

Turning on the shower, the director let the cold water flow over his head, down his back. He examined his torso. *Where'd I get those bruises though?* He could remember the cameraman sleeping on the pool table – the Mama-san had thrown water over his head to get him to move. *Hadn't the soundman been dancing?* He squeezed his eyes shut against a vague image of the room, the shrine, the girls. *Had there been some kinda struggle? Nah,* he decided, *I'm probably imagining things.* But what he could remember, for sure, was the fat policeman's big red face, laughing, always filling up their glasses, the girls sitting on his knee: *hell, you have to give it to them, they sure know how to take care of guests.* The director soaped himself gently. *Speaking of good manners – what happened to the actor last night?* He hadn't come out with the rest of them, something about seeing the waterfall, said he would join them later on; left him sitting at the table by the river talking to the ladyboy. *What did they have to talk about? Faggot.* The director snorted as he dried himself– *maybe the actor was doing research for his next role. Kiss of the Spiderwoman!*

Dressed, the director opened the door of the bungalow. The sun was already high. He wandered down to the river's edge. Two young women were fishing in the shallow water, casting small nets in a graceful arc, their sarongs folded up like knickerbockers to reveal slim brown legs. *Thai women really are the business*, thought the director, making a mental note to tell one of the cameramen. *Who could blame a man for falling in love!* The director snapped his fingers. *Of course! It's a great idea for a film*, he thought, *foreign man comes to Thailand, falls in love with a bar girl, rescues her from the brothel… It's perfect – but how would I pitch it? A meeting of cultures, of different lives, different realities, crossing boundaries… It's new, it's modern, love in the global village! The distributors will lap it up. I'll get on to the producer today – didn't the Chief say I could use the phone any time?* Turning round, the director strode off towards the reception desk of the guest house.

As he passed the actor's bungalow, the door opened slowly. The ladyboy hairdresser stepped out, fiddling with the fastener on his skirt. The actor stood framed in the doorway, one hand hanging on to the door jamb, towel wrapped around his waist, yawning, rubbing his broad chest with the other hand. He caught sight of the director and grinned.

The Way to a Man's Heart

What else to do? agonized the Chief's wife, *I can't confront him directly!* She had no evidence, and he would only twist her words again, giving them a meaning never intended, making her look unreasonable, foolish. She couldn't bear another scene. *But he hasn't been home in five weeks and three days now*, she fretted, *and hasn't bothered to phone once in all that time!* Phoning the station made her feel sick: heart clenched, blood thumping in her head, fingers trembling over the buttons, she always pictured him sitting at his desk, the hard line of that handsome jaw, smoke curling up from a cigarette in one hand, leaning forwards to pick up the receiver languidly with the other. She shivered and closed her eyes. *It's never his voice at the end of the line, anyway, oh no, that idiot sergeant always answers instead, asking me how I am – as if my well-being was any concern of his!* Then she would be informed the Chief was out of the station or in an important meeting, not to be disturbed... She had left more than a dozen messages.

For the past ten days she had locked herself up in the big suburban house, cancelling all appointments: the hairstylist, the dressmaker, a grand charity luncheon. She had even forsaken her usual trip to the temple to make merit on Buddha day, sending the maid with a basket of offerings instead. *Won't the merit*, she reasoned, *trickle down somehow?* She had stopped answering the door, instructing the maid to tell visitors she was in Bangkok. She was worried that he might call at any time, so she shouldn't leave the phone – he might even turn up in person, unannounced. *He did that once before*, she remembered, *just after we were married*. He'd wangled a few hours off duty, surprising her with a gold bracelet: she still had it wrapped up in red tissue paper in her jewellery box upstairs. She hadn't thought about where the money must have come from to buy it, not in those early days. *He must have loved me, surely, back then?*

The first time it happened she tried to deny it, making up her own wild excuses for the late nights, the smell on his clothes, the woman who kept phoning, and his endless, careless lies. But it all added up, of course. Still young then, slim and smooth-skinned, she had caught the train back to Bangkok, running home to her mother; "Why," she had asked, "am I not enough for him?"

"A married couple," her mother had explained, gazing into the distance, "is like an elephant. Men are the front legs, women the back. Where the front legs lead, the back follow, offering support. Men are different, they have different *needs*; it's only natural they should want a change sometimes. Just like food – do you think they want to eat the same dish day-in, day-out?"

She had sobbed then and asked to return home, but her mother was imperturbable.

"Don't be weak," she admonished, "don't ruin your future. If you want to win him back, give him a son. He's sure to look after you then, no matter how many other women he picks up along the way. Being born a woman is the result of bad karma, and giving birth is the best way to correct it. A son can ordain as a monk, a son is a woman's ultimate source of merit, a son will never turn his back on his mother!"

But sons – and daughters – were not forthcoming. Oh, she'd tried. Tried for fifteen years, swallowed remedies, followed strict diets, made persistent merit, visited countless temples, shrines and fortune tellers, but still she didn't conceive. She went for tests, biting her lip and staring at the ceiling as old men in white coats poked and prodded inside her, shrugging their shoulders, finding nothing wrong. She was normal, they said, a little nervous perhaps, but healthy.

Maybe, she had dared to suggest to her husband one day, maybe *you* should go for tests? He had laughed in her face at that, clutching her arm too tightly as he pulled her towards him, whispering in her ear: it was *her*, not him, she was frigid, barren, all dried up – he said he wished he'd never married her, and had avoided her side of the bed ever since.

The lack of children became a chasm of longing. She turned to good causes to fill it – refugees, orphans, fallen women – growing plump on charity luncheons as she subsided into middle age. She took a measure of comfort in the money – there was no shortage of that, it seemed – spending it on heavy teakwood furniture, silk clothes, a liveried chauffeur, rubies, sapphires and emeralds. Then came the scandal that had shamed them: dark accusations, closed doors, muffled voices, half-truths and sleepless nights, her father's intervention and her husband's transfer up to the little village. He had only just managed to retain his rank. Now he was away from her all the time, and she could only imagine what he did.

She had heard of wives who sought revenge, drugging their faithless husbands, killing them or cutting off their sexual organs while they slept. *In fact*, she mused, *wasn't there a case like that in the village last month?* Panit, the maid, had told her about it. The wife, if she remembered correctly, was given a long prison sentence. She shuddered. *Such measures*, she told herself, *are all very well for poor country folk, but imagine the scandal if I did something like that! Anyway, I don't want to kill him; I don't even want to hurt him.* She wanted him to love her again.

It was a last resort. She would never have thought of it herself: it had been Panit's suggestion. The very idea frightened her – it seemed so coarse and unnatural. *And dangerous too,* she thought, *what if it goes wrong and he falls sick? What if he finds out? But Panit said if we are careful, really careful, then all will be well.* The maid swore she had heard of faithless men who became besotted with their wives afterwards, so jealous at other men's attentions that they wouldn't let their wives out of their sight – *imagine that!* She indulged the sudden fantasy: her husband's adoring gaze at finding her waiting on the sofa as he entered the room. She got to her feet and walked over to the mirror, in thrall to her own reflection, simpering, mouthing silent words of affectionate greeting to an imaginary husband, who smiled back gently, embracing her in his strong, protective arms. *What if it were possible?* She picked up the little bell and rang for her maid.

* * *

The Fortune Teller crouched at the cave's mouth, watching Sergeant Yud pick his way back down the hill in big, black boots, clumsy over rocks and stones. *The second time already*

196

this month, he thought, *how many more times will there be?*
He shook his head, turning back inside the cave. *What had the
Chief called it, according to Yud? Rent!* Reaching into his shirt
pocket for an old briar pipe and tobacco, he looked round the
cave, the old sleeping mat in one corner, a small bundle of clothes
and books, and the shrine near the front. *Rent? For a cave?* He
laughed bitterly and sat down on the bamboo mat in front of
the shrine, staring at the space where the silver statue of Shiva
had been. Shiva, the Hindu god, six-armed, who danced on the
head of ignorance. A businessman had presented it to him the
year before as part-payment for calculating an auspicious day
for the opening of a new business. The man had come all the
way from the city to consult him. The Fortune Teller clicked his
tongue. Now the statue was gone, tucked under the sergeant's
arm. The Chief was a keen collector, Yud had explained, red-
faced, as he left the cave.

The old man turned the briar pipe over in his hands. He ran
his finger over the small fracture along the bowl, across his own
rough engraving scratched into the wood with a knife: "1948".
It was such a long time ago, that time of great hope, that time
of dreams which almost came true. Independence for Burma,
independence for the Shan State. His position had pushed him
to the vanguard of change: born into a princely family, his father
was a *sawpha* – a chieftain, a local leader. But after a few years
of inept government, the Burmese military prevailed, crushing
any hopes for an independent Shan State. His father had died
in prison; his own choice had been exile. From a bright palace
high in the mountains of Lashio to this dark cave in Thailand.
He stuffed tobacco into the pipe and lit it, watching the thin
smoke curl upwards.

No one had ever asked him for papers before the arrival of the Chief. He'd been here for more than thirty years: had walked all the way from Lashio, barefoot, a bag slung across his chest with nothing in it but his astrological books and the old briar pipe. He had begged for food along the way, exchanging amateur predictions for the odd bowl of rice and curry. On the ninety-ninth day of walking he'd found the cave: an auspicious number. The villagers were friendly and the cave's outer chamber was warm and dry. No sign of bears. The people didn't ask much about him; once they found out his profession the questions mostly concerned themselves. What number should I buy to win the lottery, on which day should I marry, when will I have a son, does my husband love me, how can I catch a younger woman? He spent the years studying books, consulting other masters. He learnt how to draw birth charts, read the tarot, sacralize amulets in special ceremonies, and apply beneficial tattoos. Most of the local men wore his indelible marks on their forearms to protect them from mishap: a row of letters from the sacred alphabet, the garuda fighting the snake, the lizard with two tails.

He had delved deep into powerful mysteries to learn his trade. He knew the secret words that could turn a tiger's tooth into a powerful talisman for wearing around a man's waist to increase his strength. He spent days covering tiny scrolls of *sa* paper with magical drawings folded into homemade bamboo pendants that had protective powers. He could cure a person whose life-soul has fled their body in fright, exposing them to sickness and ill-fortune. The villagers paid him what they could for his services: a kilo or two of rice, tobacco, a new shirt, sesame oil, sardines. His advice was sought during floods, droughts, epidemics, cases of spirit possession and plagues of widow ghosts: people turned to the old Fortune Teller in times of trouble, for only he could invoke the heavenly divinities to appease malevolent spirits. He was their Brahmin priest; what need then did he have for papers?

But the new Chief had rooted him out quickly, sending Sergeant Yud to summon him to the station. So many questions during that first interview: where had he learnt his trade, how much money did he earn, how long had he been living up in the cave? The Chief had tried to flatter him, said he was interested in buying some amulets, in learning something of the business of magic – but the old man was cagey. He knew the Chief's type.

"Do you think you are above the law?" the Chief had asked in the end, angry with the old man's silence.

"I am a poor old man, I have nothing: what could a man of your position want from me?"

"How about your papers?"

The old man had stared back at him blankly. "What papers?"

"Your ID, old man – are you a Thai citizen?"

"I have no ID; I am Shan, not Thai, I come from Lashio, I walked over here more than thirty years ago, I have no papers."

The Chief had walked out from behind his desk, right over to the chair on which the old man sat, and had leant over him, resting his hands on the arms of the chair. The old man could smell the garlic on his breath. "So you're an illegal then, a *Dai Nok*, a migrant, aren't you, old man? I could put you in prison, have you deported, turn you over to the Burmese authorities – how would you like that?"

199

Remembering the threat, the Fortune Teller stood up and stretched, going over to the cave's mouth to knock the burnt tobacco from his pipe. *What will the Chief take next*, he wondered, *as rent, or tax, or whatever he chose to call it?* First it had been smaller pieces: a few penis amulets, the gold coin medallion with the picture of King Chulalongkorn; then a wooden Buddha statue presented to him last year by Sia Heng; and now the silver Shiva. Valuable pieces: the Chief would sell them, he knew, just like he had sold the ancient relic found by Gop at the old shrine. The Fortune Teller shook his fist at the village down below. *That Police Chief*, he fumed, *is nothing more than a good-for-nothing thief!*

* * *

"I swear to you madam, it's what I heard – he's very skilled!" The maid opened her pretty eyes wider.

"But what if my husband finds out... what if someone tells him we've been up *there*... at the cave... what then?"

"Easy madam! You can say you were after your horoscope: nothing unusual in that, is there?"

The Chief's wife gazed into the mirror, thinking. "I suppose..." She spun round to face her maid. "But it means *seeing* him in the village, he was so angry when I went up last time, you've no idea Panit..."

Panit nodded, laying her hand gently on her mistress's arm. "I know madam but if you don't mind me saying so, it's the perfect chance – you can use whatever the Fortune Teller gives you there and then – no need to wait for the Chief to come home to the city!"

"Tell me again, Panit, what did you hear?" The Chief's wife sank down weakly on to the sofa.

"It was Mother Pensri, madam – you know, the woman who sells lottery tickets up in the village. *She* told me. I've known her a while: her daughter Kwan is my friend – she works in that big fruit-processing factory here in the city. Last winter Mother Pensri came to work in the factory for a few weeks: we got talking one day when I was visiting Kwan on my day off." Panit paused for breath, shifting her weight from one side to the next where she had knelt on the floor by the sofa.

"Go on, go on."

"Well, Mother Pensri was just telling me how she had to go back home because her husband wasn't well, something about a ghost, I can't quite remember – anyway, we were all laughing about it, about men, husbands, you know... and *she* said what women needed to get their husbands back on track was some... em..." Panit's voice dropped to an excited whisper. "Some magic!"

The Chief's wife drew in her breath sharply, leaning forwards. "And then?"

"I thought she was joking! But then she started to tell me all about this oil, this *namman phraaj* – it comes from *corpses* – and how it's just the strongest love potion in the whole world... and I thought, *aow*, these country folk! They still do all that! But I pretended I wasn't shocked, of course, then I asked her, straight out – where would you get such a thing these days?"

The Chief's wife raised her eyebrows. "Where?"

"She said it was easy enough if you knew the right person to go to and I asked did she know such a person and she said, yes, she did!"

The Chief's wife stood up and wandered around the room, picking up objects then laying them down. "Oh, I don't know, Panit. It sounds dangerous! What if something were to happen to my husband – what if he were to fall sick? I couldn't bear it! Especially knowing it was all my fault!"

Panit stared up at her employer with beseeching eyes. "But madam – we've tried everything else!"

The Chief's wife shuddered, remembering what they'd tried. A few months ago, at Panit's anxious prompting, she had prepared a special meal for her husband, his favourite fish curry, and had mixed some of her own female secretions into the dish. He was raising the first spoonful to his mouth when the phone rang. Grabbing his car keys he'd gone straight out, leaving her sitting at the table with the uneaten food. He didn't come home until the next morning: the curry turned sour and had to be thrown away. The next time Panit had pulled some moss from the temple wall to mix into a spicy soup, but he had turned his nose up, hadn't even tasted it – said he'd gone off the dish! It was almost as if he *knew*. He fancied an omelette instead, wandering off into the kitchen to teach Panit, he had said, a lesson about cooking. She hadn't dared follow him; she hated to see him angry, those veins on his neck standing out, his dark eyebrows knitted together. Panit was frightened of him too.

"I just want you to be happy madam. All this staying indoors isn't good for you, you look pale and thin madam."

"Do you really think I've lost weight Panit?" asked the Chief's wife, walking back over to the mirror.

"Definitely madam! It'll be the first thing the Chief notices when he sees you, I'm sure of it! Now," she said, gently insistent, "shall we get ready and call the chauffeur, madam?"

"Yes, Panit, yes – let's go ahead and do it!" cried her boss, peering at her face in the mirror, sucking in her cheeks, turning her head to the side to check the effect. "I'll go and get changed right now!"

* * *

City accents, thought the old man, getting up from where he had been sleeping on the mat; *who's come to visit me now?* He rubbed his face, reached automatically for his pipe, peering at the two women who stood just outside the cave. They looked out of breath, clearly not used to climbing. The Fortune Teller yawned. The women were no doubt after horoscopes or a tarot reading. The young, attractive one, dressed simply in jeans and a blouse, came forwards, putting her palms together in front of her chest and bowing.

"Good day, Wise Grandfather! Do you have time to speak with a good lady who has travelled all the way from the city to consult you?" She turned round to indicate the middle-aged woman standing behind her, in dark sunglasses, a straw hat and a well-cut trouser suit of black silk.

The Fortune Teller grunted, nodding towards the bamboo mat. He walked over stiffly to sit down first. The two women crept over to the edge of the mat. The young one slipped off her rubber sandals, kneeling at the back of the mat to bow three times to the statues on the shrine. The other woman bent down to remove a pair of tight, expensive-looking leather shoes, glancing nervously round the cave before sitting down. The old man cleared his throat.

"Well?" he asked, folding his arms.

The two women exchanged glances, and the maid nodded at her employer, eyebrows raised. The city woman pulled off her sunglasses and hat and took a deep breath, fixing her eyes at a spot on the floor as she spoke.

"My husband," she began in a trembling voice, "is…" Her voice trailed off.

"It's alright madam – you can tell him!" hissed the maid.

"My husband is… unfaithful, has… has a minor wife… at least, I *think* so. No, I'm *sure* he has."

The old man sighed wearily, reaching for his pencil and paper. "What day were you born on?"

The woman leant forwards, raising one hand. "No, you don't understand. I don't want my horoscope. I need… I need something… to bring him back to me. I heard that you do that, help people, I mean…"

The old man put down his pencil, looking up. The woman's face was pale under heavy make-up, her plump fingers twisting around the face towel she held in her lap. Behind her the maid nodded anxiously. The old man shook his head firmly. "I don't do that kind of thing."

"But Wise Man," cried out the maid, a note of desperation in her voice, "we have heard that your magical powers are most potent, most effective, in bringing a married couple back together!"

The old man raised his eyebrows at the maid, turning back to the other woman. "If you were a man," he began, "I could help you: I could give you a tattoo, a talisman, to win a woman's heart. But the only recourse open to a woman who wishes to win the attention of a man does not require my blessing." He lowered his voice. "Take some of your *fluids* and mix it with his food. That should do it." The old man turned his head away, staring out at the cloudless afternoon sky.

The woman let out a sob. "It didn't work... oh, you don't understand: my husband is too powerful! He wears many amulets, carries dozens of talismans to protect him: I've tried it and it didn't work! I need something... something stronger!"

"What is your husband? A tiger? Some great soldier?"

"No," whispered the woman, barely audible, "he's a Chief of Police."

"He's the Chief here in the village!" blurted the maid, unable to resist.

The old man's face was impassive. "I see," he said slowly. "The Chief. I've had the pleasure of meeting your husband already. Several times." He relit his pipe, puffing slowly. "Your husband is very... charming."

"Too charming! And handsome: he seems to always look young and now I am too old, too ugly!" The Chief's wife fumbled in her handbag. "Look, I can pay you, however much you want!" She brought out a bundle of five hundred baht notes from her purse.

"It's not a question of money, daughter. It's a question of whether it's... appropriate... for a woman to use such measures to win the love of a man."

"Do you mean to say you have... the substance that I'm looking for?"

"Perhaps." The old man rubbed his chin, thinking. He had never used it, never even given it to a man to use on a woman before, let alone allowed a woman to use it on a man! Normally women only had recourse to their own secretions, or to the moss that grows on temple walls. A man out to ensnare a woman, on the other hand, had many options: he could wear amulets to increase his charm, draw special diagrams whilst thinking intensely of the woman he desired, or sit close to her whilst smoking a cigarette, drawing the smoke deep into his lungs, reciting a silent spell, then enveloping her in exhaled smoke. If that didn't work he could always scoop up some earth with his toe and rub it on the top of his head, invoking the goddess of the earth, Mother Thoranee, to help him win his bride. But *namman phraaj*? No one had asked for it before today, and certainly not a woman! The old man cracked his knuckles one by one, staring at the empty space on the shrine where his Shiva had been.

"Just name your price!" said the woman, spreading the pink bank notes in front of her into a fan.

"Five thousand," said the old man, thinking how he could use the money to buy another statue. "Wait here."

Fumbling for the matches in his pocket, he got up from the mat to light an oil lamp. The two women clutched hands, staring as he started towards the back of the cave. He squeezed through the narrow opening from the first chamber into the second and disappeared from their sight. The smell inside the second chamber was stale and acrid; bats twitched and squeaked overhead.

He held the lamp high, ducking past the looming stalagmites and stalactites: awkward, bestial shapes that flickered and came to life for a moment before melting back into darkness. *Where did I hide it?* He squeezed his eyes shut, trying to remember. It was so many years ago. *Yes*, he remembered, *that's it: the turtle's head!* He cast his eyes around the chamber. *There it is!* He picked his way over to the big rock, fashioned by millennia of dripping water into the vague form of a turtle. Bending down, he reached his hand under the head, pulling out a small bamboo container. Taking off the lid, he looked at the tiny glass phial inside: the oil still perfectly intact. He'd been young and inexperienced at the time, and had thought he couldn't afford to miss exploiting such a rare chance. She was called Mali Foi Thong – a woman who had died the most inauspicious death of all, in childbirth. Such deaths produced the most potent *namman phraaj* in the world. He'd watched over the coffin for days, waiting until the villagers were distracted by gambling, by preparations for the funeral feast, taking his quick, precious chance to approach the corpse, grasp it firmly in his arms, hold a flickering candle under the chin to extract the dangerous liquid from the skull. He had heard the screams of the baby Gop from outside as he struggled with the cadaver of the mother: it was almost as though the newborn child could sense the act being committed... He shivered, putting the bamboo lid back on. *What's the worst*, he wondered, *that could happen? The Chief might fall sick and die?*

The two women had remained exactly where he had left them, bug-eyed, gawping at him as he squeezed back through. A gecko cleared its throat before letting out its distinctive call. The Chief's wife started in fright, the maid tittered nervously. Looking at them crossly, the Fortune Teller laid the bamboo container down on the mat and pushed it towards the Chief's wife.

"There's more than enough in the phial. A few drops in his food. Preferably on a Saturday or a Tuesday. And it has to be you who puts it in." He fumbled in his bag for an old jotter, leafing through the pages, tearing one of them out. "And recite this prayer over the food before you serve it to him."

The woman leant forwards to pick up the sheet of paper with one hand, pointing at the container with the other. "Is it... is this really?..."

The old man sighed, nodding impatiently, wishing the women would go, take the oil with them and leave him alone. He shuddered, clutching the small penis amulet around his neck.

"Do you want it or not?"

"I'll take it," said the woman, snatching up the bamboo container. The maid clapped excitedly behind her. The Chief's wife counted out five thousand baht, holding the notes between her palms as she bowed to the floor in front of the Fortune Teller three times. He pushed forwards a silver bowl to receive the money.

"Thank you, Wise Grandfather." The Chief's wife dabbed her cloth to her cheeks and forehead, moving backwards on all fours to the edge of the mat. She stood up, fumbling at the clasp on her shoes, grabbing the maid's arm to steady herself. The two women scurried out of the cave.

"And remember," he cried after them, "Saturday or Tuesday!"

It was Tuesday.

* * *

The chauffeur stopped at the gate to the compound, waiting for the uniformed guard to come forwards and offer his brisk salute to the Chief's wife in the back of the car, then reach into his sentry box to raise the barrier. The suburban development – "Green Hill Estates" – was very secure. They had reserved one of the houses whilst the estate was in its planning stages

– the Chief knew the investor well and was owed some favours, so he had received an extraordinary discount. The house, he reminded his wife when she dared to complain about the quietness, the loneliness, was worth a fortune now. The Chief's wife gazed out the back window of the Mercedes at the outlines of the huge concrete houses set back from the road, embedded in well-tended gardens. Fairy lights lit up trees, sprinklers watered perfect lawns. The houses looked like enormous birthday cakes in the evening light, frilled with big balconies, elaborate porches, painted a uniform, sickly pink and white.

The car swung into her drive. Her own garden was dark, no lights had been switched on and the pale house loomed behind the shadows of a row of young palm trees. *Why*, she wondered, *are the lights not on? What is Panit thinking? Off gossiping with the neighbour's maid again, no doubt!* Then she saw his car, parked at the end of the drive. *He's come home*, she thought eagerly, *unannounced! A surprise visit then, at long last!* She reached a hand up to her hair, hoping it would do, reasoning that it had been washed and set only the previous day. Her suit was a little crumpled, but surely he wouldn't notice and she could always run upstairs and change. She took a deep breath and exhaled, letting out a soft moan of excitement. She coughed to cover it up. "Park the cars away in the garage before you bring in the shopping bags," she told the chauffeur, getting out of the Mercedes, "and find Panit, tell her to switch on the lights!"

The front door was unlocked, the air-conditioning inside cool. As she kicked off her low heels she saw his shoes in the entrance hall: black leather. The faint smell of polish made her stomach flutter. Fumbling for the hall light, she went into the darkened lounge, peering at his favourite armchair. There was no sign of him there. *Maybe*, she thought, *he's upstairs. He might be showering, tired after the long, twisting drive down the mountains.* He always drove himself, not trusting anyone else and preferring to be in control. She loved watching him drive, his strong right hand on the steering wheel, the other resting on top of the gear stick, which he rubbed over gently with his palm. She padded up the staircase in her stockinged feet, listening for the sound of running water, the click of his cigarette lighter. She pushed open the bedroom door softly. The quilt cover was still smooth, the en suite bathroom was empty, and no clothes had been thrown on the floor or over the chair. *Where*, she wondered, *can he be?* She crossed over to the window, sliding open the glass door to stand on the balcony. The lights were on in the garden now, and the water in the swimming pool was perfectly still and inky black. In the distance came the faint sound of the neighbour's children playing in the next house. She peered down at the garden. When they first moved in he would often stand there in the evening, smoking one last, endless cigarette before coming to bed. She would lie waiting for him, switching out her bedside light when she heard his footsteps on the stairs. Lying back, she would arrange her hair, her nightdress, bring one leg up, throw one arm back casually as though asleep already. Eyes tight shut, she would listen to him brushing his teeth before sinking down on to the bed beside her. Before long he would start to snore and she would turn over on to her side to lie wide awake, worrying, wondering why he didn't touch her anymore.

But, she determined, *it will all be different now. The* namman phraaj *will work. And the fact he has come home like this, unannounced, can only be a good sign! All my effort, all my waiting, rewarded at last.* It had been so awkward that day, a few weeks ago now, accidentally on purpose meeting her husband in the village after coming back from the Fortune Teller's cave. "What on earth are you doing here," he had barked at her, "snooping on me? Don't you know how busy I am?" She had tried to reason with him – it was only to visit the Fortune Teller, she claimed, to have her astrological chart mapped, her cards read, she had heard he was good. "Why don't you come with me next time," she had gabbled, "get your own cards read?" He had laughed then – "Don't worry," he said, "I've met the Fortune Teller already, he and I are the best of friends." That had worried her: what did he mean, the best of friends? And all the while the bamboo container had been burning a hole in her handbag. She'd so nearly done it. He'd gone out of the office to talk to Sergeant Yud, leaving a bowl of half-eaten noodles on his desk. "Go on madam!" Panit had urged, nodding at the soup bowl, "what're you waiting for?" She had fumbled in her bag for it, and was just about to take the stopper out of the glass phial when he came back inside to tell her crossly that the chauffeur was waiting outside the station, so they should leave now to get the worst of the journey over before nightfall. She could still see him sitting behind his desk, the spoon and chopsticks lifted to his mouth as she turned to go. So close! She had been angry with herself for missing the chance – not realizing then that she would get another opportunity so soon.

But where is he hiding? She stepped back inside, sliding the door shut behind her. She checked all the other bedrooms, just in case. *Is he playing a game?* she wondered. *Maybe he's going to jump out at me, fold me in his arms, kiss me passionately on the lips, running his hands up and down my body?* She smiled, thinking that maybe he would do just that after she had given him some *namman phraaj!* Going back downstairs, she stood in the hall, listening. A light shone from under the door of the kitchen. Panit was in after all. *I should go and speak to her,* thought the Chief's wife, *tell her to fetch some beer for him, some whisky and ice. Yes, everything should be perfect. Then he can have his dinner! I can ask Panit to cook something spicy – a tom yam soup – the chilli will cover any taste the oil might have.*

She moved quickly down the length of the hall. As she reached out for the door handle, she heard a muffled cry from the other side. She opened the door a few inches, the overhead strip light making her blink. Warm, sultry air wafted out, carrying the smell of deep-fried garlic. She could see one end of the long wooden table. It was his black pistol she noticed first, laid down on the end of the table, next to the chopping board with a half-sliced onion on it. The thick stone pestle was lying next to the empty mortar. She opened the door another inch. The familiar brown jacket of his uniform was slung over one of the chairs. Another cry came, louder this time. She pushed the door wide open. It looked like her husband... the white cotton vest, his broad back. He was half standing, half lying across the other end of the table. Panit was underneath him, her blouse pushed up, his hands on her bra, her breasts. His mouth was over hers, muffling her strangled sobs.

The Chief's wife did not scream. She crept towards the table, the heat from the room already sticky on her back. She kept her eyes on him, fumbling blindly with her hands at the table's edge. Panit struggled under his weight, one arm flailing out weakly.

Her hand hovered briefly over the pistol. He always slept with it under his pillow, just in case, he said. She had thought he was joking, in the beginning. Her hand moved away from the gun, choosing the heavy pestle instead. She was behind him now. "Come on," he was urging, "come on Panit, why won't you let me taste your new recipe?" She held the pestle high in both hands, squeezed her eyes shut, and brought it down with unexpected force on the back of his head.

The Banyan Tree

Gop kindles the argument late one November night, shuffling past the moonshine stall, clutching to his chest a small branch.

"What have you got there Gop?" calls Lai.

Gop hesitates, muttering under his breath, the street lamp casting a yellow glow around his shaggy head.

"Give him a cigarette; he wants a cigarette," says Uncle Nun.

"Why don't you give him a drink," guffaws Sergeant Yud, "maybe it'll loosen his tongue! Hey Gop, what numbers have you got for Wednesday's lottery?"

Gop keeps his head down, face hidden, cradling his booty.

"It's a branch," says Uncle Moon, moving towards him to proffer a cheroot. "He must have pulled it from the banyan tree, look at the shape of the leaves."

Gop snatches the cheroot with his filthy fingers and turns to go.

"What's that you say?" shouts Yud, "three and four?"

The drinkers hoot with laughter. Uncle Moon shakes his head, glancing up behind the morning market, squinting at the outline of the huge tree against the moonlit sky. He tries to change the subject, wagging his finger: "A hundred men could stand under that tree's canopy, you mark my words."

Uncle Nun, the expert, scoffs. "More like two hundred! What do dustbin men know about trees? Farmers know better!"

Uncle Daeng agrees, laughing softly, licking his lips. Sia Heng, a rare visitor at the moonshine stall, takes off his huge ruby ring, laying it down beside his glass. "A thousand," he cries with firebrand confidence; "I'll bet my ring on it!"

Sergeant Yud rubs his fat hands together and clatters down from his stool. The past two weeks have been one long holiday for Yud and the other officers, what with the Chief mysteriously indisposed in the city. Crossing the road to Gimsia's shop, he raps loudly on the shutters, disturbing the light doze of Mother Pon as he calls for a small notepad in which to write down all the bets.

"Nearest guess wins the jackpot!" he cries, crossing back over.

"I'll bet fifty baht only eighty men could fit under the tree!"

"A hundred baht says one hundred and twenty."

"I'll bet five hundred on two hundred men: that's how sure I am!"

Sergeant Yud licks the stub of his pencil, scribbling numbers down furiously. Across the road, Mother Pon watches from the doorway. She shakes her head and steps back inside, clattering down the shop shutters.

"What's all that about?" calls Gimsia from his old deckchair in the back shop.

Mother Pon sighs. "Those men! No respect." She pulls her sarong tighter around her waist. "That's their problem, they have no respect for anything."

"What on earth are you talking about now, woman?" Gimsia peers at her over his reading glasses, shuffling his newspaper.

"Gambling."

Gimsia shrugs.

"Not just any gambling! Gambling on the old banyan tree. That's not right, I tell you, not respectful. The old banyan tree is..." she waves her hands around, "...*sacred*."

Gimsia grunts and disappears behind his paper. Mother Pon folds her arms over her chest, glancing at the clock, frustrated. It's ten o'clock: too late to go out and find someone to talk to. *And where*, she wonders, *is Dee? Out again, goodness knows where!* It's the gossip she minds. Mother Pon shakes her head, purses her lips and goes upstairs to lie wide awake on the bed, checking next Wednesday's forecasts in the lottery magazine. She sighs, unable to concentrate on the dreams, predictions and mathematical pyramids, laying down the magazine to stare out the window at the cold white moon, low in the clear sky, filtering through the great banyan tree's branches in the temple grounds.

Gop is crossing the rice fields at the edge of the village to climb the steps to the old shrine. Too many men at the moonshine stall to sleep peacefully in the *sala* tonight. The rice is full in the paddy, harvest is about to begin, and the jasmine fragrance of the grains is filling the night air. The end of the rains: the start of the short winter season.

The men at the stall shiver, feel the night air nip bare arms, ordering more whisky to keep out the chill as they clamour to place their bets.

* * *

The light from a solitary moped winks and blinks from halfway up the mountain road, cruising slowly down. On the back of the bike Kwan, Mother Pensri's daughter, clutches Dee for warmth. She is home from the city for the weekend.

"Will you tell them tomorrow then?" shouts Dee from the front.

Kwan buries her face in Dee's warm back. Old friends have no secrets. They grew up in each other's yards, walked hand in hand to the village school, hunted frogs down by the river, fished side by side over the old wooden bridge. They left together for the city: Dee to study at university, Kwan to work in the fruit-processing factories, canning *lamyai* from the thousand orchards flanking the great city on all sides.

"*Tho-oei* Dee, I don't know how I can! It'll break Mama's heart. It was bad enough when I pulled out of the beauty contest at Songkran! She has such different plans for me, you know... a husband, a bit of land, house, children..."

Dee stops the moped at their favourite viewpoint on the mountain road. Kwan dismounts, crouching by the road's edge, staring out across the valley, arms hugging her knees. The village lights twinkle below. Dee sighs, turning round to sit sideways on the moped seat. He pulls off a red woollen hat and pats at his hair.

"But you can still have all those things, just not *now*, not *here*. Look, they have to know eventually. If you're really sure." Dee's voice drops low. "Are you really sure?"

Kwan nods, trying to pick out her house from within the cluster of lights. The moon is so bright that she can make out the *chedi* in the temple grounds, the statue of Mother Thoranee wringing her hair, the great banyan tree.

"Then they'll get used to it: they have to. Look at me! If my dad can accept me as a *gathoey* then..." Dee laughs strangely, throwing his hands up in the air.

Kwan turns round to face him. "Wasn't easy though, was it?"

Dee shrugs. "You can only go halfway into the forest, Kwan; then you're coming out the other side, no? And it's OK, now he recognizes my incredible *flair for business*!" Dee tosses back his fringe. "I'm not what he had in mind, but at least I bring in money. And I don't have to pretend to be something I'm not."

Kwan pulls her jacket round her body. "I'll speak to Mama first, tomorrow."

"Good. Then you'll come to the salon, tell me what happened?"

"OK."

"Come on, better get you back home." Dee straddles the moped, kicking it into life. Kwan gets ready to climb on the back, but her eye is caught suddenly by a movement up in the forest, rustling, a light amongst the trees.

"Sssh Dee. Look, up there, somebody's moving."

Dee peers up. "Hunters most likely. Tribal people." He slips the bike into gear. "Or *ghosts*," he adds in a comic tone, "come to make us pay for our sins! Get on, or I'll leave you with them!" He whoops over his shoulder as they begin their descent into the valley, the sound of the engine overwhelming the slow, faint whine of a chainsaw at work deep in the thick forest beyond the road.

Not far away, Jamu fastens the buttons on his tribal jacket, listening to the chainsaw. He switches off his torch. There's nothing in his traps tonight anyway. He stands still, eyes closed, locating the sound. About two kilometres away, to the north. He knows the spot in the forest, can even guess at the particular clump of trees. He pockets the torch, moving soundlessly through the jungle night towards the sound, sure-footed over roots and tubers, a swift, silent shadow amongst the trees. Jamu wants to see.

There are five men, three lamps, two chainsaws. One tree is already down, and another one is in the process of being felled. Two men work on the fallen tree, sawing it into sections. The men work quickly, dividing and stacking up logs. Jamu crouches behind a tall clump of bamboo, at the edge of what is becoming a clearing in the forest. The teak they have cut down is only forty years old, not even a hundred feet high. Not yet fully grown, but old enough for the wood to have darkened, its oil is so bitter and poisonous that no insect will attack it – which is one of the reasons why it is so valuable to man. The air is heavy with the aroma of wood dust. One man strips branches and twigs from the logs with an axe. Large leaves and feathery white flowers litter the ground. *When the men have finished*, Jamu thinks, *I'll collect the leaves, take them back home and dry them out...* He can weave them into strips on bamboo frames to thatch a new roof for his house. Jamu shakes his head. His village is on high ground and will be safe, but if villagers and outsiders carry on cutting down all the trees, then the valley is in danger of flooding.

"Get a move on," says one of the men, "we have to finish tonight." He stands over the others, watching, edgy. Dressed in combat trousers, he clutches in his hand a government issue walkie-talkie. On the back of his khaki jacket are the words ROYAL FORESTRY DEPARTMENT. Jamu recognizes him. The other men nod, do not speak or look up: they are Shan, illegal migrants from across the border. Jamu has seen them before too, down in the village, working on the construction site of the large wooden guest house on the banks of the river.

The young novice monk sighs, resting his bamboo broom against the massive trunk of the old tree, watching the pile of leaves he has swept up shiver and resettle with the morning breeze. Hot tears prick the backs of his eyes. He sits on one of the twisted roots under the shady canopy, his back resting against an intricate structure of columns, as though he is inside a cool, dark room. The Abbot won't spot him here. He brushes an arm over his eyes. *All I took was a packet of dried noodles!* He was so hungry last night; couldn't sleep for the gnawing pain in his stomach. He'd sneaked out from under his mosquito net while the other monks snored, tip-toeing into the temple kitchen. He could have taken anything at all: rice, curry, bananas – even condensed milk – but no, all he took was one packet of instant noodles. *It was hardly anything at all!* Carrying the noodles over to the pond, he'd sat there crunching them gloomily, occasionally feeding the big old catfish. He could hear his father's voice over the wall; the Sergeant's great laugh was booming out as he sat drinking and having fun at the moonshine stall. The next thing he knew, the Abbot's hand was on his shoulder. He'd turned round and seen those eyes just staring at him, filled with disappointment. *Again.*

The novice gazes at the low wooden platform on the ground in front of the tree, at the stubs of candles, incense, and the remnants of offerings. It's mainly girls who bring these offerings. There's an old Hindu belief that the tree houses the spirit of a goddess who can help them meet the man who will give them children. He picks up a leaf, holding it in his palm, tracing the veins on its oval breadth. He peers closer. The leaf is covered in

221

tiny black spots. He drops it, picks up another: the same black spots. Another and another: all the leaves are afflicted. He reaches above his head to one of the lower branches and plucks, his heart beating. The same! Throwing the end of his saffron robe over his shoulder he runs into the main hall, clutching one of the leaves, to find the Abbot.

Inside, the Abbot is in consultation. Mother Pensri's daughter Kwan sits before him on the polished wooden floor, head bent over palms pressed tightly together, as the Abbot repeats a benediction. He shakes a few drops of holy water over her head.

"*Saddhu, saddhu, saddhu,*" concludes the Abbot.

Kwan bows to the floor three times, moving backwards on her knees from the Abbot and the Buddha statue until it is polite to stand up. Her basket of offerings is empty, her expression tight and drawn. The novice waits until she has found her sandals at the door before approaching the Abbot, who hands him a silver bowl filled with food. The novice takes the bowl and, glancing down, winces as he sees a packet of dried noodles.

"Take these to the temple kitchen." The Abbot waves his hand to dismiss the novice.

"Venerable Abbot," begins the boy, "there's something I have to show you."

The Abbot sighs, rubbing a hand over the stubble on his head.

"It's about the tree, the old banyan tree," The novice holds out the evidence. "Look at this leaf, Venerable Abbot. I think the tree's dying!"

The Abbot takes the leaf and turns it over in his hand. He stands up stiffly, knees cracking, holding a hand out to the novice for support as they cross the hall. Outside, the sun is already breaking through the slight mist, and the morning market is in full swing over the temple wall. As they approach the great tree, which is girdled in an orange monk's robe as a mark of respect, the Abbot's lips are pressed together. Kwan is kneeling on the grass in front of the tree, a lone, tiny figure under the huge canopy, hands clasped, praying under her breath. She lights a candle and two sticks of incense. The Abbot and the novice wait until she stands up and turns to go. She bows her head respectfully as she passes them.

The Abbot moves closer to the tree, staring up, examining the evidence. Even he doesn't know how old the tree is. Older than the village, older than the temple. He knows from the ancient manuscripts that the Abbot who founded the temple chose this site because of the banyan tree: the symbol of life, the protector of the Enlightened One. The original host tree is completely obscured now, smothered by epiphytes – lateral branches that have absorbed water from the air and grown down to the ground to take root. *New growth on old*, he contemplates, *first the tree, then people, a village, a temple. On and on it goes. Cause and effect. Everything interconnected, interdependent.* The Abbot gazes at the leaves. Sure enough, many are covered in spots. He reaches out a finger and rubs it across a portion of the main trunk. A skin of pale green mould comes off on his hand.

Behind him, next to the statue of Mother Thoranee, hovers Kwan.

"What is it, Venerable Abbot? What's happened to the tree?"

The Abbot does not answer. He sucks the air in through his teeth and lets out a sigh. Head down, hands clasped behind his back, he walks in the direction of the main hall, leaving Kwan and the novice to stare after him.

"What is it?" Kwan turns to the boy.

"The tree is dying," says the novice in a mournful voice, lip trembling. The dried noodles are swelling in his stomach.

Kwan covers her mouth with her hand, walking quickly towards the temple gates. Outside, on the main street, she catches sight of her mother leaning her bicycle against the lamp post by the morning market. Mother Pensri is staring at the first stall, which is piled high with enormous, misshapen green fruits. *Jackfruit*, Mother Pensri is thinking: *a special dish for Kwan*. Kwan loves the pink flesh fried with shallots and sweet plum tomatoes, topped with crispy garlic, chilli and coriander. The dish will go well with the pumpkin stalk soup she plans to make.

"Mother Pensri! Mother Pensri!"

She turns round. Mother Pon is crossing the road from the shop, arms folded over her chest.

"Guess what I heard last night!" Mother Pon opens her eyes wide. "Those men at the moonshine stall, making bets, would you believe, on the old banyan tree!"

Mother Pensri frowns. "Was Nun there?"

Her friend nods.

"Who else?"

"Oh, the usual crowd: Pan, Daeng, Moon, Yud... and, now let me see, Sia Heng was there too."

Mother Pensri shakes her head. "I'll have a word with Nun."

"The bets were getting really high! Sia Heng even gambled his ruby ring. It was Sergeant Yud, *of course*, who started a book.

I'm going to speak to Mother Nong: maybe she can convince him to call the whole thing off. It's not right!"

Mother Pensri agrees, looking over her shoulder at the market stalls. "Maybe," she says, "we should take a leaf from Mother Suree's book..." She grins, making a snipping movement with her fingers.

"What's going on?" asks Aunty Wassana, approaching the market with her barrow, little Boo trotting at her heels.

"We're discussing the men. Gambling on the old banyan tree!"

"*Aow*!" Aunty Wassana lets the barrow legs rest on the road, eagerly leaning forwards over the handlebars. "Who? When? How much?"

"Oh, I'm sure it'll blow over." Mother Pensri turns away, anxious to buy the best jackfruit before someone else does. The market is busy. Hill tribe women crouch over mats near the entrance, selling red beans, clumps of tobacco, wild mountain plants bound into bunches with bamboo twine. *I could buy some of those plants*, thinks Mother Pensri, *to mix in a special salad dish for later in the afternoon... hmmm... ground peanuts, shallots, deep-fried pork skins...* The old Fortune Teller is down from his cave to buy tobacco, negotiating with the hill tribe women. A few migrants huddle round the moonshine stall. Lai pours out drinks, bleary-eyed. The Forestry Officer sits with them, brandishing a banknote. The workers look sheepish, exhausted, clothes covered in wood dust and grime. One of them sports a makeshift bandage round his hand. The Forestry Officer urges them to drink up, promising a breakfast of barbecued chicken and sticky rice.

Mother Pensri looks over and sees her daughter standing at

the temple gates. *Good girl*, thinks Mother Pensri – *getting up early to make merit at the temple even though it's not a special Buddha day.*

"Kwan, Kwan, come and help me choose a jackfruit!" she calls, leaving Mother Pon and Aunty Wassana to gossip about the gambling.

"What's the matter?" she asks, seeing Kwan's downcast face.

"*Tho-oei*, Mama. It's the tree."

"What tree?"

"The old banyan tree. The leaves are turning black."

"What do you mean, turning black?"

"It's dying; the old tree is dying."

Mother Pensri spins back round to Mother Pon and Aunty Wassana. "Do you hear that?" she cries out. "Those silly men and their gambling! Our banyan tree is dying!"

The Forestry Officer glances over, curious. Heads look up, peering at the branches above the temple wall. A few people start towards the temple gates. The Shan workers down their drinks, drifting after the others. Soon half the village is gathered in the temple grounds, clustered around the tree, picking off leaves, rubbing their hands up and down the bark, exclaiming at the green mould that sticks to their fingers. Everyone has an explanation. It's because of the late rains that year. It's because of red ants. It's because the ghost of Mali Foi Thong is trapped inside the tree. Mother Pon grips Aunty Wassana's arm, whispering in her ear.

"I think we should call a meeting. The Housewives' Group. No point leaving it to the *men* to solve this. We can meet in the shop, tonight, at six o'clock. Tell everyone you see today at the stall."

Aunty Wassana bristles slightly, crushing the leaf she clutches tightly in her hand. *Why can't the Housewives' Group meet at her house? It's much more spacious*, she fumes, *than Mother Pon's shop.*

Standing apart from the throng, the Fortune Teller hangs back, staring up at the tree's outline against the blue sky, aghast, pipe hanging loosely in his hand. This is his worst fears realized. *I should never*, he thinks, *have sold that* namman phraaj*!* Ever since hearing the gossip about the Chief's mysterious accident, the Fortune Teller has been filled with foreboding.

In the main hall, the novice flits from window to window, fluttering around the Abbot, who chants steadily in a loud, monotonous voice, drowning out the sound of the villagers' clamour.

* * *

Daeng is working his way around the orchids growing on what was once his old rice field, watering the strips of coconut shell that nourish each plant, as the car draws up. He is surprised to see the Police Chief. The latest story going round is that the Chief fell downstairs and hurt his head. Daeng's boss, the Forestry Officer, emerges from his big teak house to greet the visitor, bowing over his hands. The Chief returns the bow and the two men slap one another on the back. Daeng walks over to refill the watering can. His new job is much easier than farming his own field and worrying all the time about debt. Selling his land to the Forestry Officer was a smart move: it had paid off the bank loan, and the regular weekly income keeps his wife quiet. He's becoming quite an expert on orchids too. As he waits for the can to fill, he peers over at the house. Through the window he can see the two men clinking whisky glasses. He licks his lips. The Chief looks his usual self; no sign of a plaster or bandages or anything. Daeng chuckles, thinking of the expressions that must have been on Yud's and Pan's faces when the Chief first walked back into the station: *they must have got a shock all right!* He walks back over to the wooden frame, covered in shady netting, that houses the hanging orchid plants – in the wild they grow on trees, exotic parasites that clutch and cling around trunks and branches, stealing moisture from the host. Many of the orchids are in bloom, ready for cutting, with their fantastic, delicately striped and spotted blossoms of pink, purple, yellow and white. The most beautiful will be packed in fancy cardboard boxes, transported to the city and sold at the airport. Business men, politicians, rich foreigners, the Forestry Officer explained on Daeng's first day, buy them as gifts for their wives.

Inside the house the Forestry Officer points with his glass to the table, where a stack of boxed orchids lie. "Want one?" he asks the Chief. "For a special lady?"

The Chief nods, thinking of a slim waist and a pair of red shoes. His long absence means that his minor wife might need a little chasing, coaxing, spoiling. It will be an enjoyable game of cat and mouse. He crunches an ice cube between his teeth. "Is everything ready then?"

"Almost. Wood's stacked in the jungle, ready to move. Three truck-loads. About 200,000 baht's worth. What about the buyer?"

The Chief laughs. "No shortage of buyers, I can assure you. It's more a question of whether we can supply the demand. Have you got drivers yet?"

The official tilts his head towards the window. "Guy outside is driving one of them. Sia Heng's providing me with two more: cousins or nephews or something."

"Good. We need to get the convoy moving tomorrow night. The Queen is visiting the city in a couple of days, last thing we need is hassle from all the extra security. We have to get the trucks to the city outskirts before dawn. You know the address. Phone me when you get there." He walks over to the window, gazing outside. "Nice little business you have here. Quite the horticulturalist, aren't you?"

"A man has to make ends meet. Can't exist on the wages the government pays, now can we?"

The Chief throws back his head, laughing, holding out his glass for a refill.

"Must admit, you had me worried, Chief. What happened? Three weeks and not a single phone call! I was beginning to think you'd been rumbled."

The Chief smiles strangely. "Truth is, I had some kind of blackout. One minute I'm in my house, minding my own business, next thing I know everything goes dark and I wake up in bed, head thumping, wife hovering over me with a bowl of soup!"

"Too much whisky?"

"I just can't remember. Wife says I fell against the kitchen table." The Chief shrugs. "Must have been the maid's cooking." He pats his stomach firmly. "Stronger than ever now. Haven't felt better for years." He laughs again, a little too loudly.

* * *

From the balcony of the main hall the Abbot frowns. Below him, women cluster around the tree, a flurry of cheap print sarongs, thin white candles, incense. Dee sits at the centre, a queen bee, hands dipping into baskets of blossoms as he constructs garlands of jasmine and bright orange marigolds. None of the women can make a garland as quickly as he can. The wooden platform in front of the tree is surrounded by trays and plates which are littered with banana leaf offerings – tiny paper flags, cake, puffed rice, pieces of fruit – while the air is heavy from all the incense sticks lit around the tree. The tree's lowest branches are smothered with garlands. Underneath the outermost branches a folding table has been erected, on top of which stands a cardboard money tree. Each woman stops at the table to make a contribution, reaching under waistbands and bra straps for tightly folded banknotes: ten, twenty, fifty baht notes are smoothed out carefully and fastened to the branches of the money tree. The Housewives' Group has chosen to organize a merit making ceremony, a *tod kathin*. A representative from the Group, yet to be chosen, will travel to the city tomorrow morning to present a special offering at the great temple of Doi Suthep. The women have heard the Queen is to visit the temple too, an event that will draw devotees from far and near. There will be merit in abundance. Only merit can save their great tree now, damaged and hurt as it is through the disrespect shown by their menfolk. Why else would the tree fall sick?

Mother Pensri, seated at the table, is anxious to be chosen to deliver the offering. Her daughter, Kwan, left that morning on the first bus. There were cross words all weekend. Mother Pensri pulls her cigarettes out from under her blouse. She can still hardly bear to think about it. *Hong Kong! Kwan will have to fly in an airplane. And the cost! Twenty thousand for the passport, another thirty thousand for the visa and work permit. Three thousand for the flight.* Mother Pensri draws the smoke deep into her lungs, turning a blind eye to Mother Nong's disapproving glance. *Fifty-three thousand baht,* she broods, *where am I to get all that cash from?* She goes over her daughter's words again and again.

"Just think Mama, I'll be able to send money home every month: you won't have to sell lottery tickets anymore, you can build another room on to the house, get a proper bathroom..."

Mother Pensri knows Kwan is only thinking of her parents. She's a good daughter. But this is not what Mother Pensri had planned. A pretty girl like Kwan could have her pick of husbands.

"But I don't want to get married, not yet," her daughter had said. "I want to save some money first, work abroad, see what life is like somewhere else."

But is it safe? frets Mother Pensri. *What if the job the agency has promised turns out to be something else?*

"I've seen the brochures, the pictures. Each girl is matched with a Chinese or European family; it's just housework, some cooking, looking after the children. Room and board included so I can send home all my wages. I've been taking English lessons, Mama: the woman at the agency is going to try matching me with a British family – who knows, I might even get to visit England!"

Mother Pensri puckers her brow. Hong Kong, England... As far as she's concerned, Bangkok is too far. But Kwan is stubborn: her mind is made up. And Mother Pensri has promised to help her raise the money for the agency fee. *At least*, she thinks grimly, *I have a head start*. The money from Uncle Nun's sword is still folded away in her underwear drawer.

"*Ficus benghalensis*," booms a voice, startling Mother Pensri.

The women turn round to stare at the Forestry Officer and the Police Chief, who are standing with folded arms at the perimeter of the tree's canopy, a straggle of men gossiping behind them. Sergeant Yud is at the Chief's elbow, red face sweating profusely in the afternoon sun. The women hum and bristle.

"What do they want?" hisses Mother Pon in Mother Pensri's ear. "Haven't they done enough damage?"

"*Ficus benghalensis*," repeats the Forestry Officer, nodding at the Chief. "Must be about two hundred years old, quite a specimen." He takes a few paces forwards, then bends to one side as Uncle Nun tugs at the sleeve of his jacket, makes to whisper in his ear. The official looks confused for a second then his face breaks into an appreciative smile. "How many?" Tilting his head on one side, he sizes up the old tree. "Three hundred? What do you say, Chief?"

"Mmm?" The Chief is not really listening, glassy eyes fixed upon the huge tree before him.

"Apparently there's a bet on. About how many people will fit under the tree's canopy."

Sergeant Yud pushes forwards, eager as a puppy. This is his chance to get back into the Chief's good books. "Two-to-one says two hundred, sir, that's the odds, sir!" He produces the clammy notebook, fumbling in his pockets for a pencil. The Chief shakes his head, turning his attention to Yud.

"How can you?" cries Mother Pon, moving towards the sergeant. "It's your gambling that's made the banyan tree fall sick in the first place!"

"Just wait a minute," calls Mother Nong, pushing forwards, "that's my husband you're talking to!"

"*Aow*, ladies," says the Chief, amused. "We'll deal with the bet later. Yud, put that book away. I've brought the Forestry Officer with me today to provide an expert opinion. Why don't you all move aside, that's right, and let him have a good look at the tree? Come on ladies, make some room."

The women fall away to the sides as the Chief and the Forestry Officer press through, tip-toeing around the offerings choking the ground. The official examines the leaves, peering closely at the green mould on the trunk. The two men confer in low voices, heads together. The villagers murmur to one another. After a few minutes, the official turns to them, hands clasped under his chin, mock serious.

"Milibug." He unclasps his hands, pointing vaguely at the sky. "It's taken hold. And small wonder. Look at all this... this *stuff*." He indicates the ground, the offerings, with a grand sweep of his arm. "You'll have to stop all this. You're killing the tree. No more incense or candles. Carbon monoxide. Forms a layer on the leaves, so they can't *photosynthesize*. Without photosynthesis," he concludes, "the tree will die."

The men nudge one another, nodding. Sergeant Yud wags his finger over at the women. "This is your doing," he calls out, "nothing to do with us!"

"A few candles?" says Mother Pon. "Incense? But it's us who care for the tree, worship it, want to protect it."

"Suffocate it, more like!" Uncle Nun cries.

Mother Pensri glares at her husband from behind the money tree. Dee stands up, brandishing a half finished garland.

"What about these?" he demands. "I suppose they're *strangling* the tree to death, are they?"

"Unnatural!" shouts a male voice from the back of the crowd.

"*Gathoey*!" cries another.

Mother Pon grabs her son's arm, trying to pull him back. It's too late. Dee seethes forwards with his basket of blossoms, tossing them over the crowd of men who hoot in derision. Uncle Nun catches a marigold and sticks it behind his ear.

"*Aow*, look at me," he shouts, prancing in front of the others, "I'm a ladyboy too!"

Dee runs out of the temple gates, chased by his mother. Sergeant Yud and Sergeant Pan have pulled out the little black notebook and are herding the rest of the men under the tree. Many of the offerings are pushed to one side. The Chief and the Forestry Officer wander away, deep in conversation. All this hullabaloo is the perfect cover for what they are planning to do. Later on the Chief will order Lai to shut his stall, and will instruct Gimsia and the other shopkeepers that no alcohol is to be sold that evening. Tensions are too high, he will explain. If he can get the village into bed early, there will be even less likelihood of anyone noticing any unusual traffic later on that night.

The Abbot stares over at the racket, brow furrowed, absentmindedly pulling at a loose thread on his robe.

* * *

Uncle Daeng wipes his sweating palms down his trouser legs. It's an eight-wheeled truck: long, heavy and noisy. Manoeuvring it along the mountain road is no easy task; the twisting road with its steep inclines has him changing gear constantly. To stall would be disastrous; Daeng has been having nightmares all week of how the truck would slip backwards, pulled by its great weight over the mountain, crashing down with him trapped in the driver's seat. He clenches his hands round the wheel, grits his teeth, and concentrates on the tail lights of the truck ahead. The money he is being paid for this one job is enough for his wife to finally open the fried noodle stall she has dreamt of. *I'm doing it,* he tells himself over and over, *for the sake of my family. It's only a bit of wood, after all. It's not like I'm transporting drugs or anything.* Daeng glances into the side mirror. *Why,* he reasons, *I used to cut wood down from the forest for my own house. Back then nobody made a fuss.* But nowadays everyone is supposed to only buy wood with a government stamp. *And at those prices,* Deang reasons, *it's no wonder so much illegal logging is going on!* Most of the villagers have spare wood stacked away in their yards, under rice barns, nailed hastily on to existing walls. It's a small investment, insurance against ill health or loss of income. Daeng shrugs. He doesn't even know exactly where the logs have come from: his job was to collect the truck from behind his boss's house. The wood was already stacked high on the back of the trucks, secured with heavy chains. He and the other drivers had covered the loads with a layer of garlic.

Daeng is almost at the village now, and can see the two street lamps. Past the rice fields, past Uncle Nun's house. Past his own house, Gimsia's shop, Lai's moonshine stall, the morning market. All closed up. He glances over at the temple: a single oil lamp burns under the old banyan tree. Heart thumping, Daeng imagines he sees the figure of a man, cross-legged under the tree. He shudders, fixing his eyes straight ahead, driving on, past the *sala*, where Gop lies sprawled over his pile of booty. The sight of old Gop is comforting. He shakes his head. The figure under the tree must have been his imagination playing tricks! Everything is quiet. Everyone is asleep. He hasn't told anyone apart from his wife about this job. The truck slows to first gear, then stops before the old wooden bridge. The river gleams beneath in the moonlight. Daeng puts on his jacket; the air up in the mountains will be cold. He swings down from the cab, lights a cigarette between cupped hands and disappears into the bushes: nerves have upset his stomach.

Under the tree, the Abbot has opened his eyes. He stands up, staring over the temple wall at the three sets of tail lights disappearing into the night. He sniffs the air, recognizing the distinctive aroma of garlic. *Garlic?* thinks the Abbot. He inhales again: there's another, familiar smell beneath the garlic that he can't quite place. He scratches his head, pulling his old yellow towel over his shoulders.

For the past few nights, since the discovery of the tree's strange disease, the Abbot has been trying to meditate under its sickly branches, unsure how best to proceed. The tree, he knows, cannot be allowed to perish; it's a banyan tree, after all: the tree that sheltered the Buddha as he attained enlightenment. It is the tree of life, of refuge, of immortality. *It's my duty*, thinks the Abbot, *to protect it. But how? If the tree's sickness really is biological*, he reasons, *then steps will have to be taken to cure it: pesticides will have to be purchased and applied, a fence built around the tree to defend it. But what if the malaise is spiritual? What if the women are right to blame the men? Gambling is a sin, after all. But how*, he worries, *can I take sides? Isn't the Sangha above politics?*

The Abbot looks back at the tree. A sick leaf falls from one of the branches. *Impermanence*, he contemplates, *decay*. Sleepy, his eyes gaze unfocused at the statue of Mother Thoranee, who is twisting her long black hair over the earth. He rubs his face, his mind a muddle. *Could it be milibug? The Forestry Officer is an expert, after all... or maybe I should invite a guest monk to deliver a sermon about the evils of gambling...* He hears one of the trucks stop. *Garlic*, considers the Abbot, *who transports garlic at this time of year?* Wide awake now, he limps stiffly through the temple gates, down the road to where the truck sits parked by the bridge. The driver's cab is empty. The Abbott clambers up the side of the truck and digs one hand deep into the layer of garlic, catching the loose thread from his monk's robe, tearing off a strip of cloth on a hard surface as he pulls aside the bundled cloves. Blinking like a newborn, he inhales with deep breaths the unmistakeable smell of newly cut teakwood. *So much of it! Three truckloads...*

He hears a cough from the bushes at the side of the road, footsteps rustling through the grass. Panicking, the old man beats a tottering retreat, back to the sanctuary of the temple, robes flapping.

* * *

Mother Pensri wriggles on the narrow seat and checks through her belongings again: *clothes and toiletries in the fake leather bag on the rack, a huge packet of deep-fried pork skins (much tastier than the ones sold in the city market, and Kwan can share them with the other factory workers); lunch (sticky rice and chilli paste) and an empty plastic bag, just in case.* The bus journey sometimes makes her queasy. She pats her stomach anxiously, feeling for the bump in the pocket of her girdle. She is carrying a lot of money. *It's just as well*, thinks Mother Pensri, *that Kwan is meeting me at the bus station. You can't be too careful in the city. Thieves and scoundrels...*

The money is folded into two bundles. One is for the *tod kathin* ceremony up at Doi Suthep temple. Mother Pensri will go to the city market later to buy two dozen sets of best quality monk's robes to present at the great temple. When she and Mother Pon had collected all the banknotes pinned to the money tree they counted several thousand baht. It was a good amount, in spite of all the unpleasantness at the temple the previous day. The women were all relieved when the Chief called a curfew; the last thing the village needed was the men getting drunk and causing trouble again. But Mother Pensri still wasn't speaking to Uncle Nun, and had left no food behind for him in the fridge.

The other bundle of money is for Kwan. Mother Pensri has sold the ruby pendant she had been saving for Kwan's wedding day. Sia Heng gave her a fair price for it. In her bag she has packed her old wedding silk too. If Kwan needs more money then Mother Pensri will sell it. Added to the sword money, she has raised enough for Kwan's expenses. *What else*, she thinks, *could I do? Maybe Kwan is right to want more.* Mother Pensri settles back and looks round the bus. It's quite busy: a few tourists, loud and long-limbed, legs poking awkwardly into the aisle; some tribal women, on their way back to their villages after selling food and tobacco at the morning market. Mother Pensri narrows her eyes at their tunics and sniffs: the smell of clothes dried over wood smoke. She turns right round, glancing at the back of the bus. The Abbot and the young novice – Mother Nong's boy – are on the back seat. *Where*, she wonders, *are they going?* Mother Pensri leans over and peers down the aisle.

"Venerable Abbot," she calls over, "are you going to the ceremony at Doi Suthep too?"

All the other passengers turn to stare but the Abbot only shakes his head. Mother Pensri shrugs and pulls herself back. The bus crawls up the mountain in first gear. Mother Pensri's ears pop as she stares out of the window. It's winter now: her favourite season. Up on the mountain a light mist threads through the tops of thin pine trees. She can see for miles, right across from this mountain to the next, green, thick with forest and jungle. The news reports are always going on about deforestation but Mother Pensri can't see any sign of it here. There had been some terrible floods and mudslides in another province the previous year. *Over a hundred people died*, she recalled. The papers had said it was because of all the logging: no trees meant there was nothing to stop the rainwater eroding the soil, sweeping everything up in its path.

One of the tribal women calls out to the driver, who pulls up the handbrake, screeching to a halt by the side of the road. The bus boy jumps down to wedge a block of wood under one of the back wheels. A narrow footpath winds down from the side of the road. The tribal women gather up their belongings and get off. Mother Pensri watches them sling sacks and bags over their shoulders and start the walk to their village. She is surprised to see the novice alight too, putting his hand out to help the Abbot down. *What business do they have in the middle of nowhere*, she wonders, *and what's in the cloth shoulder bags they are carrying?* The bus pulls away before Mother Pensri can ask. She reaches for her bag of sticky rice instead. It's been almost two hours since breakfast.

The Abbot lays his hand on the boy's shoulder and stares across the valley. The sun is halfway up the sky, melting through the mountain mists. The village lies below, the river snaking through it, the houses and shops an indistinguishable scattering of grey and brown dots. Blink and you might miss it amongst the lush green and purple landscape.

"Where are we going, Venerable Abbot?" asks the novice. He is confused, and a little worried about the old Abbot. This morning, after the alms round, the Abbot took him to one side, gave him a pile of old robes, and told him to tear the robes at the seams into long strips.

The Abbot looks down at the boy. "What is the Second Precept, little mouse?"

The novice blushes, staring at his bare feet. "To abstain from stealing, Venerable Abbot."

"Do you see the forest?" The Abbot points ahead. A faint path leads off from the main path to the tribal village. "That's where we're going."

"Are we going to meditate?"

"No."

"Venerable Abbot, what are these old monk's robes for?"

"You'll see."

The Abbot walks a few steps forwards, halting at a young teak tree near the side of the road, two or three metres tall. Spindly branches stick out from the thin trunk.

"A sapling," says the old monk in a whisper, laying his hand on the tree, "just like you."

The novice follows the Abbot into the forest, watching his feet, anxious about snakes, scorpions, fierce red ants. He still doesn't understand. He worries that the trip into the forest is some elaborate penance for stealing the dried noodles. The forest grows thicker and darker. Birds with brilliant blue tails flash through the treetops, and butterflies flit up from bushes. On and on they walk, the Abbot following the trail of leaves trampled underfoot. Monkeys laugh in the distance, cicadas drone, bamboo creaks in the breeze, while underfoot the dry leaves crunch. Suddenly the forest opens out into a scar of cleared land: hot sun hits tree stumps, dead grey branches and curled-up brown leaves. The Abbot clicks his tongue against his teeth. Moving on, he stops in front of a survivor, a teak tree, gnarled and bent. The Abbot nods at the novice.

"And what is the First Precept?"

"To abstain from taking life," answers the boy, watching the old man reach into his bag, from which he pulls out a length of orange cloth. *Why are we here*, thinks the boy, *and what are these torn-up robes for? Is the Abbot going to mark the trees in case we lose our way in the forest?*

The Abbot begins to chant an ordination chant, winding the monk's robe around the tree's girth, securing the ends in a single, indisputable knot. He glances round at the boy, beckoning him to do the same, moving on to the next tree, and the next. The novice fumbles in his bag and pulls out a piece of sacred robe. He finds a tree and winds the cloth around it, stumbling over the ancient Pali chant. The Abbot smiles and nods as the novice ties the knot.

On and on, hour after hour, tree after tree is consecrated, until the sun slips and the day disappears and the moon gleams above a pale snake of orange robes spreading across the jungle, bandaging the darkly silent trees.

* * *

Daeng folds the money in half and tucks it into his trouser pocket. His head feels light, a little dizzy. His hands tremble slightly. He lets out a long breath. It's over. The wood is delivered, stacked now inside the large warehouse just outside the city. It's early morning, a grey dawn glowing through the mist. Daeng walks away from the warehouse towards the main road, his services no longer required. It should be easy enough to get a lift into the city. He'll catch the midday bus back home to the village. First he wants to visit the famous city market and buy some folding tables and chairs for Mother Noi. The equipment for her fried noodle stall is almost complete. Last week Daeng cut a piece of wood and painted a sign to hang over the stall: "Mother Noi's Special *Phad Thai*."

Inside the warehouse, the Forestry Officer is counting through the piles of wood.

"Sixty-two, sixty-three, sixty..." the official hesitates, drawing his fingers back from the teak. A scrap of torn orange robe clings to the cut wood. *How did that get there*, thinks the Forestry Officer, horrified, *I would have seen it while we were cutting, stacking, unloading...* He pulls the cloth free from the wood, heart thumping. *Could we*, he groans, *have inadvertently cut down a consecrated tree?* Legs weak, he stumbles across the warehouse to the little office, sitting down heavily on a chair. He lays the scrap of robe on the desk and stares at it for a while before reaching his hand out to pick up the phone.

Epilogue: Lottery Day

Uncle Nun yawns, throwing back the blanket, shivering in the cold morning air. Getting up quickly, he pulls on his trousers and shirt, and makes his way into the kitchen, looking in the fridge, under pot lids, in bags and in cupboards for something, anything to eat. It's no good. Mother Pensri was so angry with him before she left for the city that she has cleared the kitchen of anything tasty. All he can find is lime leaves, curry paste and sour tamarind. She has even hidden the dried noodles and eggs.

Every time he tried to apologize she found another reason to shout at him: he was lazy, he was untidy, he drank too much, he didn't care about the banyan tree, he didn't care about Kwan and he didn't care about her. Uncle Nun sighs, stomach rumbling. He fumbles through his pockets for change, and finds nothing. There's no point even looking for his wallet: his wife is much cleverer than that. He trots back into the bedroom, kneels on the bed and tugs at the little cupboard door built into the headboard. It's locked, of course, and Mother Pensri carries the key to it around her neck. He returns gloomily to the kitchen, resting his elbows on top of the fridge, gazing at the calendar on the wall. The King stares back at him disapprovingly. Uncle Nun glances down at today's date which is circled in red. Wednesday, the first of December. *Tho-oei*, thinks Uncle Nun, rifling around in the little basket on top of the fridge, *it's lottery day and she's been too busy with the Housewives'*

Group and the tree and this business about Kwan to collect her usual bets. He finds her lottery notebook and takes it out to the balcony, flicking through the pages. All her regulars are listed in a neat column at the front. *Would it get me back into her good books,* he wonders, *if I went round all her regulars and took their bets?* He stuffs the notebook into his trouser pocket, smoothes down his hair and pulls his woolly hat over his head. *I'll surprise her,* he thinks, *with the commission when she gets home!* He chuckles to himself, hastily washing his face and brushing his teeth in the backyard. *And I won't go to the whisky stall tonight either,* he resolves, *I'll stay at home and we can talk over this business about Kwan going abroad.* Excited now, Uncle Nun grabs Mother Pensri's bicycle and pedals out into the road in the direction of the morning market, calling out to everyone he sees.

"Lottery tickets! Anyone for lottery tickets! What about you, Mother Nong?" he cries, braking suddenly, almost knocking his neighbour down. "Any lucky numbers today?"

Mother Nong waves a basket of food at him. "Can't you see I'm on my way to make merit?"

"What about Yud?" says Uncle Nun, "he usually buys a few, doesn't he?"

"Sergeant Yud," declares Mother Nong, "is already at the station. It's almost eight o'clock."

Uncle Nun grunts, changing course, and pedals off in the direction of the police station. The officers are lined up on the lawn outside the station, and Sergeant Yud has just raised the red, white and blue flag on the flag pole. The government sponsored morning radio broadcast from Bangkok booms over the village from a loudspeaker attached to the station roof.

Inside the station, the Chief is shut in his office, in the middle of an important phone call.

"Look," he is saying, through gritted teeth, "there are more important things to worry about than a scrap of cloth. The wood has to be sorted *now*." He runs his hand through his hair, listening to the voice at the other end of the line. "What do you mean, bad omen... there's no such thing as... no, no I don't believe... look, I can't talk now..." He slams the receiver down and reaches into his desk drawer for a bottle of whisky. Beads of sweat shine on his forehead. He loosens the top buttons of his uniform jacket and breathes deeply. The nausea started last night, in the middle of what was supposed to be a romantic reunion with his minor wife. Each time he tried to kiss her, each time he began stroking her smooth skin, a wave of sickness and revulsion gripped his guts. In the end, even the sight of her was turning his stomach, and he had to send her home. *What's wrong with me*, wonders the Chief, pouring himself a glass of whisky with trembling hands. He can't think straight this morning. Even the wood doesn't seem that important: the Forestry Officer can deal with it. He swallows the whisky in a gulp and grabs his car keys. *I need to go home*, he decides, *I'm not well, I need... my wife...*

As the Chief is clattering down the balcony steps, eight o'clock chimes out the loudspeaker. Trucks, mopeds and bicycles come to a halt as the strains of the national anthem begin to echo over the valley. Market vendors stop trading, schoolchildren stand to attention, hands clasped behind their backs. The policemen salute. The Chief doesn't stop. He gets into his car and slams the door shut. The car roars into gear and screeches out the station, speeding out of the village towards the city. Sergeant

Yud lowers his hand as the national anthem comes to a close, raising his eyebrows at Sergeant Pan. Pan shrugs. The halted traffic moves on.

"Yud!" shouts Uncle Nun, over the station wall. "Want a lottery ticket?"

"Tell you what," answers Yud, lumbering over, "I'll take the last three numbers: two-three-seven. Fifty baht."

Nun notes it down. "Did you have a dream?"

"No, heh, heh, it's the Chief's license plate. He drove out here like a man possessed!"

"I guess that's as good a sign as any," says Uncle Nun, pocketing Yud's fifty baht. He hands Yud a small slip of paper and runs his finger down the list of names. "Seen the dustcart?"

Sergeant Yud jabs his thumb in the direction of the morning market. "It went past a few minutes ago."

Uncle Nun nods, turns the bicycle round and pedals off, past the school, the district office, the newsagents, the green papaya salad stall and Aunty Wassana, who is busy plunging noodles into her huge pot of soup stock. Gop sits outside the market entrance, laughing to himself as he sniffs cabbage leaves. Uncle Nun dismounts, resting the bicycle against a tree. The dustcart is parked across the road, outside Gimsia's shop.

Inside the market, Mother Noi is packing up. Her tray of fried pumpkin isn't finished yet but already she has short-changed two customers – one of them Mother Nong – and has forgotten to put peanut sauce in several orders. Daeng won't be back until the afternoon bus: around four o'clock. Until then she won't know if he's safe.

"Mother Noi!" calls Uncle Nun, pencil poised over the notebook. "Any numbers for the lottery?"

Mother Noi puts her head on one side, considering. "Five and one, please. Twenty baht." Fifty one: her husband's age.

Uncle Nun writes down her bet, handing her a strip of paper which she tucks carefully into her apron pocket. He moves on, stopping at all the stalls to ask for numbers. Grandmother Gaysuda, who dreamt last night about her late husband, puts half her day's earnings on the date he died. Aunty Wassana chooses sevens and nines: she has her own system of working out lottery numbers, which she refuses to share with anyone else.

By the time Uncle Nun has worked his way through the market, he has more than a thousand baht in his pocket. *That's a hundred baht commission already*, he thinks, grinning to himself as he crosses the road to Gimsia's shop. He spots Uncle Moon inside, sitting on one of Dee's new salon chairs. Mother Pon is on one of the other chairs, peeling garlic on top of a magazine on her lap.

"*Aow!*" cries Uncle Nun, brandishing the little notebook, "who's going to buy a lottery ticket from me today then? This could be your lucky day!"

Mother Pon clicks her tongue against her teeth. "I've had it with gambling," she says, not in the least prepared to forgive Uncle Nun for the way he made a fool of Dee in the temple the other day. "Look at the damage it's done to our banyan tree."

"*Tho-oei*, Mother Pon! And that wouldn't be a *lottery* magazine under all those garlic skins, would it now?" laughs Uncle Moon. He winks at Uncle Nun as Mother Pon gets up, flouncing into the back shop. "My usual bet, Nun: a hundred baht on the number five to come up." Moon takes a swig of whisky before pulling the note from his shirt pocket. Number

247

five is Uncle Moon's lucky number. It reminds him of Mali and that little strawberry birthmark, about the size of a five baht coin.

* * *

At four o'clock in the afternoon, Uncle Nun climbs on to his favourite stool at Lai's moonshine stall. He's already had a shower, combed his hair and put on a clean shirt. He's made the bed, swept the house and put plenty of water in the fridge to cool. He has time for just one Widow Ghost while he's waiting for the bus to arrive. *Surely*, he thinks, *I deserve it?* There is two hundred and five baht commission from Sia Heng in his pocket. So far, he hasn't spent a single baht. Grandmother Gaysuda gave him a bag of leftover coconut cakes for breakfast, and Uncle Moon treated him to a bowl of noodles at midday. Mother Pensri, he knows, will come back from the city laden with purchases from the city food market. He licks his lips, anticipating something special for dinner. *Deep-fried red snapper*, he wonders, *barbecued tiger prawns… or maybe some delicious Chiang Mai sour sausage…*

Everyone looks up, as everyone always does, when the bus from the city turns the corner by the police station, tooting as it trundles down the street. The buses are getting busier now that winter is here again; and many of the seats are filled by farangs who have heard about the valley and its little villages, charming views and welcoming local people. Besides all the rucksacks, the bus roof is laden with several other large packages, wrapped up in cardboard and string, containing six folding tables and two dozen folding chairs. Uncle Daeng had to pay extra to the bus boy for his trouble, and has been worrying all the way that the ropes are not tied tightly enough to keep everything in place.

Mother Pensri starts to gather up all her belongings as the bus screeches to a halt outside the morning market. She looks out the window and sees Uncle Nun by the roadside, shielding his eyes from the sun as he searches up and down the bus windows for his wife. *Home*, she sighs wearily, *at last*.

Acknowledgements

I would like to thank Mike Stocks for his editorial flair and his faith in my writing, Andrew Radford for his enthusiasm and conviction, the Scottish Arts Council for their bursary and Alma Books for taking a risk. Heartfelt thanks are also due to my fellow writers in Glasgow for their support and encouragement, my sister Fiona for her tireless campaigning and – last but certainly not least – Mark for putting up with me so patiently during the whole process.

The narratives in this book spring from a blend of personal observations during twelve years of living in northern Thailand, my imagination, and the incalculable influence of novels, newspapers and scholarly articles. Mary Beth Mills's excellent chapter in *Bewitching Women, Pious Men: Gender and Body Politics in Southeast Asia* (University of California Press, 1995) inspired the widow-ghost idea, whilst B.J. Terwiel's book, *Monks and Magic* (White Lotus, 1994), was an invaluable reference on Buddhist and animistic rites.

.